The Poison Oracle

By the same author

SKIN DEEP

A PRIDE OF HEROES

THE SEALS

SLEEP AND HIS BROTHERS

THE LIZARD IN THE CUP

THE GREEN GENE

THE LIVELY DEAD

KING AND JOKER

WALKING DEAD

ONE FOOT IN THE GRAVE

A SUMMER IN THE TWENTIES

The Poison Oracle

Peter Dickinson

PANTHEON BOOKS, NEW YORK

All rights reserved under International and Pan-American Copy-
right Conventions. Published in the United States by Pantheon
Books, a division of Random House, Inc., New York. Originally
published in Great Britain by Hodder & Stoughton Ltd.

Library of Congress Cataloging in Publication Data

Dickinson, Peter, 1927-
The Poison Oracle.

I. Title
PZ4.D5525B3 [PR6054.I35]   823'.9'14   73-18716
ISBN 0-394-71023-1

Manufactured in the United States of America
First Pantheon Paperback Edition 1982

Note on Translation

THE LANGUAGE OF the marsh-people cannot be translated directly into an English word-for-word equivalent. All the sentences that appear here are paraphrases. I have used archaic word-orders to do this, because the language is somewhat of that nature; colloquialisms do exist, but are used only when speaking to children, or occasionally when wishing to imply that an adult is behaving in a childish manner. For those who are interested, here is a specimen of how the language actually works: The formal greeting on page 59 "Thy buffaloes may rest in my wallow" consists of the single word-accretion Kt!urochaᴚʜa'yghᴀralocht!lin. This accretion has three roots of relationship: -och- comes twice and implies the relationship of property rights, linking in the first case Kt!u which is the locative of K!tu, a wallow, with -aᴚ- which is the first person root unmodified by any clan stop; the -r- in this section is meaningless, a euphony insert. The second -och- links -ghᴀral- (the plural form of gᴀral, a buffalo) with -t!in which is the second-person-singular suffix tinʜ, modified with a ninth-clan stop and closure. The central relationship of permission is expressed by -ʜa'y- where the y is a breathed uvular semivowel modifying the normal permissive root -ʜa//- to show that the permission is not to be taken for granted as this is merely a formal greeting.

I have also translated the Arabic into slightly formal English, as that is how the language is usually spoken in Q'Kut, compared with the rest of the Arab world.

One

1

WITH AS MUCH passion as his tepid nature was ever likely to generate, Wesley Morris stared at Dinah through the observation window. He thought she looked incredibly beautiful, leaning against the heavy wire mesh on the far side, and watching the main group with that air of surprise which Morris knew to mean that she was apprehensive. She looked healthier than most of the others; her coarse black hair had a real sheen to it, and her eyes were bright with vitality.

The others were in a listless mood, though they ought by now to have got over the shock of their arrival; only Murdoch's baby showed much life, making little exploratory forays away from his mother. Sparrow was gazing with sullen intensity at the air-conditioner; perhaps its thin whine got on his nerves; he couldn't know how carefully it had been adjusted to produce a temperature and humidity at which he would thrive. The rest merely lolled and slouched. The darkening caused by the one-way glass in the observation window softened the concrete tree-trunks and metal branches, and gave the whole scene the look of a forest glade. Morris was both pleased and disturbed by this illusion of nature.

"Sparrow looks pretty unintelligent," murmured the Sultan.

"I don't know," said Morris.

"In fact I think he looks decidedly thick. Thicker even than Rowse."

"You can't judge them by Dinah—she's exceptional."

"So what? If she chooses one of the thick ones . . ."

"It doesn't work like that. The odds are she'll be completely promiscuous—she's just made that way. When she has kids you'll never know who the fathers were."

The Sultan knew this perfectly well, but something in his heredity or culture made it hard for him to imagine a set-up in which the males were dominant but did not have exclusive rights to individual females. (Morris had to keep explaining the point to him.)

"Then we ought to start weeding out the thick ones," he said.

Morris recognised in his tone the dangerous moment when a notion was about to harden into a fiat.

"We don't know which *are* the thick ones yet," he protested. "I'll try to set up a few tests, if I can think of how to do it without mucking up the whole idea. We've got plenty of time—Dinah won't reach puberty for at least a year, so . . ."

"Can't we speed it up, my dear fellow? Listen, down in the marshes they know a few things that your puritanical scientists have never caught on to. Some of the local aphrodisiacs . . ."

"Certainly not," snapped Morris.

When the Sultan sighed several hundred-thousand-poundsworth of rubies shifted on his gold-robed chest, and the folds and dewlaps of his large face took up the lines of tragedy. Only the little, hard eyes remained bright. Morris stared sourly at his employer. There were not many amusements in Q'Kut, but the Sultan managed to keep himself happy; and one of his favourite games nowadays seemed to be forcing Morris to draw the line somewhere and then tricking him across it. There'd been the ridiculous business of drugging the white rhino to take shavings off its horn; and rebuilding several cages to make this concrete glade and then filling it with near-wild animals; if he now insisted on doping Dinah's feed with nameless filth there was only one way of preventing it, and that was for Morris to give up his ten thousand dollars a month and take Dinah back to Bristol. Supposing the Sultan would let him out of the country. Or her.

"Look," said Morris. "The whole point of this experiment is to simulate natural conditions as nearly as we can. I was against it, as you know, but now we've set it up I'm going to do my damnedest to make it work. But who's going to pay the slightest attention to our results if it comes out that half our apes were high on local dope?"

8

"I have read that male gorillas have a very low sex-drive," said the Sultan. His reading was patchy and his memory more so, but a point like that was likely to stick in the mind of a man conscious of the twenty-six children in his women's quarters, and the unimpeachable impotence of the eunuchs who guarded them.

"Chimpanzees are different," said Morris.

"I'm glad to hear it. Murdoch's baby looks quite bright."

"They usually do."

"What shall we call him? I am so out of touch."

"Berlin?" suggested Morris.

"He must be getting on. Isn't there a psychologist with a name like a Dutchman?"

"Eysenck? He isn't Oxford. I suppose you could endow a chair for him, but . . ."

"The camera, man!" snapped the Sultan.

Morris pressed the starter button of the fixed camera which covered about two-thirds of the grove, then checked how much film there was left to run; when he looked again through the window he saw that Murdoch's baby, in one of its forays, had strayed within Dinah's reach and she had grabbed it. Now she had it face down across her thigh and was beginning to peer and finger among the hairs along its spine. Through the glass they could not hear its little whimpers, but Murdoch's scream was clear enough as she rose from her torpor and rushed over at Dinah, who with equal speed, still holding the baby, flung herself up the wire mesh and leaped for one of the central trees. Murdoch followed her route and, having both arms free, had almost caught up when Dinah swung to the next tree, dangled for an instant from one of the metal branches, and simply dropped. She fell heavily on Sparrow's back, let the baby fall and clutched to steady herself at Sparrow's neck.

Certainly Sparrow was in a nervous state. He shot across the floor just as if he were starting a male chimpanzee's charging display, but with Dinah still clinging to his back like a rucksack with one strap broken. Murdoch snatched up her baby and rushed with it to the furthest end of the cage, where she stood for a while chattering angrily at the group, until she settled to possessive grooming of the much-groomed infant. Meanwhile Dinah had

9

let go of Sparrow, who, having reached the end of the cage and tried in vain to wrench a metal branch from a concrete tree, came charging straight back at her, swinging his right arm as if he were twirling a club.

By all jungle rights she ought to have cowered out of his way, probably presenting her rump to him. But as the main relationship in her life had been with Morris her experience of male domination had been, to say the least, mild. Besides she always had a tricky temper when you removed from her a toy with which she had not finished playing, and no doubt that was how she thought of Murdoch's baby; so she stood her ground and hooted back at Sparrow. Morris hardly noticed the glass of the window slide up.

Sparrow halted in the middle of his charge and began to bounce up and down, chattering back. Now both arms were swinging, and Dinah was losing confidence. Suddenly, close at Morris's ear, there came a sharp whoof, and in the same instant Sparrow made a three-foot leap, straight in the air. When he landed he stood stock still, peering with horror at the shiny dart that now protruded from his right thigh; a wary hand came down and plucked it out. He inspected it with glazing curiosity for several seconds before he crumpled to the floor.

Dinah, still snickering with fury, came forward and pissed on the fallen body, a reaction of a sort that Morris had never seen from her before—nor did he remember reading about it in any of the literature. Rowse, whose lethargy had been partly alleviated by the drama, came slowly over and grunted warningly at Dinah, who this time had the sense to retreat. Rowse pinched Sparrow experimentally three or four times, then returned to the group with the express purpose of dislodging old Cecil from his place against a tree and thus establishing himself as leader of the group. The window slid shut. Morris stopped the camera and turned to the Sultan, who was standing with the squat spring-gun cradled on his arm, waiting smugly for applause. Behind him his enormous black bodyguard, Dyal, grinned with simple pleasure. And behind *him* the stuffed gorilla they used for target practice grinned too, with simulated fury.

Morris's fury was real.

"Christ!" he said.

"You must mean 'Allah!'" said the Sultan.

10

"I mean," said Morris slowly, "how the hell do you expect Dinah to integrate naturally with the group if every time there's any kind of confrontation her opponent collapses at her feet? This experiment is your idea, not mine, so for God's sake get it into your head that the whole point of putting her down there at all is to let her begin to find her place in the social hierarchy. You want her to mate and have a baby. How's that going to happen if every time a male looks at her he suddenly falls flat on his face?"

"It was a good shot, don't you think?" said the Sultan. "He was bouncing up and down, but I got him just in that big vein that runs down inside the thigh. In fact it was a perfectly beautiful shot. He went out like a light, didn't he?"

"It was a complete fluke," said Morris.

"Oh, come, these guns aren't as inaccurate as all that."

"What's more, it was high-grade hooliganism. You're a bloody trigger-happy . . ."

His anger tailed away in the knowledge that it would be an error actually to call the Sultan a wog to his face. His Pacific Majesty got a kick out of a relationship in which Morris was the only man in all Q'Kut who could speak to him without subservience, but he also possessed a generous ration of his race's cunning for avenging an insult.

"I really must protect my investment," said the Sultan. "After all, I am paying Dinah ten thousand dollars a month."

"You are paying me!"

"Of course, of course, my dear fellow. I do apologise. I'm a bloody trigger-happy wog. Hello! What gives?"

From the doors of the zoo a wheezy flute tootled. Dyal made a clucking noise in his throat and strode off down the inspection gallery. The Sultan handed Morris the empty spring-gun, picked up the old one which he used for practice, swung round and fired from the hip at the stuffed gorilla. Instantly the dart (also an old, expended one) was there, glistening in the middle of the bare, heroic chest. The Sultan reloaded and fired again. By the time Dyal returned the gorilla was wearing a precisely spaced row of darts from his windpipe to his midriff, like buttons on a fancy waistcoat. Dyal whispered a few words. The Sultan nodded. Dyal waved to the jet-black eunuch who had appeared by the doors, then strode away to the gorilla to retrieve the darts.

11

The eunuch beckoned to someone out of sight. After a brief pause a white-robed Arab crawled round the corner on hands and knees. He paused, raised his splendidly bearded head and looked down the vista to where his master stood. Doggedly he lowered his head and crawled forward. Long practice had made him expert in the knack of not kneeling on his beard.

By Morris's side the spring-gun whoofed. He turned and saw that Dyal was now decorating the gorilla's chest with a neat row of medals, while the Sultan watched critically. Their backs were towards the crawling man.

"For God's sake!" whispered Morris.

The Sultan turned and looked unimpressed at the new arrival.

"Can't you let him off?" whispered Morris. "My nerves won't stand it! He'll have a heart attack before he gets here!"

"What will you bet?"

"For Christ's sake! OK, for Allah's sake!"

"We'll make a believer of you yet," said the Sultan. All the same he called in ultra-gracious tones to let the man know that he was, this once, permitted to approach his sovereign with the gait of a fellow human. The man rose, bowed deeply and came impassively forward. Looking at him Morris was conscious that he had somehow managed to lose yet another minor engagement with his employer. Akuli bin Zair, major domo of the Palace and effectively Prime Minister of Q'Kut, was not exactly an enemy of Morris's, but he was not the man to appreciate any departure from ancient custom. Although they had never had any conversation apart from the stateliest compliments in classical Arabic, Morris knew bin Zair to be a bigoted opponent of any kind of Westernisation, especially when it took the form of research into the linguistic abilities of unclean beasts. He would certainly not have come to the zoo unless he had important and urgent business to transact, and Morris wanted no part of that. It was clearly time to withdraw.

"Be seeing you," he whispered, and withdrew—backwards, because bin Zair's eyes were on him, and there was no point in offending the old gnome. And anyway it was good practice for court functions.

* * *

The palace was a fantasy, so the zoo was a fantasy inside a fantasy. The palace was square in plan—so far, so rational—but each floor was wider than the one below it, so that seen from a distance across the desert dunes the building looked like an inverted ziggurat, a giant's teetotum perched on its tiny podium, ready to topple at a breath of wind. In fact it was a fantasy of reason. That is to say the architects maintained that its absurd shape was the rational solution to building a palace in the appalling conditions of Q'Kut. It never rained in the Sultanate; the strongest wind of the locality could barely animate an anemometer; the nearest earthquake zone was a thousand miles away; so what could upset the balance? On the other hand, built as it was, each floor gave shade to the one below from the flogging sun, and the roof offered the widest possible expanse to the solar panels that provided much of the energy for the palace's gadgetry. And supposing the Arabs or the marshmen revolted, there was a remarkably small perimeter to defend at ground level. But despite all these good reasons you had only to look at the thing and see it was absurd.

The spindle of this teetotum was the lift-shaft. If you were a woman or a eunuch you entered at ground-level a lift whose doors opened only into the women's quarters. If you were a man you used the lift that backed on to this, and could reach any other section of the palace. If you were a white rhino, you used the big bleak service lift, which had doors at either end and so could reach any part of the palace—but the arrival of the current rhino had strained the machinery and it was still waiting repair. There was also a stairway running beside the lifts, but as the architects had lacked the ingenuity to prevent this from passing through the women's quarters it was barred by locked doors at several points. The zoo occupied a third of the top floor of the palace, so when the men's lift was out of order Morris could only reach his work from his living-quarters, two floors below, by being blindfolded and led stumbling up several flights by scimitar-toting eunuchs. Luckily this lift was going through a good patch.

The visitor to the zoo came out of the lift into a lobby, on the far side of which were the double doors of the zoo itself. Beyond these a very short passage finished in the inspection gallery, which ran at right-angles to it across the entire width of the palace.

This was a straight, tiled passage, as wide as a small lane. Against the wall that held the doors stood cases of zoological specimens, none of any interest whatever, and a few stuffed animals. On the other side the wall was pocked by the regular pattern of the rectangular inspection windows and the knobby excrescences of the fixed cameras. The visitor could watch the animals, unseen by them, through the polarised glass; here he would be standing about eight feet above the floor of the cages. Alternatively he could walk round to where a parallel gallery ran in front of the cages, at their own level. Down there he could be inspected as well as inspect, for the inner wall was the wire-mesh front of the cages; the outer wall was all glass, enabling animals and visitor alike to gaze, if they chose, eighty miles eastward across the glaring sands. At dawn the rising sun shone horizontal into the cages, but within an hour it was hidden by the final brim of the palace roof.

These two galleries were joined at either end by transverse passages, set far enough in from the outer walls to leave space for store-rooms at the southern end, and at the northern one for Morris's office and surgery. Morris, whom we left reversing along the upper gallery, felt his way round the corner into this northern passage, stopped, muttered under his breath, turned and walked down a short flight of steps into his office. He was still muttering as he reloaded the spring-gun with a fresh dart containing a chimp-size dose of anaesthetic and clicked it into the rack beside the spare gun. He shut the doors of the gun-cupboard, turned right outside his office and walked round into the lower gallery. Going this way he came at once to the front of the chimpanzee glade.

Before Morris's arrival, eighteen months ago, the zoo had had the highest mortality rate of any in the world; monotonously the smuggled orangs had died, and the target gorilla was only one of a sad series. Typically, the Sultan was not interested in owning small, manageable animals; so there had always been empty cages. The glade had been constructed by amalgamating five of these, with the dens behind them, leaving the concrete tree-trunks to support the roof. Some of the metal branches were supposed to extrude oranges at the touch of a button, but few of these worked; occasionally Morris had crept in, like Santa Claus, in

14

the dead of night and tied bunches of bananas to the lower branches, but the chimpanzees took this phenomenon for granted and were no more interested than when he dumped their fruit on the floor through the usual chute—part of the plan was that they shouldn't connect humans with food.

Now as he came round the corner he saw that the scene had hardly changed. Sparrow was still inert on the floor; Rowse had succeeded in dislodging Cecil and was now carefully grooming him to show that there was no ill-will; and Dinah was still separated from the rest of the group, but had picked the dart up and was edging her way innocently round the cage with the clear intention of prodding it into Murdoch. But when Morris clicked his fingers for her attention she came rushing to the door, with the dart poised to jab at him. He hoped that this was her experimental urge showing itself, and not malice.

He backed off, extended his right hand palm up and flapped his fingers towards himself several times. He regarded manual sign language as unscientific, but for day-to-day living with a chimpanzee a quick way of saying "Give me that" is essential.

Dinah took hold of the door with both feet and one hand and rattled it hard. Morris made the give-me sign again. Dinah stopped shaking the door and hung considering. She obviously wanted to be let out of the cage, but realised that the dart held better bargaining power than that; she might even guess he was going to let her out anyway, so giving him the dart for nothing would be a waste. At any rate she smacked her huge lips together several times, returned the give-me sign, then stuck the fingers of one hand in her mouth: "Food."

With a sigh Morris knelt by the door, unslung his satchel and spilt the coloured chips of plastic into its lid. Dinah panted with pleasure and squatted down inside the bars to join the game. Morris sorted deftly through the pile, chose the counters he needed and poked them through the door to form a line just in front of her.

large blue triangle:	first conditional
white square:	Dinah
yellow circle with hole:	give
yellow square:	thing with no name

15

blue square:	(to) Morris
small blue triangle:	second conditional
blue square:	Morris
yellow circle with hole:	give
green/blue striped square:	banana
white square:	(to) Dinah

Dinah peered at the symbols as though she were much more short-sighted than in fact she was, sniffing along the line of them in a rhythmic quick-time. She laid the dart down on the yellow square to confirm its identity, but kept a firm hold on it while she did so. (Morris had never cheated her in her life, and could hardly imagine circumstances in which he might be forced to do so, but the possibility seemed to remain vivid in her mind.) She chattered thoughtfully to herself for a few seconds, then made the give-me sign and gestured towards the satchel. Eagerly she picked out the blue/white striped square that meant grapes, then hunted fastidiously until she found the little black triangle they used for the connective conjunction. She added them right at the end of the line and studied her revised message; clearly she realised there was something wrong with it, but it took her some time to discover what, twelve symbols being near the limit of sentence-length she could cope with. At last she moved the second white square to the end of the sentence.

Immediately Morris snatched up a red circle, larger than most of the others, and slapped it down on the floor.

red circle: negative

He was shocked. A banana *and* grapes! Her victory over Sparrow had given her inflated ideas.

She lurched away from the door and chattered up and down the wire mesh. The other chimpanzees eyed her sidelong, like xenophobic villagers watching one of their girls flirting with a passing hiker. On her second return to the door she sulkily removed the green/blue square and the black triangle. Morris considered a moment: to give in would be a depraving act, but it would stem from the Sultan's trigger-finger, an organ beyond anyone's control; and anyway the Sultan was paying for the grapes, at around three pounds a bunch. He found a green circle and replied.

green circle: positive

He fished back through the bars all the counters except the second, third and fourth of his original sentence; obediently Dinah passed him the dart. As soon as the door was open she snatched at his hand and smacking her lips tried to drag him along the corridor. The other chimps, stirred by her food-noises, came ambling over; Morris only freed himself just in time to prevent the crowd of them bundling out into the corridor. Rowse picked up the yellow circle with the hole in it and bit it in two, but after a couple of chews spat out the gnawed fragments and handed the other half to Cecil to try. Morris retrieved the other two symbols and closed his satchel.

As soon as he was on his feet Dinah made a leap for his shoulders. He hitched his arm contentedly under her buttocks, adjusted himself to her weight and walked on down the corridor; by going the long way round he could cast an eye over the rest of the zoo, and also avoid passing the Sultan and bin Zair. The polar bear was swimming, huge in its tiny pool; he paused and watched it with vague guilt; but for him it would have died months ago, and though he did not believe that its soul would have gone to roam the dazzling ice-floes east-north-east of the Pearly Gates, he did feel that it would be better for such a creature not to exist than to be cramped in this mean, expensive prison. Only the Sultan would then have imported another polar bear. He was proud of owning the one that held the world record for nearness to the goddam equator.

Dinah still had the memory of grapes on her mind's tongue, so Morris walked on when she hooted in his ear to remind him. There were several things that combined to console him for the complex indignities of Q'Kut—the ten thousand dollars a month, the Sultan's erratic friendship, the excitingly strange and wonderful language of the marshmen, the absence of serious personal relationships and responsibilities—but Dinah was more important than any of these things. He was glad that the gradual process of integration into the society of the new chimps didn't seem to be spoiling her relationship with him.

As he waited for the lift that would take him two floors down to his own living quarters he realised that it would have been a bitter blow if she had preferred Sparrow's company.

2

Dinah ate her grapes with slow, concentrating enjoyment, perched up in her nest and peering at each one like a jeweller inspecting an emerald for flaws. Prince Hadiq, accompanied by the usual weedy Somali slave carrying the *Batman* comics, arrived for his English lesson before she had finished. He looked at her for some seconds while he fought with words.

"I am . . . want . . . the grapes . . . above," he muttered.

"I would like some grapes too, please," corrected Morris. He tried to sound patient, but his residual bad temper over the shooting of Sparrow came clearly through.

The Prince pouted. His fine but childish features became set as he started on the construction of another sentence. Morris found the process agonising to watch. He could never achieve imaginative sympathy with anyone, even a clever child like this, who could not pick up a language in a few weeks, so he swung away and looked through the window as though he was interested in the unappealing view.

There was only one hill in that part of Q'Kut, not counting dunes. The palace stood on its summit, ninety feet above the dead levels where the marshes seemed to bounce and heave in the glaring noonday heat. In the foreground the new concrete of the airstrip blazed like a white-hot ingot, painful to look at despite the double layer of tinted glass. But everything else that Morris could see was coloured the same sulky khaki and wavered before his eyes as the heated air rose in different columns above reed-bed and mud-bank and water-course and lagoon. Q'Kut was one of those places where you expected to see further by night than by day; when the heat-haze condensed into dew Morris could usually make out the black line of the hill ranges, ninety miles away on the borders of the tiny sultanate, but now he couldn't even see the nearest stand of giant pig-reed three miles beyond the air-strip.

"You are give me better honour unless I tell my father will make you flodge," said the prince all in one squeaky breath.

"Flogged," corrected Morris automatically. But he had seen the child's reflection in the tinted glass, and the misery of pride made inadequate. Morris hated that sort of thing, hated being exposed to it. And the prince would never have allowed him to see it direct. Really, it wasn't a bad shot at a very complex conditional sentence—passion finds its own expression. Morris turned with a sigh, put the palms of his hands together, lowered his head respectfully and spoke in formal Arabic.

"Serene rivulet of the fountain of power and wisdom, it is many years since thy father honoured me with the undeserved gift of his friendship. No man knows the heart of another, but I have learnt some of thy father's ways. If thou wast to go to him complaining of my insolence, he would not satisfy thee, but he would invent some subtle manner whereby thy complaint could be used to diminish both thee and me. Is it not written 'Ask not of the King that which the King cannot give, for thereby is his glory the less.'? Therefore let us come to an agreement. When we speak in Arabic we will conduct ourselves in the manner of Arabs, among whom thou art a prince, and so shall I treat thee. But when in obedience to thy father's command we speak English, we will conduct ourselves in the manner of the English, from whom Allah has withheld the comprehension of honour."

"Their mothers are she-asses."

"In many cases thy observation is just. But when thy father speaks with me in English he condescends to answer bray with bray."

"Why may the ape feast on grapes when they are denied to a prince?"

Morris picked up the satchel.

"Dinah will get you some grapes if you ask her," he said slowly in English.

"Yes, yes," said the prince, suddenly thrilled. He was both jealous of and fascinated by Dinah. Morris sorted the necessary symbols on to the coffee-table.

"What they mean?" said the prince.

"What *do* they mean?"

"What do they mean?"

"Good. You can say the words as we put them down."

white crescent:	please
white square:	Dinah
yellow circle with hole:	give
blue/white square:	grapes
black square:	(to) person other than Morris or Dinah

"The prince must say please to the ape?"

"Well . . ." said Morris, then shrugged. It was a nice point. Neither Dinah nor the symbol language was covered by the new agreement.

"OK, OK," said the prince charmingly. Morris clicked his fingers for Dinah's attention and she climbed carefully down from her nest on top of the wardrobe, dangling from her left paw the forlorn skeleton of her bunch of grapes. The Prince arranged the symbols in a very precise line.

The coffee-table was just the right height for Dinah to read from when she was on all fours, and she did so with her usual quick sniffing sound, as though she somehow smelt the meaning. The message puzzled her. She read it three times, then with a dubious gesture offered the grape-skeleton to the prince, who backed away as if it were something the Koran declared unclean. Morris sorted through the satchel again and made a second message.

yellow square:	thing with no name
red circle with hole:	negative verb
blue/white square:	grapes

Dinah sniffed at the symbols, laid the grape-skeleton down on the yellow square and sniffed at the symbols again. She chattered a little to herself as she re-read the first message, then moved resolutely towards the kitchen door, where she stopped and glanced at Morris over her shoulder. He made a "Go" gesture to her.

The buzzer sounded as soon as she broke the beam to the photo-electric cell. The prince laughed. She looked back and Morris made the "Go" gesture again. With a nervous leap she was gone.

"She is not take?" asked the prince.

"No, she will not take anything. But please will you give her a few of the grapes when she comes back?"

"I give," asserted the prince, ". . . a few."

Morris smiled. The boy was his father's son, in his quick calculation of the possible profits of generosity. Dinah emerged with the stalk of a bunch of grapes clenched in her fist and offered them to Morris, who had the negative red circle ready and showed it to her. She sniffed again at the message on the coffee-table, frowning; then, with the same hesitation and doubt she often showed in the early stages of learning a new skill, she offered them to the prince. He carefully broke off a twig of grapes and handed them to her. She smacked her lips and leaped for her nest with them.

Morris got up and stopped the buzzer. For a moment he thought there was something wrong with his ears, but the prince, too, was frowning and staring at the ceiling.

"Aeroplane!" he said, first in Arabic and then in English.

"Big!" he added after a few seconds.

Morris nodded. Q'Kut was not on any conceivable route from anywhere to anywhere. The air-strip's only users were the Sultan's executive jet and the old Dakota that flew in such luxuries as grapes and apes. The sweating Italians who manned the oil-derricks, up in the hills on the far side of the marshes, had their own strip, but by the sound of it this plane was aiming to land here. Already the prince was crouched against the window, craning for a sight of it.

"Lo!" he squeaked in Arabic. "See! See! See!" he added in English.

Morris strolled over, uneasy, but could see nothing because of the overhang of the floor above. He knelt to bring himself to the prince's level and immediately saw the big red and blue plane whining away with flaps down and black smoke streaking from its four jets. The prince bounced with the thrill of it.

"Am coming!" he squeaked.

"It is coming. I hope to God not. The strip's too short."

But the wings tilted sharply. Now the plane was curving towards the south, showing all its upper half to the glare of the sun; the curve tightened and the gap between the machine and the marshes grew less and less. Now, by sleight-of-air, the plane seemed to vanish for several seconds as it pointed straight towards the palace; and now it was a slant dark line in the wavering sky, jerking among the erratic thermals. At last the pilot levelled for the runway.

"Christ!" said Morris, "he'll never make it! Those things need thousands of feet!"

Burnt rubber smoked behind the braking wheels. Some of the tyres seemed to be tearing themselves into strips. The huge plane hurtled down the concrete towards the dunes, bucketing as the pilot fought to hold it steady. A wing tip almost touched the ground. The plane slewed, still doing about eighty mph. When it was sideways on half the undercarriage collapsed, but the machine went sliding along the concrete. The blind, tiny panes of the flight deck smashed all together, blasted out by an inexplicable small explosion. The prince squealed. Morris shut his eyes, though he knew flames would be invisible in that sunlight.

The telephone rang.

Morris opened his eyes again and stared at the scene. The plane lay still, thirty yards from the end of the runway, with its tail towards the dunes and its near wing resting on the concrete. Still no flames. The symbol of the rising sun stared from the tall tail fin. The telephone was still ringing, so he picked it up.

"Morris, old fellow?"

"Yes, it's me. What the hell was all that about?"

"A slight emergency. I need your help. Would you be kind enough to go down to the runway and greet any survivors?"

"Survivors?"

"Some buffoon was sitting in the cockpit with a live grenade in his hand, but it looks as if he dropped it in the landing. There ought to be somebody alive in the cabin, though, so I'd be terribly grateful if you . . ."

"Me?"

"Pick up a walkie-talkie as you go and tune in on channel A. We had radio contact with them, but its gone dead. The thing is, old fellow, that this is one of those hijack jobs—Palestinians, but they made a mess of it."

"I'm a zoo-keeper, dammit!"

22

"By this word we, Pacific Sultan of Q'Kut, Lord of the Marsh-lands, etc, etc, appoint our trusty and well-beloved companion Wesley Naboth Morris to the office and privileges of Foreign Minister of Q'Kut, for such period as shall please us. Thanks be to Allah!"

"Balls."

"Look, Morris, I need you. It's got to be someone who speaks Japanese, for a start. And someone I can trust, to go on with. You won't need to take any decisions—I'll be on Channel A."

"Something's happening."

The emergency door at the root of the tilted wing opened, and a figure walked precariously out and down the slope.

"There *are* survivors, you see," said the Sultan softly. "Carry on, Morris—Dyal and I will have you covered from here. Don't get out of sight."

"Oh, all right," said Morris.

"I'm afraid you'll have to walk. Before the radio went dead they said just one man, on foot, to meet them."

"What! In this sun!"

"Take a brolly-man. He won't count."

"Oh, all *right*!"

Morris snapped the phone down. He found it hard to compose himself enough to explain in courteous Arabic to the prince that their lesson must be postponed. Before he had finished that Dinah chattered nervously at him from her nest, and he realised that he hadn't time to dispose of her. He'd have to take her along. He clicked, and she came rushing over. Thoughtlessly, as if for reassurance in this daunting and unwelcome task, he took her hand and led her out.

3

Sweat streamed in prickling rivulets all down Morris's skin. He walked slowly, to lessen the risk of heat-stroke and allow for the pace of the brolly-man behind him. His sunglasses were not quite big enough to eliminate all the glare from the side. He felt a fool, and frightened.

"Testing, testing, one two three four," he said.

"My dear fellow, I know you can count," hissed the expensive gadget in his shirt pocket. "I've got her bang in my sights. By Jove, that's what I call a figure!"

The walkie-talkie smacked its metal lips. Warily Morris peered across the concrete furnace—he still had a hundred yards to go. He wished that the hijackers had allowed him to come in a car—the bullet-proof one would have done fine. The girl posed on the wing had a nasty-looking gun at her hip, which distracted Morris's attention from what the Sultan considered her finer points. She was dark-haired and brown-skinned, slim in her blouse and jeans. Visor-like sunglasses hid her eyes, but her nose had a hawkish look. Her stance was tired but confident, quite different from the deflated exhaustion of the dozen people who stood grouped before her on the concrete, covered by her gun.

Dinah whimpered and tugged at Morris's hand to be carried. It was too hot for that—but then he realised how the concrete must be burning her feet and picked her up. She clung to his side, shading her eyes against the glare.

"Stop," called the girl in Arabic. "That is near enough."

She had the words right, but her accent was appalling. She called again as Morris came on and waved the gun his way. Then she tried French, which she spoke even worse. Morris became more confident as he approached. It was too hot to shout over distances.

"I insist that you stop," she said suddenly in perfectly good English, clipped and officer-like.

Morris walked on until he was about ten feet from the wing-tip, where he and the girl and her captives formed the points of an equilateral triangle. He took the sweat-towel which the brolly-man carried, folded it and put it on the ground in the shade of the brolly. Thankfully he dumped Dinah on it, then turned and bowed to the captives.

"His Pacific Majesty the Sultan of Q'Kut conveys his greetings," he said in Japanese. "He is honoured to receive you in Q'Kut."

The captives stiffened with surprise and hope. Several of them returned his bow. He turned to the girl.

"Is anybody injured?" he said in English.

"No," she snapped. "Who are you? What powers do you have?"

24

"My name is Doctor Wesley Morris, and I am Foreign Minister of Q'Kut. I am also in radio contact with His Majesty."

"Fine," she said. "You can tell his nibs I . . . we want a new plane, with a pilot, and food and drink. We demand these things in the name of Arab solidarity, for the liberation of Palestine."

Morris muttered into the walkie-talkie.

"Yes, yes," answered the Sultan. "A pilot? See if you can find out what happened to the other one. And there ought to be three guerrillas."

"Get on with it," snapped the girl.

"Listen, Morris," said the walkie-talkie, "I'll have to back these goons up to keep my Arabs quiet, though privately I say pooh to Palestine. But the oil company is run by a rabid bunch of absentee Zionists. I want no part of any of this. They only landed here because some idiots at Karachi tried to shoot their tyres out and got a fuel pipe as well."

"Get on with it," said the girl again. "Or I'll shoot that chimp to show I mean business."

"His majesty is an ardent supporter of the Palestinian cause," said Morris, "but regrets that he has no plane or pilot available."

"He can have one flown in," said the girl. "We'll get back into the plane and wait—I don't think it's going to catch fire after all."

"In that case you will all die of heat-stroke," said Morris.

"Don't give me that," said the girl. "Come on you lot."

"This is a comparatively cool day," said Morris. "To-morrow will probably be twenty degrees hotter."

He turned to the captives and asked in Japanese whether any of them knew whether the air-conditioning was still working. There was a mutter among the group. A square, blue-suited businessman moved to one side and allowed Morris to see that there were two diminutive air hostesses standing among the men, limp little rag dolls in pretty kimonos.

"We think the air-conditioning is now broken," said one of them. "We think also the pilots and two of the attackers are dead. One attacker was holding a grenade with the pin drawn, on the flight deck, when we landed, and there was a big explosion before the aeroplane stopped."

The she-guerrilla's gun was now wavering vaguely from the

25

captives to Morris and back again. Morris translated quietly into the walkie-talkie and listened to the reply.

"Christ," he whispered, "that's a hell of a risk. Are you sure ...'

"Quite sure, old fellow. I'm enjoying myself."

Morris licked his lips.

"His Majesty requests you to stand quite still," he said to the girl. "He is about to shoot out the window by your left hip—for God's sake don't move."

Her mouth opened. None of them heard the crack of the rifle, only the snap and tinkle when the bullet hit the thick glass. The group on the concrete gasped and closed up, but one of the men clapped his hands. Dinah copied him vigorously.

"You see," said Morris. "I believe your companions are dead, and two first-class shots have you in their sights. Would you please put that gun down?"

She moved a long, fine finger to touch the bullet hole, as if to make sure it was not a trick one from a joke-shop.

"I must point out," said Morris, "that even by Arab standards Q'Kutis put a low value on human life."

Suddenly she crouched, put the gun on the wing beside her and covered her eyes with the inside of her wrists. The man in the blue suit stole quietly forward, reached up and took the gun, but she stayed motionless, stuck in her foetal huddle. The walkie-talkie laughed.

"Stow it," muttered Morris angrily. "And send us a few cars out, mate, and someone to take charge of the girl. You're not appointing me chief of police."

"My dear fellow, you've done it beautifully. One of those air hostesses doesn't look a bad bit of skirt either."

Morris clicked the gadget off. An absolute monarch has many powers, but he can't gloat at you if you're out of earshot. Then he walked across to the passengers, leaving the patient brolly-man to shade Dinah.

"His Majesty is delighted to announce that you are now safe," he said. "He will be sending some cars to take you to the palace, but there will be a few minutes' wait. I suggest you move into the shade of the aeroplane."

The man in the blue suit handed him the gun, which he took unwillingly. Dinah started begging to play with it as soon as he

26

reached the shade of the brolly. He switched the walkie-talkie on again.

"How does the safety-catch on this bloody thing work?" he said.

"Ah, you're back in circulation, old fellow. What model is it?"

"Don't ask me."

"Try pointing it at the sand-dune and pulling the trigger. Hold it firm, though."

Morris did as he was told. Nothing happened.

"Safety-catch on, then," said the Sultan. "Now listen, Morris. I'm sending Dyal out with the cars—he'll take charge of the girl. He's bringing robes and veils for the women—he'll be there in a couple of minutes. You've just got time to go and see whether there's anyone alive in the plane. OK?"

"I suppose so."

With extreme reluctance Morris moved towards the wing. Dinah whimpered at him and he turned. More for reassurance in his grisly task than anything else he handed the gun to the brolly-man and allowed Dinah to climb into his arms. As they went up the wing the girl didn't move.

Inside the plane the plush tunnel reeked of sweat and hot plastic and something else—fear, Morris thought. Animals can smell fear, old wives say. Dinah was certainly very clinging, and it took him some time to persuade her to let go of him and settle into one of the seats. He showed her the tilt button and left her trying to make it produce bananas.

Fear, he thought as he hesitated by the door on to the flight deck. You'd be able to set up an experiment to check whether the old wives' tale is true—group of animals with strong sense of smell—raccoons?—sever olfactory nerve of half of them—find human volunteers to be frightened—how? How? Why by putting them one side of a metal door, tell them that there may be an armed man, wounded, dangerous, on the other side, and then telling them to open the door—which, they would note, was out of shape and torn in a couple of places by fragments of grenade casing.

There wasn't a sound in the plane except for Dinah fidgeting with the unproductive button. Morris found it hard to turn the door-handle, slippery with the sweat from his own palm. When he pushed, something resisted on the far side. He pushed harder and the thing gave, reluctantly. New smells came through the crack, a warm, wet odour mixed with the stink of something burnt; but nothing moved. He put his shoulder to the door and felt the resistance slither away. He looked in, swallowing hard to keep the vomit down, and stared at the mess of blood-spattered instruments and broken glass and shabby leather and smashed men. One, two, three, four, five—five heads, anyway, though one had no face—and two of the wrenched torsos wore khaki shirts.

He pulled the door shut and stood gulping.

Behind him Dinah chattered suddenly, and he turned. She was crouched in the luggage rack, trying to take a picture of him with a miniature camera she had found.

"Morris?" said the walkie-talkie.

"I'm OK. There are five dead men on the flight deck. Two of them aren't wearing the airline uniform."

"Spendid, perfectly splendid. The cars are almost there, so you'd better come out. You don't sound too good."

"I'm OK, I tell you."

Morris clicked for Dinah's attention but she snuggled away from him on a nest of coats, hugging the camera to her crotch. He clicked again, making her twist her head to look sulkily back at him. He spread his hands, palm up, making a slight pushing gesture towards her: the I-give sign. Her expression changed to one of farcical surprise as she stared to and fro between him and her new toy, as though thinking it might be booby-trapped; then she catapulted off the rack into his arms.

Out in the furnace air he saw five of the Cadillacs sliding across the runway. He stood on the wing and gestured at them with his free arm, making four of them circle round to the nose of the plane while the fifth stopped beside the brolly-man. In the group beneath the fuselage one of the passengers was now lying supine on the concrete with a stewardess kneeling beside him and loosening his collar. Morris went hurriedly down the wing, but when he put Dinah back on her towel she scampered straight across the concrete, opened the front passenger door of the nearest car and jumped inside.

"There's a stretcher in one of those cars," said the walkie-talkie. "I meant it for the bodies, but you might as well use it for that bloke."

Morris organised a couple of the chatterbox drivers to cope with the patient, a wizened little Japanese still stertorously breathing. Then he called to Dyal who came striding over, huge and seeming blacker than ever in the hateful sun. Morris took two of the robes from his arm and turned to the air hostesses.

"The Sultan is most honoured by your presence," he said in Japanese, "and has already expressed to me his admiration of your beauty. So it is with double regret that he requests you to veil yourselves, according to the custom of the country."

Through all the weariness and disintegration their trained smiles flicked alight, like a cuckoo clock striking in a bomb-smashed house. They even started to giggle as they swathed each other in the robes. Morris walked across with Dyal to the girl on the wing. Her pose was of such abject defeat that he spoke to her apologetically.

"We're going now," he said. "We'll send out men to bring in the bodies of your friends."

She didn't move.

"I'm afraid you'll have to wear a veil till you're in the women's quarters," he went on, a bit despairingly now. But she looked up and reached down her hand for the robes. Below the sunglasses her cheeks were smeared with tears. She rose to her feet, towering above him, and tossed the robe away with an arrogant gesture

"I'm not wearing that gear," she declaimed. "That's one of the things it's all about. You can shoot me first."

From the way she spoke there might have been a vast audience gathered on the air-strip, listening to this declaration of a basic human liberty. At any rate she spoke loud enough for the walkie-talkie to pick her words up.

"Beautiful, beautiful," said the Sultan. "The two male goons arrive dead, and the female one's first act is to flout local Arab feelings. You may tell her that I have no intention of making her a martyr to fashion."

But the girl was already stalking down the wing towards the Cadillac, as though it had been ordered for her by some millionaire admirer. She was a bit nonplussed to find Dinah already occupying the front seat.

Morris watched her out of the corner of his eye as the car slid towards the palace. His own nerves were completely shredded, but the other two seemed quite cool, although Dyal's finger was on the trigger of his gun and its muzzle no more than six inches from her left breast. She seemed to relax and soften in the lovely air-conditioning, lolling against the golden silk upholstery. When she spoke her tone was adjusted to polite party conversation.

"I hope you don't mind my asking," she said, "but if you're Foreign Minister, who's that? First Secretary?"

She pointed at Dinah, who was playing with the radio controls.

"Well, as a matter of fact I'm the zoo-keeper too," muttered Morris.

"That proves it," she said. She made an elegant little gesture towards the startling shape of the palace, outlined on its hill against the ferocious sky.

"I'd already decided that whoever built that place must be absolutely giddy bonkers."

Morris was so surprised by the phrase that he turned and stared straight at her. She returned his stare, lowering her sun-glasses to do so.

Her eyes, still a bit swollen with weeping, were a pale, pale northern blue. He was too startled to speak, but his mouth twitched as though it were trying to find sentences of its own.

Two

1

In a sealed and seasonless environment, such as the palace, it
was difficult to judge the passage of time. Morris used the wrecked
aeroplane as an erratic calendar, judging the weeks since its landing
by the amount of it that remained unstolen. Despite the three
turbaned guards who sat gambling in its shade the whole machine
was gradually disappearing. The baffled engineers who had come
to study the problem of flying it back to civilisation would soon
have no problem left—the aeroplane would simply have dissolved
like an object acted upon by two powerful acids, the thieving
aboriginals of the marshes and the thieving Arabs of the sands.
Morris saw that another large chunk had been sawn from the tail
fin: that made it about five weeks since that nightmare day.
(If it has been possible for him to peer through the surface of
time, instead of seeing only the reflected past he would have
been able to watch a different process of disintegration, and used
it to measure the two weeks and two days that remained before
the murders.)

Meanwhile the haze above the marshes had steadily thickened,
as it was bound to do when the floods were at their height.
Something was happening at the marsh edge, where the first
reeds rose—a small body of men, mostly slaves, stood there.
Four of the slaves carried a blue canopy, fringed with gold.
Another carried a long pole with a wicker box at the top. Morris
fetched his binoculars and saw that a little Arab was sitting on
a carry-chair beneath the canopy; he was dressed all in
white, and his grey beard flowed to his waist; it could only be bin
Zair.

31

As Morris came to this conclusion the group stirred and bin Zair rose from his chair. Morris lowered his binoculars and saw that a long canoe was emerging from a channel between the reeds, paddled by a dozen naked marshmen, all as black as the blackest negro. Like most marshmen they were small and scrawny, and so was the man who stood near the bows holding a pole with a box at the top, similar to the one on the shore. But the man who sat in the stern, clothed all in white, looked really big, as big as the Sultan or Dyal, though his face was as black as any of the others'. He hadn't been there last year.

Last year! Time suddenly became solid and exact.

This day last year Morris had stood at the window with Kwan beside him, and the gaunt old marshman had explained the meaning of the ceremony. It was a preparation for the flood-going feast, at which the compact between the first Arab conqueror of Q'Kut and the last free ruler of the marshmen was celebrated and re-stated. According to Kwan the boxes on the ends of the poles contained the mummified right hands of the two heroes.

Morris turned away from the window. Three days after the flood-going feast last year Kwan had been dead, and Morris still missed him.

With a shrug he went to his little work-bench, unlocked a Dinah-proof drawer and took out a sheet of blue plastic. Marking out a precise row of blue crosses was soothing work, and as soon as his little jig-saw began to whine Dinah woke and filled his mind completely. She was always thrilled with excitement when Morris started to cut new symbols, and then unmanageable with disappointment if they merely turned out to be replacements for ones which she had lost or broken, or simply hidden (which happened frequently with the red circles.) She watched the cutting out with panting absorption until he gave her the first complete cross, untrimmed and unpolished, to play with. He stopped work and watched her carry it over to her toy-store. Her own collection of counters was kept in a leather bag; she shook them out on to the floor and, as usual, sorted eagerly through them just in case (Morris believed) one of the symbols meaning fruit had appeared among them. Then she set out a well-known practice sentence:

white square:	Dinah
green circle with hole:	go
yellow/white square:	bed

She barely sniffed at this before flinging herself to the curtain-rail over the door, from there to the top of the bookshelf and from there with a crash and rattle into her nest, where she shook herself a couple of times and chattered while she studied the blue cross she still held in her left hand. Then she lowered herself gently to the floor and loped back to the symbols.

She tried the cross both at the beginning and end of her sentence, removed it, replaced it first with a blue triangle which turned the sentence into one half of a conditional clause, then with the blue square which meant Morris. Morris made a few notes and returned to his crosses. He had cut them all out and was adjusting his polishing wheel when a eunuch's flute tootled tunelessly beyond the door-curtain.

"Come in", he called in Arabic, then realised that the flautist couldn't hear him so got up and pulled the curtain aside.

A black slave, grinning like an idiot, entered. Dinah leaped to her nest and crouched there, peering over the edge like a soldier in a fox-hole. The slave took the curtain from Morris, allowing him to back into the centre of the room to receive his visitor—Hadiq's mother, presumably, come for a PTA meeting—with proper formality. But, concealing though the robes were, the figure that came through the door could not possibly have been that of the Sultan's fat, worried first wife—and the pale blue eyes that showed through the eye-slits were unique in Q'Kut. Morris's mouth fell open and began to twitch, just as it had done when he had last seen her.

"I hope you're not busy," she said, glancing at the cluttered desk and work-bench, and Dinah's spilt toy-store, and the gnawed and tattered furniture.

"No, no," he said. "Come in. Sit down. The chairs are cleaner than they look."

"This bloke's got to stay too, you know?" she said. "It's that kind of scene."

"I'm used to it," said Morris. He unlocked another drawer and tossed the slave two of the sticky black cheroots he had originally

33

bought for Kwan. The slave grinned, propped his scimitar in the corner and settled down to chew them like liquorice sticks. Morris brought him a bowl to spit into.

"How will he react if I take this lot off," said the girl, feeling for the brooch of her robe.

"What are you wearing underneath?" asked Morris nervously.

"Just clothes."

"I should think that'll be OK. He's not a Moslem. That flute code is quite elaborate, but I doubt if it covers points like this. He could slice your head off, of course, but I don't know whether he's empowered to do that without consulting higher authority."

"I'll risk it."

She plucked the black, mask-like veil over her head, smoothed her hair and began to unfasten the swathing folds of the robe. As she did so she glanced sideways at Morris with a curious teasing look, provocative but not exactly sexually provocative. He half expected her to emerge wearing something to startle or embarrass him—a diving suit, or a belly-dancer's outfit with the naked skin tattooed with revolutionary slogans; but what she had on was the traditional baggy trousers, in pink silk, and a frothy white blouse fastened up to her throat with long criss-crossing laces, like a skater's boot but following a slightly shallower curve. She still looked as fit as a gymnast, though her face had paled during her five weeks out of the sun—paled till the pink-and-white beneath the fading tan made it even less likely that she was any kind of Arab. Morris decided that she was as English as himself.

She adjusted the glossy swathes of black hair, slightly ruffled by the removal of her veil. It was a tactful little gesture, deliberately inviting Morris to inspect her without actually staring. But for her eyes he mightn't have recognised her as the same girl who had stood declaiming about women's rights from the wing of the wrecked aeroplane. She hadn't exactly changed, but had, so to speak, adjusted. Her lips seemed fuller; her cheekbones showed in the softened planes of flesh; even her slightly hooked nose had somehow become less accipitrine than columbaceous; and the pride with which she held herself was the confidence of good breeding rather than any Amazonian arrogance. Later Morris was to discover how fast she could re-adapt her features

34

to any role she chose, but for the moment he was only conscious of being asked to look at an outstandingly pretty woman and feeling awkward about it.

"OK?" she said to the slave, but he didn't look up.

"I can never remember which ones are deaf and dumb," she said to Morris. "In fact it's difficult to believe they really are—the other women treat them as if they weren't there—or weren't human anyway, more like dogs. You don't mind what you do in front of them, after a bit. Where do they all come from? Africa?"

"No. Most of the ordinary slaves come from Africa, but these are marshmen from Q'Kut. It's a hereditary job."

"That can't be easy. They're eunuchs," she said, settling into the less ramshackle armchair. Morris sat down also but couldn't loll. He found himself crouched forward on the edge of his chair with his elbows on his knees and his fingers tightly laced together.

"No, it's like that," he said. "Down in the marshes there's one clan—the eel clan—who always castrate their second sons and cut out their tongues and pierce their ears. If that son doesn't survive they do it to the third son, and so on."

She looked at him with lordly disgust.

"I hate sick jokes," she said.

"I'm afraid it's true. In fact it's an essential part of the economy of the marshes, and population control."

"How horrible."

"Not much more than . . . oh, forget it."

Morris had no wish to start an argument about the ethics of terrorism. He hated that amount of involvement, and usually lost, too. She smiled at him with sweet complicity. There had been a very severe-seeming administrative officer at Bristol; she too had sometimes smiled at Morris like that, because he'd had digs in the same street as her and had seen how she dressed in the evenings, to go out with how many varied men, in what cars. Just so this girl was smiling now to establish a convention whereby that other girl—the one with the gun at her hip and the dead bodies of innocent men behind her—had nothing to do with this visit. This visit was quite different, the daughter of the big house paying a social call on, oh, the rather dull local doctor, being uncondescendingly charming, not yet mentioning whatever business it might be that the charm was expected to pay for.

35

"Do tell me about your zoo," she said.

"Well, I'm not really a zoologist. My field is psycholinguistics . . ."

"Oh."

(She meant "Oh?")

"It's rather a vague subject—it's the study of the effect of language on the mind, and one way you can tackle it is by researching into the linguistic abilities of non-human creatures. I happened to start working with a particularly intelligent female chimpanzee at Bristol, but about eighteen months ago when the Sultan was in London he asked me to come up and have dinner— we used to live on the same staircase at Oxford and got on pretty well—and I told him what I was doing. He offered me a fantastic salary to come out here with my chimp and look after the zoo as a sideline."

"What's in it for him?"

"God knows. When you're that rich you don't have motives any longer—or rather any motive is as good as any other motive, since you can satisfy them all. I think he likes having me about. And he's a bit obsessed with Oxford—he never sat his finals, you see. And if Dinah really comes up to scratch we actually might one day hit the academic headlines."

"That's a slave name."

"I didn't choose it. And I don't think of it like that."

"You think you don't think of it like that. What are you actually doing with her?"

Morris clicked. Instantly Dinah exploded from her nest to the top of the bookshelf, then sprang, whirling like a falling sycamore seed, down to his lap, where she sat pouting at the stranger.

"This is Dinah," he said. "My name's Wesley Morris, but everyone calls me Morris. I'm afraid I don't know yours."

"I've got a lot of names. You'd better call me Galayah."

He repeated the name, but couldn't help correcting her pronunciation.

"Bloody hell!" she said, flushing. "All right, call me Anne. I used to answer to that."

Dinah stopped pouting and shifted round until she could pick at Morris's shirt-buttons. She had never discovered a satisfactory way of grooming him, except in the sparse and unrewarding strip

36

of hair that circled his bald patch. This was only a sign that she would like to be groomed herself, which in turn meant that she wanted reassurance. That makes two of us, he thought, starting to pick systematically along the fur of her forearm.

"Well," he said, "currently I'm setting up an experiment to investigate Dinah's ability to cope with the idea of time."

"Animals don't have one."

"So people say. We'll see. If you'd asked me five years ago, I'd have said that animals couldn't understand or construct conditional clauses, but Premack in California taught a chimpanzee called Sarah how to, and Dinah and I have duplicated his work. So why not time?"

"I see. What else?"

"Well, the Sultan is very anxious to make a breakthrough with an experiment for which *he* can claim some credit, and his idea is that Dinah should have a baby, and then we can see how much she teaches it of what she's learnt from me."

"Will she even look at a male chimp? Doesn't she think she's human, living all the time with you?"

"We don't know, yet. She spent her first three years at Bristol with other chimps, including her mother, only coming out for tests and lessons. Since then she's lived with me, but I've never treated her as a human—I mean dressed her in clothes or let her eat with a knife and fork. She doesn't sleep in a cot, but as near as I can arrange to a jungle nest. She's got her own room—that's essential, so that I can shut her up if I have to do something without her—but it isn't at all like a human room. She even wears a leash sometimes, though she hates it. Nowadays she spends a bit of her time with a family group of near-wild chimps we've imported, and my impression is that she recognises them as being the same species as herself. For instance, one of the females was in season a few weeks ago, which meant that her sex organs swelled to a large pink mound on her rump. Dinah saw it, and spent a lot of time inspecting herself for the same symptoms."

Anne laughed and stretched. Morris found himself relaxing slightly, but when he started to lean back in his chair Dinah grabbed his hand and re-applied it to the bit of her shoulder he had been working on.

"So that's why you're in Q'Kut," she said. "For bread."

"Not entirely," said Morris. "I mean, I don't need all that money. I do like having an unlimited budget for my research, of course. On the other hand I miss the kind of colleagues I could talk things over with. I didn't realise it till I got here, but the real attraction of Q'Kut is the marshmen."

"And the marshwomen?"

"No, as a matter of fact, not. Oh, I see, you mean sexually. Not that either."

"You'll have to explain."

"Well, there are about a dozen languages left in the world which are not dialects of other languages and are spoken exclusively by a coherent group of people. By 'exclusively' I mean they are monoglots. They don't speak any other language. There's a few in New Guinea, a few in Brazil, and a remarkable tribe in the Andaman Islands called the Jarawa. There may be something still in Central Asia, but I doubt it. But the Q'Kuti marshmen are easily the largest and most uncontaminated of such groups, apart perhaps from the Jarawa. From a psycho-linguist's point of view, Q'Kut is the most exciting place in the world."

"It doesn't look it."

"No, but the marsh language . . ."

"Can you speak it? How the hell many languages can you speak? You hissed away in Japanese, didn't you, that day I came? Can you speak Chinese? Have you read Chairman Mao in the original?"

"I've only read his thoughts," said Morris, rather bowled over by this sudden spate of eager questions, and afraid that it might signal a metamorphosis to some other role, terrorist or vamp or ardent student. He felt better able to cope with her as she was.

"That's great," she breathed.

"I don't know. I mean, you can understand a language without understanding what somebody is saying. That's one of the things psycholinguistics is about."

"Please go on about that," she said, politely laying the ghost of Chairman Mao.

"Oh, well, the marshmen have a very interesting language. It contains a number of unique elements, but it lacks a number of other things which we would regard as normal, if not essential. For instance, there are no words and no grammatical structures with which to formulate notions of cause and effect. It can be done, but you have to go a long way round, using very clumsy expressions to achieve it. There are almost no general nouns, either. You see, the marshes are a closed world, in which almost everything is *known*, and has its own name. They have a few general nouns for things that seem to them mysterious, such as foreigners and particularly witchcraft. But you can't say 'plant', for instance. You can't even say 'reed'. You have to name the particular type of reed."

"That must make life difficult."

"They get along. Then there's another aspect of the linguistic-cultural nexus that particularly interests me. You speak the language in sentences, but the sentences are made up not of words but of word-accretions . . ."

"Like those long words in German?"

"A bit like that. But all the word-accretions are constructed round roots of relationship . . ."

"Cousins and things?"

"Not that kind of relationship—or not only. We tend to build up our sentences round verbs. That's to say our central notions are notions of action. They accrete their words round particular roots which describe the relationship between the various parts of the accretion. Their central notion seems to be a notion of everything's position in a very complicated network of relationships."

"Isn't cause and effect a relationship?"

"Yes, of course it is, but I didn't say that they had ways of describing all possible relationships—only the ones that seem to matter to them. For instance they can use a single syllable to express a particular personal obligation which it would take us several sentences to attempt to describe. But the thing about cause and effect is that it's a relationship of such enormous power—I mean for us it is *the* relationship—it's what verbs are about—that if you admitted it into a system like the marshmen's I think it would destroy it—destroy the language, and thus, ultimately, the way of life. I must admit that I find the whole problem of relation-roots absolutely fascinating."

39

"That's funny. It doesn't sound really your thing."

"Oh?"

"Well—oh hell, I suppose this is rude—but you don't look as though you related to anything much, except Dinah."

With extreme care Morris parted a fresh section of the short, almost bristly hairs and peered at the line of greyish flesh below.

"It is arguable that the looker-on sees most of the game," he said in as distant and donnish a voice as he could contrive.

"That's what I mean," she said. "You sit up here in this glass fortress, miles from anything that's actually happening, teaching a monkey conditional clauses. That's all done with, that way of life. You can't know what it's like, what it's about, what it *means*, until you've been part of it. I bet you don't even go into the marshes if you can help it!"

"I don't go at all. I was taught the language by an old man called Kwan, who was the previous Sultan's bodyguard. He used to arrange for the singing boys who sometimes come for state occasions to sing me a lot of their songs, which I taped. But he died just under a year ago, and as far as I know the only other person in the palace who speaks the language is Dyal, the present Sultan's bodyguard."

"There are some in the women's quarters. I think that's what they must be. I hadn't realised."

"There ought to be eight of them, very black, tattooed with different patterns under their eyebrows."

"I haven't looked that close. They keep to themselves, and—I oughtn't to say this, but they really stink."

"I believe they rub themselves all over with rancid buffalo milk."

"It smells worse than that. The Arab word for them means . . ."

"I know."

"I'm glad it's only buffalo milk. Why eight?"

"Well, there's a slightly odd arrangement down in the marshes. I'm not an anthropologist, so I don't know if it's unique. There are nine clans, eight of which conform to a pattern you do find elsewhere. That's to say they all have different fishes or animals for their totem, and strict rules about which clan you have to sell your sisters' daughters to, and so on. Each of those eight clans provides the Sultan with a wife. That's who they are."

"What about the ninth?"

"They're quite different. They provide the Sultan's bodyguard, but they're set apart in a lot of other ways. It isn't just that they're so much bigger than the others that they look like members of a different race—they're expected to behave differently, too. They never lie, for instance . . ."

"How do you know?"

He laughed.

"I don't, of course," he said. "It's just that they haven't got a totem animal, but where you'd normally get a totem-reference in a song, with the ninth clan you get a reference to their truth-telling. I'm so wrapped up in the songs that I hadn't even considered that that might be a polite fiction. Anyway, they're also set apart by not marrying. They steal women from the other clans, but as they haven't paid for them it doesn't count as marriage. There's quite a bit of feuding among the other eight clans, so a lot of men get killed and the survivors are polygamous, but they're all very strict about adultery. Kwan said that if they discover a couple in the act the woman is drowned and the man made to take poison; but if he's a warrior of the ninth clan they let him off scot free. They don't even demand the bride-price from him. They just drown the woman."

"Jesus!"

"I don't think it's always as bad as that. They've got to be caught in the act, for one thing; and I've got a tape of a song about a ninth-clan warrior who took a man's wife and defended her from the man's family until she was too old to bear children, and then she drowned herself and he poisoned himself with his own spear."

"This still goes on?"

"Drowning women? Yes, I should think so."

You cannot groom a chimpanzee to her satisfaction without careful scrutiny of every millimetre of flesh that is exposed as you move the hairs, so Morris had been talking without looking at the girl. The quality of this new silence made him look up.

The ghost of Mao was back at her elbow. She was sitting straight up in the chair, square-shouldered, pale-cheeked, her pretty mouth a hard slit. Her angry Wedgwood eyes held his.

"You sit here," she said, snipping the words apart with bright

41

emphatic teeth, "teaching an animal tricks while there are people down there living like . . ."

She was trapped by her own rhetoric, by the use of the earlier noun. She changed gear.

"You've never been down there, even," she said. "You don't know what it's *like*. You just wait here, snug as a bug in a rug, learning it all second hand."

"That's right," said Morris. "Perhaps I prefer to work that way, so perhaps it's lucky I can't."

"Can't?"

"Uh-uh. One, the Sultan wouldn't permit it. Two, if I tried the marshmen would skewer me through with poisoned spears."

"Oh."

"They aren't isolated by accident. They chose to be isolated. It's all in the Testament of Na!ar."

"Go on."

Morris picked up Dinah's limp hand and studied it, as though he thought a secret might be hidden in the strangely non-human lines that criss-crossed the human-seeming palm.

"As far as I can make out," he said, "all this basin was once fertile and was inhabited by the ancestors of the marshmen. There are songs which seem to imply that. Then the sands encroached and they retreated into the marshes. It probably took centuries. Then—quite late—the Arabs came, and they fought. The marshes are pretty well impregnable, so it was stalemate until the last of what I think must have been the ruling clan of the marshmen, a hero called Na!ar, managed to ambush the chief of the Arabs, Nillum ibn Nillum. They killed each other, but seem to have reached some sort of agreement before they died. Or perhaps their followers reached the agreement, and put it back into their mouths to sanctify it, if you see what I mean. Anyway, it's all in the Testament, which is a perfectly marvellous epic song-cycle embodying the treaty; and the main effect is that the marshmen acknowledged Nillum's heirs as their overlords, and in return he gave them the right to kill any of his followers who trespassed into the marshes . . ."

"No feud? No blood-money?"

"The Sultan would pay that, but in fact it doesn't happen. There hasn't been anything to go into the marshes for, until recently. The Arabs don't even water their camels here if they can help it, because the water's so full of diseases. There's probably every known form of bilharzia down there, and quite a few unknown ones. I'm always astonished that they manage to produce specimens as magnificent as Dyal and Kwan—the singing boys and the musicians are all weedy little runts."

"The women are tiny too," said Anne. "But why didn't you get them to teach you? That might have persuaded you that you ought to *do* something about those people, instead of just sitting here."

Morris shrugged, stuck his lower lip out, pulled at it, retracted it. Dinah, who had been peering into his face to see whether he would carry on grooming her, imitated his grimace but made it ludicrous by the extreme size and elasticity of her own lips. The girl laughed and became a social caller again.

"I don't know," said Morris seriously. "I didn't think of it. I suppose I ought to learn the women's language, which is a bit different, supposing they'd teach it to me. But as for *doing* anything, I don't know. I mean, all I know is that it's not up to me to make moral decisions about other people's lives. Of course I agree that some of the things that happen down there seem unspeakably vile—there's a lot worse than I've told you—but . . . well, take these blokes . . ."

He nodded towards the eunuch in the corner, now nibbling cheerfully at his second cheroot.

"I've never seen any of them looking at all unhappy. Admittedly I can't even bring myself to think what it was like when they were . . . you know . . . *done*, but now they seem perfectly content. And Kwan always talked about life in the marshes as if it were a lost paradise. Last year, when the boys were singing the Testament at the flood-going feast I saw his face streaming with tears . . ."

"But all you really know is what one man has told you. One *man*."

"I suppose so. But there's something else. I was telling you about the language—well, in fact the whole verbal culture is as rich and sophisticated as anything I've come across—certainly anything that exists among illiterate people. It's not just the language, it's the way they use it. I've never heard anything to

43

touch the songs, which range all the way from little blessings for the birth of a calf to great chanted epics. Those are perfectly marvellous. You get a basic story, but inside it you get dramatic sections, and love lyrics, and witches' spells—there's a lot of witchcraft in the marshes—but it isn't a hotch-potch, it's shaped and coherent, quite fit to stand up beside anything I've read in Western literature. Anyway, I'm quite certain that as soon as you started tampering with the culture, bringing in outside influences, pop music (I mean, look what's been happening in Java, for instance) Cairo radio, Bible societies, all that, you'd kill the culture dead in a generation and the language in two. Look, half the world these days seems to tear its hair out and beat its breast if a rather dull species of bird is in danger of extinction. It seems to me much more terrible to risk the death of a language."

The unaccustomed energy of Morris's speech seemed to unsettle Dinah. She shrugged herself free of his inattentive hands, slid off the side of the chair and loped over to her toy-store. Knowing her as well as he did Morris could see that this was only one of her typically devious feints. She had decided that Anne was not a hungry predator and was therefore worth investigating, stealthily, from the flank.

"Is that Bruce's line too?"

"Bruce?"

"Your Sultan. I always call my blokes Bruce. It keeps them in their place. In fact I know an Anatolian village where they now think Bruce is the English for 'darling'."

"Oh . . . er . . . I didn't know."

"Why should you?"

"Um. Well, if you ask him he just takes the line that he has an hereditary obligation, and that's that. He takes it seriously, anyway. I mean, there's much more comfortable places he could live, but he stays here ten months of the year."

"I know. The women spend most of their time grumbling and discussing what they're going to buy next time they go to Paris. How rich is he?"

"I don't know. Enormously, but I don't know how enormously. He told me he couldn't afford to buy a Concorde. It wasn't the capital expenditure, it was the upkeep. But that's his sort of joke."

"Did you see the emerald he gave Simoko when she left?"

"Simoko?"

"That's a funny thing about this place. It's just one building, but there's such a lot going on in it that people only a few rooms away haven't any idea about the dramas happening in your bit. Simoko was one of the air hostesses—the plain one, too sweet—and she and Bruce had a passionate five days; they kept at it just as if the world was ending, and when the plane came to fly the Japs out he gave her an emerald as big as my thumbnail. You could have bought a Phantom with it. It was rather funny—the other women weren't at all jealous, even the real wives. In fact they loved it—something to gossip about. But if Bruce can afford that sort of thing, why doesn't he do something for the marsh-men? I bet there isn't a school or a clinic anywhere. What about his hereditary obligation?"

Out of the corner of his eye Morris could see Dinah beginning her flank attack, pushing a couple of building-bricks with deceptive aimlessness across the floor. He kept his gaze on Anne so as not to spoil the fun, and saw that her indignation was again simmering up to a full revolutionary boil-over.

"There are clinics and schools for the Arabs," he said quickly. "There's a young Parsee doctor who goes round the tents in a very up-to-date mobile unit, and the Sultan flies in teachers during the winter, when there's steady grazing up in the hills which means that the kids stay all in one place for a bit. But he won't let anyone touch the marshmen—I don't think he'd be very pleased if he knew how far I'd got with the language."

"It seems bloody selfish to me."

"Ung. Well, I expect you realise that most of his money comes from the oil company. Apparently their geologists decided that the richest fields were probably under the marshes, but he wouldn't let them drill there. He still won't."

Dinah had left her bricks and was creeping in behind Anne's left shoulder.

"The Sultan's manner is very deceptive," said Morris. "He really is very superficially Westernised. His Oxford accent and his slang and the gadgets in the palace are all a sort of parody of our civilisation—at least half-deliberate—a way of having what he wants of us and rejecting our values at the same time.

Anyway, I'm not sure he isn't right about the marshmen. We're all rushing along, faster and faster, like water in a river before a cataract, dragging the developing nations along with us. It might be important that there are a few totally undeveloped peoples, so undeveloped that they don't get involved when we go over the edge. It really isn't an untenable attitude, but if you adopt it you've got to go the whole hog. Those Jarawa I was talking about aren't the only tribe in the Andamans, but all the others have made vague contact with the rest of the world and either been assimilated or died out—dying out's more usual in fact. The Indian government won't let anyone go near the Jarawa, not even anthropologists—that isn't because they're enlightened, it's because the Andamans are an important naval base. But the result is that they're still totally isolated—different—themselves—and it *is* just possible that the future of mankind might lie with them. Or with the marshmen here."

She was about to retort, but was distracted. During the last sentences of Morris's harangue Dinah's face had emerged above the tatty chintz of the arm of Anne's chair, the ludicrous arch of her brows expressing wonder and surprise as her brown clear eyes gazed first at the glossy black hair, then at the soft-skinned cheek, and last at the lacy promontory of the bosom. Suddenly her dark arm snaked forward and two fingers probed at the white curve. Anne barely recoiled. She looked down and laughed kindly.

"Hello, future," she said.

It is uncomfortable to find oneself liking, however momentarily, somebody of whom one disapproves with all the poor passion at one's command. Morris distracted himself by watching Dinah, and immediately wished he'd had a camera going—it was a perfect example of her quickness that she should at once recognise in her own nature an element that she shared with this stranger but did not share with him, for she was peering sideways and down at her chest and feeling with her fingers the area round her own nipples. It would have been anthropomorphism to say she was dissatisfied, but to a comical extent she looked it.

Anne, still laughing, reached out a careful hand and started to tease at the fur on Dinah's nape. Dinah was entranced. For a few seconds she stayed where she was, hunched like a man in a

46

shower to relish the process; then she skipped on to the arm of the chair, took Anne by the wrist and moved her hand to a place on her ribs which she seemed to think needed attention. Anne, Morris could see, did instinctively what he himself had only learnt to do by watching Hugo van Lawick's films.

"You ought to have trained as a vet," he said.

"Oh, Mummy always has a dozen dogs in the house. And my father behaved as though our education was complete when we'd learnt how to groom a horse. But they'd have thought vets a bit beneath us. Will you do something for me?"

She had chosen her moment beautifully, establishing a deliciously cosy relationship with Dinah, slipping in a quick reference to her real social superiority to anything Morris knew, then asking. She mightn't be brainy, but she was cunning.

"Ung?" he said.

"Are you still Foreign Minister?"

"I think so. I'll know to-morrow, when I see where I'm sitting at the feast."

"Can you fix me a passport?"

Morris said nothing, but stared at her gloomily, pulling his lip. She and Dinah made a charmingly posed contrast, both beautiful examples of their species, absorbed in their simple task: it was difficult to imagine refusing either of them anything. Really, this girl was a hundred years out of date. The roles she wanted weren't being written any more—barging about the middle east, meddling in native politics, upsetting everybody, landing in some fracas far beyond her and then expecting to be rescued by a British Naval Party under the command of a snappily saluting little snotty. Now she was expecting Morris to come to the rescue.

"Haven't you got one?" he said.

"I've had my British one withdrawn, the sods. I've been getting about on a Syrian travel document, but I think Bruce has impounded it. A Q'Kuti passport would be just the job."

"Ung."

She stopped grooming Dinah to look at him with the same speculative glance he had seen earlier. She was calculating his price. Not money, not sex . . .

"The point is," she said, "I don't think Bruce is going to let

47

me go. Ever. We're having a wild time together at the moment, but it can't last. And when it's over . . . He hasn't said anything, but I've been listening to the women . . . sometimes he's taken a fancy to a dancer from Dar or somewhere and had her flown in for a week and given her a present and sent her home . . . they talked about Simoko as if she was one of those. But they talk about me as if I'm one of *them*—you know, there's several old women there who were Bruce's father's girls—they've been shut up in the women's quarters for years—when it was only a sort of mud fort. OK, I'm enjoying myself right now, but I've got work to do."

"Exactly," he said.

She stopped grooming Dinah and swung round at him like a gun on a tank turret.

"Who made you judge in Israel?" she snapped. "Slavery for life, is it?"

"I don't know . . . nobody . . . I'm not a judge . . . to set you free, either."

"As far as you're concerned I'm just another monkey in Bruce's zoo? And you're one of *them*?"

She made a gesture, vivid with passion, towards the oblivious eunuch. Dinah parodied it. Anne didn't laugh this time.

"I don't know what I think," said Morris. "I'm not very clever at either/or situations, I'm afraid. As a matter of fact I don't really approve of the Sultan keeping a zoo here at all; but since he insists on having one I try to make it tolerable for the animals. And, well, I suppose you're better off here than you might be in prison."

"Which is where I belong, you think?"

"I tell you, I don't know!"

Slowly she swung back to Dinah.

"Sorry, sweetie," she said. "We got interrupted."

They returned to the silent ritual of grooming. Morris felt a twitch of jealousy that they should seem to understand each other, instantly, so much better than he understood either of them. Hell, there were things he could accomplish which this girl could never begin on—he began to run his mind over the probable grammar of Dinah's exploration of the future tense.

"What were you saying about to-morrow night?" said Anne.

"About this feast, I mean, and knowing whether you were still Foreign Minister?"

It was uncanny how smoothly she flipped herself back into the unruffled stream of polite chat.

"Oh," said Morris, "well, there's this feast. Theoretically it's held when the floods begin to recede, but it doesn't work out like that . . ."

"It's probably something to do with the moon. Like Easter."

"Yes. Well . . . you know, you ought to go and listen to some of it. The Sultan gives this feast—it lasts six hours—and in between the courses boys from the marshes sing the Testament of Nalar. There's one clan—the rock-dove clan—where all the boys have to learn all the traditional songs. Really it's an astonishing performance, especially if you know that they aren't allowed to sing them after they've reached puberty. Why don't you make friends with the marshwomen? They could explain. You see, there's a special gallery with a pierced screen where the women can sit if they want to . . ."

When she had gone, mission unaccomplished, Morris settled again at his work-bench; the whine of his fine-toothed saw, the hum and fizz of his polisher discs, the small feeling of accomplishment as each blue cross took on an almost professional finish—these should have been soothing, but despite them he felt irritated and disappointed. Dinah, too, was suddenly tiresome. Quite soon he had to give up his work to try to occupy both their minds with education.

It didn't go well. Morris kept thinking about Anne, and perhaps Dinah did too. He was surprised, almost alarmed, by the strength of his wish that she had stayed longer, and how his original awkwardness and resentment in her presence had changed to liking. If the Sultan had known, he would have been full of jeering innuendoes, but . . .

Dinah suddenly swept a row of six counters off the coffee-table and squatted sullenly, waiting for some kind of reproof or punishment that would give her the excuse for a tantrum. When it didn't come she shuffled off to her nest, stuffed her mouth with shavings and went to sleep.

Morris picked up the scattered counters and then sat crouched forward on his chair, poking them around at random and thinking about himself. This was not a thing he often did in any analytic way, because he considered his own personality rather null and unrewarding; he spent much more time speculating about Dinah's character, or the Sultan's. But now he was struck once more with a kind of resentment of a trait in his own nature which seemed to make it impossible for him to enjoy the company of suitable friends and colleagues—suitable in the sense that his mother had used when she selected suitable children for him to play with; all his life the people he had got on with had been quite wrong for him, hopelessly out of his sphere, or even morally corrupt—a raffish collection of High Tory squirelings at Oxford, that ruthless fat Dutchman who smuggled orangs and talked about nothing but guns, the Sultan, Kwan, and even this murderess.

> Lucky are they, beyond earth's common lot,
> Whose friends amuse, whose enemies do not.

Sometimes he had considered this trait to be a reaction of his mother's insistence on suitability, but since he had been in Q'Kut he had come round to believing that it was a phenomenon of western civilisation, and that there were probably a lot of people like him in existence in countries where all recognisable cultural structures had withered or exploded into fragments. Living among Arabs, whose ancient culture had the strength of its own narrowness and so was only now beginning to collapse, or listening to the songs of marshmen who still knew the exact function of every man, every buffalo, every reed-channel in their universe, he had come to understand as a tangible reality what had before been only an academic commonplace, that the great thing is to *belong*, know what you belong to, and your place in it, to accept it and be accepted by it. But not any old grouping would do—it had to be of a graspable size, to contain its own inner structure, to give at least the appearance of permanence. A desert tribe, or a mining village, yes; the Pan-Arab nation, or some bloody great industrial union, no. Old bin Zair knew what he was, and where he belonged, but Morris had been unable to accept his own native culture. It had none of the desiderata—it was too large, too boneless, too impermanent. So quite unconsciously he had refused to accept his role in it, by refusing to accept people apparently like himself who *had* accepted their roles; and in the end he had escaped to Q'Kut, to the highly unsuitable roles of zoo-keeper and Foreign Minister, acceptable because of their very absurdity.

Morris thought about these matters erratically, poking the symbols into meaningless messages as he did so; in the end he got cramp in his left haunch, rose to ease it and rambled round his room full of a vague inner smugness at his own isolation. I am heroically alone, he thought. There is no one remotely like me in all Q'Kut.

Stooping to clear the counters away he saw that the last message he had made actually meant something, if you could call it a meaning:

> blue square: Morris
> brown circle: has qualities of
> black square: person other than Morris

(The brown circle did not exactly mean "is". It had been mainly used in an earlier stage when Dinah had been learning about qualifiers—Morris would present her with a banana and a yellow play-brick and a sentence to say or ask what they had in common.)

All right, he thought, all right. I probably did it subconsciously. It doesn't mean anything.

But as he tidied the counters away he wondered whether in fact Anne too had chosen her role as a rejection of the non-culture she was supposed to belong to. Her roles, rather, because that was the alternative course. You could choose, like Morris, to be a quietist and wash about where the tides drifted you; or you could actively seek roles, the more extreme and violent the better, switching them as the mood took you, wearing mask after mask to hide the lack of features behind. Perhaps even the vet-despising, dog-owning Mummy was an invention, a beauty spot on such a mask—there had been something a little off key about her very first line in the role—absolutely giddy bonkers. Hmph.

He wondered what she would make of the flood-going feast, if she bothered to go and watch it from the women's gallery.

51

2

Quite unreasonably Morris had expected the boys to be the same three that had sung the Testament last year. They wore the same white clay masks whose lips were set into a permanent pout to allow room for the funnels that made the young voices resonate, but they were three different boys. The main singer's voice was less limpid than last year's but he sang with greater drive and drama, even with a slight harshness that contrasted well with the softer voices of the younger pair. Their naked black bodies were striped with ochre designs. They sat cross-legged, motionless on a patterned reed mat in front of the throne, while to either side of them the little orchestra of their fathers and elder brothers thumped and clinked and gurgled at their tuneless instruments.

The wonderfully ornate passage about the preparations for Nillum's boar-hunt came to an end in an onomatopoeic flourish of hoofbeats and horns. A vast series of dishes piled with spiced rice and mutton was carried in to the hall. The audience—petty sheikhs and their cousins, random brigands, senior palace courtiers, a party of town Yemenis on some unexplained mission, several groups of litigants who had arranged their cases to coincide with a famous free meal but whose real interest was in camel-theft and water-rights and blood-money—maintained for the most part the extraordinarily dignified silence with which they had listened to the singers, not one word of whose song any of them could have understood.

The Sultan spoke affably to a small fat sheikh. The leader of the Yemenis listened, nodding. Akuli bin Zair scratched his ribs, pulled his beard and turned to Morris, who was evidently still Foreign Minister, to be sitting so near the throne.

"Your excellency is entertained by the squealings of the savages?" he asked in his high, tinny voice.

"I like the songs," said Morris.

"I have made a film of the performance of one of our dancing boys, one of the Hadahm. He is very beautiful and can do strange things. Your excellency must come to my quarters to see it."

"The pleasure would be as great as the honour," said Morris, who had in fact often been forced to watch the smutty contortions of young male prostitutes which seemed for some reason to delight and amuse quite respectable old Arabs. He himself detested them, so switched the subject back to the marshmen.

"I saw yesterday, from my windows, the ceremony at which the tribute was brought," he said, gesturing at the odd little pile of offerings in front of the singers. "What do you do with them when the feast is over?"

"The spear is burnt, always. It is a sign that the killing of each other is finished. The boar-tusks we put in a chest, as we did even when the Sultan's father lived under tents. That is how it has always been done."

"You mean that if you were to count the pairs of tusks in the chest, you would know how many years ago the ceremony first started?"

"No doubt," said bin Zair. "However, some may have been lost or stolen."

"Even so, I expect you could have the oldest ones carbon-dated."

"You think the matter important?"

"It is not for me to say. I am always interested in such matters. But if, for instance, there were to be some question about the validity of the treaty, then it might be useful to be able to prove its antiquity."

Bin Zair sat pulling his beard and looking at Morris with his old, bloodshot eyes.

"The matter shall be looked into," he said at last. "I trust, excellency, that all your animals are in beautiful health, and the slaves attending to them with care."

Morris blinked. So abrupt a change of subject is not common in polite Arab conversation, nor had bin Zair ever before evinced the slightest interest in the zoo. No doubt the old man considered that the new Foreign Minister was in danger of regarding his post as other than merely honorific. But in fact there had been a tedious little dispute about the number of helpers needed in the zoo—the sort of problem that in a place like the palace could only be settled by high authority, but which was in itself too trivial to bother high authority about, and so never got settled. Morris explained. Bin Zair nodded non-committally. The meat came round. A litigant sidled up and began, with ridiculous circumlocution, to sound bin Zair out on the possibility of helping his case along with a few bribes; Morris turned away and pretended to adjust the tapes of his recorder, ready for the next episode of the song. Out of the corner of his eye he saw that the Sultan was starting on his second bottle of "sherbert" (bottled on the Heidsieck estates in Rheims, but re-labelled in Aden.) At last a soggy little drum began to revive the echo of the hoof-beats, and hands as black as insulated cable slid over the strings of two little harps, producing a tuneless, shivery whispering. Morris started his recorder. The music, if you could call it that, died. The boy in the centre threw back his head and sang.

Last year Morris had regarded this passage as a disappointing one, after the reverberant nastiness of the scene in which Na!ar's grandmother's second brother had gathered and prepared the poisons, and the barbaric clutter of the preparations for the hunt. This time he listened with increasing absorption to the sparsely ornamented lines that brought the two heroes together for their necessary deaths.

One of the traditional adornments employed by the makers of the marsh songs was a patterned arrangement and modulation of the successive relation-roots; even an apparently artless lyric would on inspection turn out to contain, for instance, three sections, the outer two using a series of roots in the same order and the central one reversing them. There was none of that in the description of the duel. Word-group after word-group clustered round the same root, the strong (or willed) transitive. The groups themselves were unusually short, the nominal and adjectival elements always the commonest of many possible synonyms, inflected very straightforwardly—straightforwardly, that is, for a language in which it was possible to inflect the nominal element "cheese" so that three syllables meant "the first-pressing cheese made last drought from the milk of my elder brother's three-year-old buffalo". As the heroes closed, the language became drier still.

Nillum rode by the reeds.
His servants and his friends were far behind him, ·

54

Hunting a different boar.
Hidden in the winter reeds Na!ar waited.
His spear-thrower was hard in his hand.
The tip of his spear glistened with fresh poison.
He moved like a fisherman,
An old fisherman who creeps to spear a quick fish.
Nillum rode by the reeds. He reined in his horse.
Na!ar sprang up. He threw his spear.
He shouted with joy to see it fly straight.
Nillum heard the shout . . .

Of course the story carried the listener through. Cynical calculation? If your material is all blood and drama, it's a waste to put frills on it, because no one will notice them? But to a man of Morris's temperament the whole passage seemed to prove that he was listening to the work of a truly potent artist, a forgotten savage who had understood the essential nature of action, its drabness, the perfunctoriness of muscle-movements compared with the salivating torments of anticipation and the long, rich pastures of regret.

The expressionless clay mask chanted on. The voice of the main singer was expressionless too, telling, as if in a stone frieze, the precise cruelties that the two heroes dealt each other until both were dying.

Na!ar dragged himself through the reed-bed
Using only his arms.
The barbs of his own spear held fast in his liver.
The spear-shaft caught and dragged among the reed-roots.
Where clear water gleamed he lay still.
He saw the piebald horse wallow away, saddle empty.
He saw Nillum kneeling in the water.
He felt the poison-creatures beginning to suck up his soul.
Words then Na!ar, shield of the people, spoke.

Morris thrilled to the grammatical surprise, though he was ready for it, the sudden, rare null-root, the expression of general and involuntary action, contorted almost to the end of the longest word-group for many minutes. He was quite sure that the effect was intentional: the fight itself had been a personal matter between two men, moving their own limbs at their own will; but now a different power stirred in Na!ar's dying mouth, as large and impersonal as the movement of the floodwaters or the return of day, for which the null-transitive root was invariably used. A series of heavy strokes on the slack-stringed harps seemed to underline the effect and at the same time to usher in another procession of dishes to fill the interval before the cryptic exchange of oaths and absolutions that actually embodied the ancient treaty.

Shivery and sighing Morris switched his tape-recorder off. In an attempt to protect his inner silence from any idiot who might want to break in with gossip or comment he pretended to be absorbed in the ridiculous architecture of the Council Chamber.

Even the Sultan was a bit ashamed of the Council Chamber; he would never explain quite how it had been designed, but Morris's own theory was that the architects had been told to go to Oxford and Cambridge and produce a large room that combined all the most striking features of various college dining halls—though it looked as though they might have strayed into a few chapels as well. In some ways they had been ingenious, adapting the idea of a music gallery to make the place whence the women could watch from behind a screen (carved into a uniquely eclectic Gothic-Arabic design) their lord gobbling. No use had been found for the pendulous great nodules of plaster that hung from the fan vaulting—unless there were secret switches that enabled the Sultan to release them like bombs on to the unwelcome guest. The stained-glass windows had to be lit by an electric sun, because the chamber had no outside walls. The chandeliers were certainly very fine. But everything had somehow been thrown out of proportion partly (Morris suspected) because the Sultan had at a late moment decided to add a few feet to the dimensions here and there, and partly because of the tables. Perhaps it is impossible to design a room which will look right when all the furniture consists of one low throne, a lot of cushions, and five enormous black oak tables only eighteen inches high; Morris was actually beginning to wonder about this as he came out of his trance when the persistent litigant on the far side of bin Zair belched so loudly that he woke himself up. Bin Zair turned pointedly away from him, so could hardly avoid addressing Morris.

"I will come and see the animals to-morrow morning," he said. "Thus we will settle this matter."

"I am your debtor already," said Morris.

"It is convenient," explained bin Zair. "These Yemenis are slave-merchants; thus I can buy what you need, or order it if they do not have the stock in hand."

He was turning away but the litigant, quite unrebuffed, was still there waiting his chance. Bin Zair half rose from his cushions so that he could resettle with his back completely towards the man, which brought him directly opposite the tape-recorder.

"What is the machine?" he asked.

Morris explained, adding that he already had a tape of the Testament, but that the quality was poor as last year he had been sitting further away.

"And what use do you make of these howlings?" asked bin Zair when he had finished.

"I have learnt the language. I find it very interesting."

Bin Zair nodded like a grave goat.

"I have lived all my life at the edge of the marshes," he said. "But I have learnt no more of their language than is needed for various ceremonies."

"You have been busy with greater matters, no doubt."

"Perhaps."

At last the litigant rose and stalked away. Bin Zair bowed with great politeness to Morris but closed the conversation, which was a relief. As Morris settled to brooding on the passage they had just heard, he realised that it had been at this point in the feast last year that he had seen Kwan's lined face glistening with tears, glistening like the spear in the song and the other spear which lay crosswise on top of the primitive offerings, its point looking as though it had been dipped in the blackest of black treacle. He wondered to whom else, now, the song had such a fierce meaning—none of the Arabs; not the Sultan who, Morris already knew, claimed to speak the language when in fact he had only an ill-accented smattering; Dyal, of course, and the new black giant sitting on the mat behind Prince Hadiq on the far side of the room; Morris himself, in his academic way;

and (strange, strange) the eight women whom Morris had never seen, sitting up in the screened gallery, stinking of rancid milk. For them, perhaps, each syllable meant the stench of the lagoons, and the smoke of dried buffalo dung filling reed huts, and fevered babies muttering in the moist dark, and flighting duck, and home.

3

Dinah was having trouble with the concept of time. At first, though clearly puzzled by the blue cross being a different shape from any of the other nouns, she naturally attempted to identify the symbol with the egg-timer. Morris had anticipated this, and produced a square counter divided into blue and red along the diagonal.

blue/red diagonal square: egg-timer

He had also prepared a couple of other blue-diagonal squares, one for the clepsydra he intended to make out of a coffee-tin, and one for the kitchen timers he had sent for. He thought that Dinah's first move would probably be to try and use the blue cross as a general noun to cover all transparent objects—glass always fascinated her. That wouldn't be too hard to correct by producing the other gadgets—but then she would try to use the cross as a symbol for "gadget".

Morris was watching her build one of her untidy towers of play-blocks, and thinking of carefully timed processes which did not involve gadgets, when the curtain was pulled aside. Dinah fled to her nest.

"Hi," said the Prince. He looked grave. There was someone in the corridor behind him.

"Come in," said Morris, not rising.

The newcomer turned out to be the large young marshman whom Morris had seen a few days ago in the canoe, and last night at the feast. The Prince produced what was obviously a very carefully rehearsed sentence.

"Friend of my father, it is Gaur."

"Gaur is welcome," said Morris, rising.

The Prince made an encouraging little nod to his companion.

"Salam Alaikum," said Gaur, stumbling over the ancient desert greeting of the Arabs.

"Alaikum as Salam," said Morris, then added in the language of the marshmen their own salute: "Thy buffaloes may rest in my wallow."

Gaur hesitated an instant, no doubt because Morris had used the special vocative for addressing a warrior of the ninth clan, but there was no place in the language for somebody who, like Morris, did not belong to the hierarchy of the reeds. In the end he settled on a strange, archaic form which Morris had only come across before in a ballad in which two men met by night and could not identify each other's status.

"Half my cheeses are thine," he eventually replied, guardedly.

"Be welcome," said Morris. "Dost thou eat tobacco?"

Gaur unsmilingly handed Morris the Batman comics and accepted a cheroot to chew, but before he had settled to it Morris saw him flinch and stare across the room. Dinah was doing her trench warfare trick again. Gaur muttered an invocation and made a curious sideways gesture with spread palms, as though he were glancing some missile to the side.

"What what?" said the Prince, like an early Wodehouse character.

"Gaur thinks that Dinah is a demon," said Morris slowly.

"What means demon?"

Morris explained in Arabic.

"The marshes are full of witches and demons," he added.

"Oh, I know it. You speak Gaur Dinah goods. Dinah is good. Speak you teach me English. I teach Gaur Arab."

Something had happened, Morris saw, to produce this erratic flow of language. Normally the Prince would have paused for a minute between each sentence, and then ejaculated it unhappily; but today he thought it no shame to be wrong. Morris explained to Gaur, but Dinah for some reason refused to emerge from her nest to demonstrate that she was a mere animal (and was she?), while Gaur reluctantly returned the cheroot to its box; his smooth young face remained impassive, but his free hand now clutched the little amulet that had hung round his neck since he was a child. At the explanation about the English lessons he merely nodded.

59

At this point a pompous little slave arrived to say that bin Zair really was going to pay his unlooked-for visit to the zoo, and trusted that Morris had recovered sufficiently from the feast to be able to meet him there; very likely this was the self-same official who had hitherto thwarted Morris over the zoo-cleaners, for he managed to fill his little message with indignities. Morris never minded about that sort of thing, but suddenly the Prince snapped, in Arabic, "Thy soles shall be flayed off thy feet before this dusk," and the slave whimpered away. Certainly the Prince was full of sudden confidence.

"We learn . . . we shall learn . . . more English with animals?" he asked.

"Fine," said Morris.

He clicked at Dinah. Gaur flinched as she came leaping to the door but his big hand did not move to his knife or to the heavy new revolver at his hip—such weapons are no use against demons —the only hope is to clutch your amulet. To calm him Morris carried Dinah. She clung close all the way to the lifts.

The syndicate of architects who had designed the palace had made their name running up swish hotels in Beirut. The Sultan's fantasies had dictated certain elements, such as the absurd external elevation, the grottoed audience chamber, several internal vistas and coups de theatre—and, of course, the zoo. But between these fixed points the architects had doodled in the light of their past successes, producing a series of plush but garish suites and lobbies. There were even meaningless side-rooms, dark and secret, which in a less teetotal environment would have been cosy little bars for lonely travellers.

But upon this characterless background the inhabitants and transients had imposed their own pungent culture. Morris had never yet met a goat trying to graze the amber pile of a corridor, but he would not have been surprised if he had. Stacks of coke-tins tended to collect in corners behind pierced mock-alabaster screens; tribesmen, wrapped in their tattered cloaks, snored and stank in random gathering-places, or played their stone-age version of peggoty in noisy groups round the indoor fountains; their tobacco, which they smoked in spent cartridge tubes passed round from hand to hand, smelt of gunpowder and dung-fires; somewhere far off someone always seemed to be boiling sour mutton-fat, but this odour was occasionally swamped by the presence of a young Arab who had been experimenting with cheap scent from Dar. They were a people who moved with great silence, while the plush decor muffled their fidgets. All the sounds in the palace seemed to come from mouths—arguments about the virtues of a strain of camels, reminiscences about old murders and raids, prayers, whisperings, greetings, snores and tubercular hawkings, and the mysterious reedy code of the eunuchs' flutes. It was a world where action was hushed but every sound had a meaning, and for that reason it suited Morris. He had even come to like the smells.

The lifts were working today. Dinah escaped from his arms for long enough to press every button on the control panel, so it took them some time to ascend the four floors to the zoo. While the slow box sighed from floor to floor Morris studied Gaur, who would not meet his glance; he was a magnificent specimen, even allowing for his having lived on milk from birth and never having drunk the wriggling waters of the marshes. His skin was so black that in the dull light of the lift the shadows on it had a bluish tinge; his face, like Dyal's, had in it only a few suggestions of Arab blood but was not at all negro—flattish, thin-lipped, high cheekboned, and narrow-eyed. He wore a white turban beneath which, Morris knew, the straight black hair would be surprisingly sparse, although it had never been cut. He would never grow a beard. (Kwan had once told Morris that he had at first felt friendly at the sight of another hairless face, and thought it very curious that Morris needed to shave to achieve the effect.)

Suddenly a number of possible explanations slid together. Morris turned to the Prince.

"I suppose the age-sets must have changed down in the marshes," he said.

Even when he turned the sentence into Arabic the Prince only shrugged and nodded at Gaur. Morris asked the giant direct.

"New men became," said Gaur. "At the flood-going."

"Would I had been there to see," said Morris—though to be honest he would rather have read about the ceremony, and perhaps watched a film of the dances. But his mild courtesy was received with a withdrawn glance that flickered for a moment

61

from him to Dinah and then away. Still, it was gratifying to have guessed right; with the initiation of a new age-set—boys "became men" at roughly five-year intervals—Gaur must have reached warrior status and so could be sent to the Palace to guard the Sultan's eldest son; and his arrival constituted an acknowledgement that Hadiq was indeed the chosen heir—with so many other products of the royal loins available, even an eldest son by a first wife needed to be constantly awarded symbols of his primacy. Gaur was a very potent symbol, with his gun at his hip and his hand on his amulet.

When at last the lift doors opened, Morris saw that the lobby outside the zoo was not empty. Two eunuchs sat on the floor playing their inexplicable finger-game; they had not, of course, heard the movement of the lift but the alteration of light made them look up and come smiling to their feet. They grinned at Dinah and made a curious wristy gesture to Gaur, but when the party moved towards the zoo doors they barred the way.

"My father is at here," said the Prince. "One woman also."

His hands fluttered through the sign language of the harem. Dinah recognised the process, though not the symbols, and promptly made her own sign to demand food. One of the eunuchs laughed, a breathy gargle. The other used his flute to blow a short message, answered almost at once by a near call and a distant answer. It was Dyal who opened the doors. Morris paused in the short corridor that led to the main inspection gallery and said to the Prince "Your father will ask how your English lessons are going. Tell him 'Not so dusty'."

"Dust was . . . dirt?" asked the Prince.

"Forget it," said Morris.

But, like almost everything else that happened that morning, the idea turned out badly. The Sultan was showing off his marksmanship to Anne, who was wearing a very English tweed skirt, a powder-blue twin-set and a double row of pearls. Only the pearls were different from what her alleged mother might have worn at a point-to-point twenty-five years ago—they were far too big. Presumably the Sultan had sent for this gear in order to gratify his penchant for the English county style, and it was amusing to see how Anne wore the clothes: not exactly to the manor born, but with the slightly exaggerated stance and gestures of a musical comedy actress of the 'thirties playing a manorial role; whether deliberately or by luck, she had hit the exact off-key note that would entrance her captor.

"Hello," said the Sultan affably. "And how's the English going, my lad?"

The Prince stammered, looked desperately at Morris and blurted out in Arabic "Not as the language of excrement."

"I should think not," said the Sultan. "Morris, you haven't been trying to muddle his wits with the marshmen's lingo, have you?"

"No . . . well . . . I mean . . ."

But before he could sort out the mistranslation they heard more fluting from the doors and another cry from Dyal. This time, of course, it was bin Zair, and the explanation about the Prince's linguistics got lost in an argument about how far the old man should be forced to crawl, with the Sultan insisting on his own ludicrous rights simply because both Anne and Morris asked him not to. He then decided that as there were now seven people in the zoo they would have a shooting match. Dyal and Gaur were summoned from the door and they all took it in turns to bombard the gorilla with empty hypodermic darts. Anne, very much in a squire's-lady fashion, attempted to put Gaur at his ease by striking up a conversation, all smiles and good-will; and despite the lack of language they seemed to get on well enough to spoil the Sultan's aim; then Prince Hadiq had the lack of tact to shoot straighter than his father; either Dyal knew better or he too was disturbed about something. Anne turned out to be a very moderate shot; Gaur started badly, never having seen any kind of gun till a week ago, but improved quickly; Morris completely missed the gorilla with two of his five shots, while old bin Zair never hit it at all and was heaped by the Sultan with the harsh traditional mockery of the desert for the feeble warrior. They tried to get Dinah to shoot, but she was unable to connect the gun itself with the sudden appearance of the darts on the gorilla's chest. In any case she had never much cared for the gorilla, who had been stuffed in a bristling pose of snarling anger. Morris found it a relief when he could at last pick her up and retreat, side by side with bin Zair, backwards from the Sultan's presence. He took the old man into his office and made the ritual coffee. Dinah settled down to trying to type on the ancient, unbreakable Remington he kept for her.

"The women of your country, are they all so shameless?" asked bin Zair.

"It is not our custom to wear a veil," explained Morris.

"Oh, I have seen the faces of women, many times. I have talked with Freya Stark. Even now there are women who work at the oil wells, unveiled. But I have not seen them roll their eyes and show a moist lip to some young savage, as your countrywoman did."

"She was only trying to be friendly."

"Among my people, if a man's sister behaved so he would shoot her, and be praised by his friends."

Morris could only shrug and pour bin Zair his second tiny cup of coffee. After this they would be able to get down to business. As so often before, he was maddened by the lack of subjects for small-talk—life in an unvarying climate made one realise how much the English owe to their crazy weather as a source of uncontroversial chat.

"What was Freya Stark like?" he asked, though in fact the lone explorers of Arabia, the Doughtys and Starks and Thesigers, filled him only with relief at not being like them.

"She wore strange shoes," said bin Zair. "Now, the women at the oil-wells are like men—and the men are like women. Perhaps you will see them when they begin to drill in the marshes."

The old man's watery and blood-shot eyes looked speculatively at Morris, as though trying to guess whether his taste ran more to manly women or womanly men.

"They will not drill in the marshes, surely," said Morris. "The Sultan won't let them."

"My master has many minds. No man can know them all."

"But the treaty—the Testament of Na!ar!"

"Is my master a child, or a lover, to turn from his path for the sake of a song? I tell you, sir, I have done what you suggested and have counted the tusks in the chest. There are eighty-two pairs. The ceremony of the tribute therefore began when my master's grandfather was a young warrior. If the treaty is true, it is yet not truly old."

"There may have been another chest."

"True. But where is it?"

64

Bin Zair peered into his empty cup like a hairy little ape looking for a fat grub in a hole. Dinah suddenly lost her temper with her typewriter and slid it angrily across the floor, but Morris hadn't time just now to start her off on a new ploy; against all his own rules he fetched a banana from the cupboard and gave it her.

"Surely the marshmen will fight," he said.

"With spears, against guns and aeroplanes?" asked bin Zair, holding out his cup to be filled.

"Perhaps," said Morris as he poured. "In the Sudan, in the south, there are tribes which have warred for ten years against the government, and have not been conquered. They too live in marshes and swamps."

"It is said that these marshes can easily be drained. They have but to build two short new watercourses through the southern hills; and when that is done, they also say that where the waters were will be good land, able to feed many cattle."

"Has he told Dyal?" asked Morris, remembering how comparatively badly the bodyguard had shot.

"A slave? Sir, will you speak to my master of this matter?"

"I will ask him, yes."

Bin Zair leaned forward, suddenly emphatic.

"Let not my master know that I have told you of it," he said. "I am old, and so speak more than I should. You must ask him cleverly, as if the thought came from your own mind. He is your friend—he will not lie to you. Now you must show me your needs."

As they rose Dinah picked up the typewriter again and threw it with a crash across the room; she must have decided it was an easy way of being given bananas. Morris clicked at her and she followed him sulkily out into the passage.

Bin Zair was a very Arab Arab, Morris found. One of his characteristics was that he was unselective about the relevance of information. He seemed to want to see everything; as a result the zoo inspection took well over an hour. For instance Morris had to go into exact detail of how the apparent cost of the equipment to purify the polar bear's water, and the labour to keep its litter clean, was negligible compared with the cost of providing a new bear every few months. Bin Zair combed his beard with thin, shaking fingers and watched the big beast pad its ceaseless figure-of-eight across the diagonal of its cage. Polar bears always reminded Morris of mediaeval barons, narrow-brained, shaped for slaughter, magnificent, useless. No doubt Nillum ibn Nillum, the Sultan's original ancestor, had been of that nature also, so the Sultan had come a long way. There was hope for mankind yet.

Far off in the other gallery the whoosh of the spring-guns sounded through the stillness.

"Must each animal have its own slave?" said bin Zair dubiously.

"No. All I want is two men who do their work properly, and do only that, and are not taken from the zoo to perform other duties. I want no more than I need. It is less trouble to use two good men than a lazy twenty. I would prefer hired men to slaves— I am not accustomed to the idea that an animal should be worth more than a man."

"I can remember a horse which my father bought for the price of three hundred slaves," said bin Zair. "Now let us consider the rhinoceros."

But at that moment Dinah raced away down the front of the cages to the chimpanzee grove and crouched chattering by the bars. One of the caged chimps answered her. She bristled and backed away, still chattering, while the deeper voice of one of the males joined in the racket. Though she was perfectly safe Morris instinctively hurried to her side.

He found the whole group more lively than he'd yet seen them. Except for Murdoch, who had retired for safety with her baby to the top of the central tree, they were all ranged along the front of the cage, chattering or grimacing at Dinah. The scene reminded Morris of an episode in some ancient *Wizard* where the town urchins mock through the school railings one of their number who has been forced to dress in an Eton jacket and be educated with the nobs. Dinah answered their jeers with bitchy confidence, as if she knew that she had indeed left the slums to join the evolutionary smart set, Man.

At the back of the cage the shiny panel of black glass slid up, and there were Anne and the Sultan leaning on the window-ledge, laughing at the scene. The Sultan beckoned.

"His Majesty is angry," said bin Zair. "You must go quickly. I will wait in your office."

"Good," said Morris. "I hope you're wrong. He looked pleased."

Even so he was slightly nervous as he took Dinah by the paw and hurried her off to the upper gallery, where he found that the atmosphere was indeed stickier than he would have guessed from that glimpse of the couple at the window. Dyal and Gaur were sitting against the wall several yards down the corridor. The Prince stood apart, withdrawn and angry, fiddling with one of the spring-guns as though, in the usual Bedouin manner, he wanted to take it to bits and put it together. Anne continued to lean on the window-sill while the Sultan turned unsmiling to Morris.

"What the hell have you been up to?" he said.

"In what way?"

"You don't seem to have taught Hadiq a single syllable of English."

"Rubbish mate! He's not getting on at all badly, considering. He just lacks confidence, especially with you standing there expecting him to spout a mixture of Wordsworth and Bertie Wooster."

The Sultan turned his head towards Anne.

"You are quite right, my dear," he said. "It is a clear proof of the need to hire properly qualified teachers for the school."

"You aren't being fair," she said. "Mr Morris is an absolute whizz at languages."

"What school?" said Morris.

"Oh, it's just a little plan we've dreamed up," said the Sultan. "Dinah doesn't seem to be making much progress either."

"Rubbish again. She's getting on fine."

"She didn't appear to be just now," said the Sultan.

"Oh, that . . . I was talking about her learning the future tense."

"There is a limit to my patience, Morris. I have gone to great trouble and expense to set up this experiment, and you dismiss it as 'Oh, that . . . ' How much time has Dinah actually been spending with the other chimps?"

"Not very much, so far. I've had to wait for them to settle down."

Morris did in fact feel mildly guilty about his having kept so

67

much to the old routine that had prevailed before the wild chimps came, with Dinah spending practically all her time in his company; but he hadn't expected the Sultan to react with such cold, bullying anger. The little dark eyes were like opaque beads in the flat, sand-coloured face. Morris, always easily cowed, was beginning to stammer reasons when Anne deliberately broke the tension.

"I'd love to see Dinah read something," she said. "Could she do that now?"

"I don't know," said Morris. "She's not in a very good mood, and in any case she's just had a banana."

"By God, Morris," shouted the Sultan, "you seem to think you own this place!"

"OK, OK, let's give it a go," said Morris. "What would you like her to do?"

He found that he too, by now, had joined in the general fit of sulks that seemed to have permeated the gallery; he had always particularly disliked making Dinah do her reading as if it were a circus trick.

"Let her fetch the spring-gun from Dyal and give it to me," said the Sultan, and without waiting to ask whether this was practicable he called to Dyal to put the gun in front of him on the floor. Morris scurried back to his office to fetch fruit for a reward to Dinah, and found bin Zair looking systematically through the files in the small cabinet. He looked up and smiled when Morris apologised for the delay.

Back in the upper gallery Dinah scampered over at the first rattle of the counters, instantly the alert pupil, teacher's pet. Morris laid out a message on the tiles.

white square:	Dinah
green circle with hole:	go
orange circle with hole:	get/fetch/take
yellow square:	thing with no name

She sniffed a couple of times at the message, which was a form they normally used for search-games, then set off towards Morris's office. Morris clicked and slapped down the red negative circle. She sniffed at it, then set off in the opposite direction,

68

along the bleak corridor towards where the two guards set. Gaur shrank visibly from her, but Dyal laughed and when she picked up the spring-gun and returned he rose and followed her. She placed the spring-gun on the floor and dubiously compared it with the yellow square. Morris added a positive green circle to the message, and she immediately began to bounce up and down, eager for the banana, then chattered irritably as he spelt out a new message.

white square:	Dinah
yellow circle with hole:	give
yellow square:	thing with no name
black square:	(to) person other than Morris or Dinah
purple rectangle:	qualifier—"big"

All might have been well—tempers been smoothed, Morris's treatment of Dinah justified, even his qualifications for teaching Prince Hadiq confirmed—had not Dyal and Gaur come to join the group; but Dinah was never very happy with the qualifying group of symbols; she knew perfectly well how they worked, but their presence in a message seemed to make the whole thing harder for her. Now she picked up the gun, trailing it by its muzzle, and studied the possibilities before her, the Sultan, the Prince, Anne and the two bodyguards. The hush of waiting became ridiculously tense, almost as though it should have been filled by a circus drum-roll. At last, with a rush, she laid the gun ungraciously at Gaur's feet and scampered back to Morris's side.

The ten seconds' silence was so intense and shocking that it seemed almost as though Dinah's mistake had some ritual significance.

"Well," said the Sultan at last, "what went wrong?"

"Honestly it was pretty good," said Anne. "In fact it was marvellous. Only she gave it to the wrong person."

"Exactly," said the Sultan, clearly so angered by her intervention that Morris wondered whether his haphazard reading had included some potted Freud.

"Give her a chance," said Morris. "She's got a tiny vocabulary, with as few nouns in it as possible, because we're more interested in her grasp of logical sentence-structure than just lists of words. I told her to give the bloody gun to a big man. That's the nearest I could get. The language doesn't contain a *name* for you."

As if to settle things he gave Dinah her banana, with which she retreated to the far wall, as though one of them was going to try to steal it off her. Morris crouched to pick the counters off the tiles, scrabbling with his finger-nails on the slippery surface.

"Whose names does she know?" asked Anne.

"Just her own and mine—these two. This black square means a person other than one of us . . ."

The Sultan interrupted, dropping into Arabic, the first time for years that he had used it, except on formal occasions, when talking to Morris.

"By God, Morris, you do me great shame. You and the ape have eaten my bread and taken from me many gifts, and yet you have not thought me worth a name of my own, to tell me apart from some slave or goat-boy!"

"I'm sorry . . ." Morris began in English.

"Let it be seen to. I will have a name. Let a black symbol be made and on it set in gold the shape of a hand, the symbol of my house."

"If you like," said Morris. "She's going to have to see quite a bit of you if she's going to learn to associate it with you, and only you."

The Sultan laughed, and reverted to English.

"She can come to the Council—we'll make her Minister of Education, eh, my dear? And Morris, old boy, you really must see that she spends more time with the other apes. Got it?"

He smiled, a jovial great genie. But his eyes were still as hard as glass.

70

Three

1

"'Holy . . . cats . . . Batman,'" read Prince Hadiq, "'. . . am . . . I . . . seeing things . . . back . . . to . . . the . . . Batcave . . . Wonder-boy . . . this . . . looks . . . like . . . wit . . . widge . . . wicket . . .' I cannot read one word, Morris."

"Is it 'witchcraft'?" asked Morris, without turning from the window. The whole tail-fin had now vanished, and some genius had contrived to remove one of the engines, but had been unable to shift it more than a few yards. It simply lay on the concrete by the wing, but no doubt time would whittle it away. The guard had been withdrawn, now that all the more easily de-tachable parts had vanished, but the thieves' work went on at its regular pace.

"Yes, witchcraft," said the Prince. "A woman is witching my father. Is witching also Gaur."

Morris turned and saw that the prince was looking up from the comic as though he wished to pursue this conversation. The lesson had not gone well so far, and any subject which would encourage the boy to talk must be pursued. He was really getting on quite well, but something—perhaps this stupid worry about Anne being a witch—had caused a slight relapse.

"Where is Gaur, by the way?" asked Morris.

"Outside the curtain," said the Prince. "We have . . . a matter to laugh . . . to laugh at, I say. Gaur tells you are a big witch, witching me. I tell this woman is a big witch, witching Gaur."

"I'm not a witch, and I don't think Anne is," said Morris. "We don't have witches in England any longer."

"If so, how this?" said the Prince, flapping his hand against the *Batman* comic.

"Oh, that's only a story—and I expect you'll find that it turns out that there is no witchcraft at all, only some kind of machinery made to look like witchcraft."

"Stupid," said the Prince, dropping the comic. "The mother of me, the Shaikhah, she tells this woman ... is a witch."

Morris smiled, but was answered by a scowl.

"You think ... I am telling woman's talk. *Wallah*, Morris, the mother of me has go ... has gone ... to London ... to Paris ... to New York. The Sultan has much women, always. She thinks OK. A man is a man. Never she tells them witching. When I am baby, she ... I speak Arab, please?"

"If you want to, but you're doing very well."

"By God, Morris, I tell you the woman is a witch. I have seen the Shaikhah mourn and weep because my father does not remember to take her to his bed when he is mad for love of some dancing girl. But never before has she told me to find her poison!"

"Speak English," hissed Morris, knowing how whispers could travel and float along the corridors of the palace. "What are you going to do?"

"I ask you. What?"

It was a great honour to be consulted over so intimate a matter as whether one should help one's mother to murder one's father's mistress. Morris did not care for great honours.

"I wouldn't do anything for a bit," he said. "I'd tell your mother it's difficult to get poison."

"But is *not* difficult. *Saqwa* is ... medicine for ... skin of camels. Gaur also. He knows many ... poisons ... in marshes."

"Yes, I see," said Morris. *Saqwa*, he knew, was usually arsenic, and certainly the songs were full of ugly deaths after feasts.

"So what I do?"

"Well, I could talk to Anne, I suppose. I expect your mother could give her a message asking her to come and see me, and I could suggest that she stops doing whatever she is doing to your father. And Gaur, of course."

"Oh, Gaur is mad only. Is mad for love. He make songs for the woman."

"Does he, by God!" said Morris. He had never taped anything

like that, the love-songs and canoe-chants and lullabies of the ordinary marsh-people. All he had in his collection was the formal music of the singing clan.

"Yes. He lies on the floor. He groans. He is mad. I tell him, unless . . . if my father hear . . . he shoot him. True."

"That doesn't sound like witchcraft."

"But Gaur is mad. My father shoot him. Will shoot him."

"I know. The thing is that down in the marshes Gaur is a warrior of the ninth clan, and that means he's not allowed to marry, but he is not punished if he takes another man's wife. So I expect it seems natural to him."

"OK. But he is mad, still. I send Dyal to you. You tell him tell Gaur. OK?"

"Fine," said Morris, who had in a vague way been waiting for a chance to talk to Dyal about the future of the marshes, without doing anything to bring such a meeting about.

"But this woman," said the Prince. "She make my father . . . send . . . other womans . . . women . . . away. Send back to tents . . . Such is great . . . great 'aib."

"A great disgrace? I see."

"Not for all peoples a disgrace. He send young woman back to tents with a good gift . . . yes, OK. She finds good husband quick, if peoples are Hadahm, Mura'ad, that sort. But some peoples tell it is a great . . . disgrace. My father knows this. He will not do it, but she is witching him."

"Yes, I see," said Morris inwardly cursing the pretty busybody for scattering the seeds of female emancipation on such unwilling ground. "Yes, of course I will talk to her. Don't let your mother poison her, though. She isn't a witch—she's just a fool."

"A witching fool?"

"Yes . . . I mean no. I mean what you are trying to ask is 'Is she a foolish witch?' The answer is no. She is foolish, but she isn't a witch."

But she's a witching fool all right, he thought.

2

When Kwan had wanted to pay Morris a visit, he used to send one of the marsh eunuchs carrying a short piece of reed, notched in the middle. Morris would break it at the notch and send one half back with the slave—the reed symbolised a spear, and breaking it was a sign of peace. Kwan used this ritual even when he was himself standing just outside in the passage; it gave Morris time to unroll the reed visiting-mat and fetch out a box of cheroots and a can of sweetened condensed milk; then Kwan would come in, settle on the mat, suck at the can, chew tobacco and talk, endlessly, never repeating himself, about old doings among the buffalo herds.

So Morris found himself off-balance when, the day before the murders, Dyal came to the door unannounced and asked in his excellent Arabic if Morris was busy. Morris had in fact been watching some film of the chimpanzees and had a slight headache because the palace developing laboratory (installed by the Sultan to satisfy a sudden fad for wild-life photography, but now also apparently used by Akuli bin Zair for his home porn movies) was erratic in its results. So Morris was glad of the excuse to switch off and open the blinds. Dinah, who had been having one of her scuttering, restless mornings, leaped hooting to her nest where she stuffed her mouth with the shavings she used for bedding and glowered at the visitor. Morris rose from his desk.

"Peace be on you," he said. "You are very welcome. How would you choose to be seated? I have the visiting-mat that Kwan used to use."

"A chair is more comfortable," said Dyal, smiling. "We have no customs in common, Lord Morris. We are both far from our own people, you in distance and I in time. So we can ignore all customs."

"All right. That chair is cleaner than it looks. Would you like coffee? Or ... er ... Kwan used to drink sweet milk and chew tobacco."

"I like weak instant coffee in a large cup, very hot."

Morris laughed aloud because this was so exactly the opposite in every way of the Arab notion of what coffee should be. Dyal laughed too, a large easy sound, showing that he understood the joke.

"But I will chew tobacco," he went on. "In this I am still a marshman. We have a root in the marshes which we chew, but tobacco is better. My brother the Sultan has made me swear an

oath not to chew it in his presence, nor to buy it for myself;
but I may take a gift of it. Thank you. Ah, yes, that is good
stuff!"

He chewed with slow gusto while Morris got the coffee ready.
The jaw-movement altered his face and gave it a less human look;
in fact for a moment he seemed to have more in common with
Dinah than with Morris. Perhaps it was this emergence of a
more primitive aspect of his guest that made Morris relapse
into marsh language.

"The floods go very slowly," he said.

"Let us continue in Arabic," said Dyal, too gravely for the
words to sound like a snub. "I cannot think easily now in the old
language. But let us omit all that coffee-talk—how it wearies me
to stand behind the shoulder of my brother the Sultan and hear
the same words spoken over and over again, by each guest, as
though they had never before been said. I prefer the manners of
you Franks. You say 'Good morning. How are you?' and then
you do business."

Morris was impressed. There was a relaxed lordliness in Dyal's
tone, and he had pronounced the English words in a very com-
prehensible accent. His bulk filled the shabby chair. He might
have been an old-fashioned Oxford don putting a freshman at
ease before his first tutorial. Kwan had had a kingly manner too,
but a whole Toynbeean cycle of civilisations seemed to lie between
their two styles of majesty.

"As you wish," said Morris. "It is only that since Kwan died I
get little chance to practise the language."

"You must speak it with Gaur. Prince Hadiq tells me that you
wish to talk to me about young Gaur."

"It was the Prince's wish," said Morris carefully. "The Prince
is both my pupil and my friend, and it is painful to him that
Gaur should be afraid of me."

Dyal's laugh made Dinah duck out of sight.

"He is not physically afraid of me," explained Morris. "But he
thinks I am a witch."

"He is a boy, a savage straight from the mud. His head is full
of old women's chatter. When a boy becomes a man down in the
marshes they do not give him a man's mind. I remember, when
first I came to the sands—before this house was built, when we all

75

lived in a big mud fort—how many childish tales I believed. Yes, I will tell him to be a man."

This was all uncomfortably abrupt. Morris had hoped to ease from a fairly detailed demonstration that he was not a witch into the next item on the agenda. Now he would have to tackle it direct.

"The Prince," he said, "also believes in the truth of witches."

"So do all sensible men."

"Perhaps. But he believes that the Frankish woman, who is my countrywoman, has cast a spell on Gaur."

"It is possible."

"A love-spell?"

Dyal laughed again like a man auditioning for Father Christmas.

"By God, boys are always the same. I remember when I came to the sands, how it was. There were four of us in the reeds, of the ninth clan, who became men that year. Before the dances we slept in the same hut, talking all night of women, the girls we had seen, or the young wives herding buffalo, and how we would take this woman or that as soon as we were made men. But then I was sent for, to be the prince's shadow, here in the sands, and here there were no women to be seen, all shut away, hidden under litters when they rode out. So I wept and groaned in the dark to think of my comrades sporting among the reedbeds. Surely, if there had then been one such as the Frankish woman walking about the fort unveiled, I would have rolled my eyes at her!"

"But what would the old Sultan have done if he had seen your eye-rollings?"

"Now, he was a man! Perhaps he would have laughed and given me the woman. But my Prince was more of an age with me than Hadiq is with Gaur, so most likely the Sultan would have sent for brides from the eight clans for his son, who would then have lent them to me."

Morris blinked but Dyal didn't seem to notice.

"As it happened," he went on, "my Prince soon went to get his learning in your country, and I returned to the marshes and waited. It was a weary three years, but I eased them with hunting pig and women."

76

"Prince Hadiq believes that the Sultan would shoot Gaur if he knew."

"It is not possible. What! Break the Bond of Na!ar for a woman!"

"Oh?"

"Have you not heard the Testament of Na!ar? Does it not say that thus is the Bond broken. Many things in that song are obscure, but those lines, as I remember, are clear."

Morris was puzzled. He remembered the passage clearly enough, but since Arabs and marshmen had continued to murder each other occasionally over the intervening centuries, he did not see how the lines could have a precise meaning. However, it gave him a lead-in to the next subject.

"Is that the only fashion in which the Bond can be broken?" he asked. "For instance, I have heard talk among the Arabs that the Sultan will soon give permission to the oil company to start drilling in the marshes, and later to drain them."

"I have heard such talk many times. The Arabs are always full of foolish stories. They think about nothing but money."

"I expect you're right. But I have listened to a lot of Arab talk, and I think I have learnt to tell the grain from the chaff. This rumour seemed to me to have some substance to it. And bin Zair has been recently to the wells—he told me so himself."

"It is foolishness," said Dyal, calm, academic, slightly bored. "First, it *would* break the Bond, as you say, and my brother the Sultan knows that. He would have talked with me about whether it was possible. Second, if the oil company came we would kill them."

"You too."

"Certainly. I am here under the Bond. If that is broken I go back to my people and fight for them, as did Na!ar, himself. And how could the oil company explore and drill when every reed-bed might hold twenty poisoned spears? They could bring machine-guns and helicopters, but there is good hiding in the reeds, and until the last male child in the marshes was dead they could not begin. Do you think these Italians would come here to work on those terms, though they were paid ten times over? There is safer work elsewhere."

"And you yourself would fight against the Sultan?"

77

"If the Bond were broken. We are each other's hostages for its continuance, but when it is broken it is my inheritance to fight for the people."

"I hope you are right, then."

Dyal had been speaking in a slightly odd fashion. Morris had once worked with a Professor who had suffered a slow kind of nervous breakdown, lasting several months, until one appalling morning his personality had completely come to bits while he was showing the Mayor round a new wing of his language department. By hindsight the Professor's colleagues had then realised that what had seemed minor mannerisms had in fact been symptoms, and one of these had been a tautness, almost an aggressiveness, in discussing the trivia of weather and county cricket, combined with a steady languor when the topic was of any importance. There was something vaguely similar in the way in which Dyal now switched from affable civilised conversation, about machine-guns and danger-money for oil-men and hereditary feuds, back to academic chat. Perhaps it was part of a boredom, already expressed, with social niceties, though he knew that his visit ought to have such a coda. But to Morris it suggested that there was more tension than appeared on the surface between the white-robed, westernised bodyguard and the naked savage who had once hunted pig and women among the reed-beds.

"It matters to you, then, whether the marshes are drained or no?" said Dyal.

"Certainly. I admire the language of the marshmen, and the songs. If the marshes are drained, all that will go."

"It has lived," said Dyal. "That is enough."

He spoke dispassionately, like a hunter discussing the necessary death of an old hound.

"Last year at the flood-going feast," said Morris, "I saw Kwan weeping during the songs."

"Yes, they are strong. I close my mind when the boys sing, but perhaps when I am old I will open it again. Kwan was a good man, and a great warrior. He killed many men. Once, before I came to the sands, he went hawking alone with the old Sultan, and the Sultan's brother sent men to attack them. They fought all day and killed seven of the men, and in the evening the Sultan rode for help while Kwan prevented the rest from following. There

78

was no moon, so Kwan stripped off his clothes and became a piece of the night. We marshmen know the smell of Arab. When the Sultan rode back with his guard in the morning he met Kwan walking unwounded out of the desert. They found fifteen dead men among the sands, eight of them killed with one small knife."

"He never told me, though he talked a great deal to me. I never even knew that the old Sultan had had a rebellious brother. What happened to him?"

"He was sent to the marshes. Our women have a trick of drowning a man, so that the drowning lasts all night. Of what, then, did Kwan speak? It is strange, for he was a silent man."

"I'll show you."

Morris rose and got out the tape-recorder. At the click of its cover Dinah climbed down from her nest and came carefully over with the curious, stiff-legged walk which chimpanzees use when they are being formal. Morris showed her which button to press and she wound the old tape off, watching with delight as the reels whirled. Then he threaded the new tape in and let her prod down with her black-nailed finger on to the "Play" button.

A mutter, a hush, and then Kwan's voice.

"The dance for a dead warrior is arranged in this fashion. First, the dead man's sister's son kills a year-old male buffalo and drains the blood into a bowl, so that the priestesses can paint the secret symbols against witchcraft with the blood on the dead man's body. Then the song-maker is sent for, who is the dead-man's spirit-brother, and he makes a song and teaches it to his sons. Next . . ."

Morris did not play this tape often, partly because he was not much interested in anthropological minutiae, and partly because it reminded him how much he missed Kwan's company. He stood staring out at the marshes, thinking of his big, gentle friend creeping naked about the desert under the stars, killing men with his knife. It took him some time to realise that something was the matter with Dyal.

Dyal was having a fit. He was sitting bolt upright in the chair, with the whites showing all round the iris of his staring eyes, with sweat all across his forehead like the condensation on a chilled coke-tin. He had a pistol in his right hand, but he clutched it to his chest just as Gaur had clutched his amulet. Morris switched the recorder off.

"Are you all right?" he said.

Dyal muttered several times and tried to speak. Then his whole body shuddered and relaxed. He lay back in the chair, wiped his brow with the back of his hand and sat for several seconds looking down at the pistol on his lap.

"By God, you have done an evil thing," he said.

"I have not done it willingly, and if I can I will undo it."

"I thought to kill you."

"Oh. Well . . . er . . ."

"A year ago Kwan lived. He was well. His eye was clear and his skin soft and black. Next day he was dead, as if by witchcraft. Now I see that you keep his soul in a black box, and summon your unclean servant to make him speak."

"He was my friend. I would not have hurt him for all the gold in Sheba. I swear to you, Dyal, that his soul is not in this box. It is only a piece of machinery. I will tell you how it works."

"Oh, I know that. I have seen such things, for bin Zair uses one in his office. But . . . but . . ."

Suddenly, awkwardly, he dropped into the language of the marsh.

"There are two worlds, and both are true. A man may throw his spear in the sun-world and hit nothing, but in the moon-world that spear strikes into his enemy's liver. To be a witch is to know how the channels wind in the moon-world, and when the floods of that world come and go. One deed may be done twice, by those who know, once in each world. The soul of a man is in his words— how otherwise can the singer make the souls of his hearers dance? You have put Kwan's soul in a box, Kwan who was my father's brother."

He spoke with a strange, jerky rhythm, which might have been caused by emotion or might have been the result of his long disuse of the language. Certainly he made two or three little slips of syntax.

"The guilt is mine, but I did not know it," said Morris. It was a line that occurred in several different songs.

"By God," said Dyal in Arabic, "I almost killed you and your ape."

"I can take Kwan's voice from the tape," said Morris. "I can wipe it off so that it will be if he had never spoken."

"Let it be done."

Morris hesitated a moment. He felt that what he ought to do was borrow a recorder from the Sultan and play the tape through once more, using the headphones and speaking Kwan's words himself. Then this no doubt invaluable account of funeral rites would be preserved. But the hell with it. He rewound the tape and set it to erase itself. The reels moved hypnotically. Goodbye, he thought. Goodbye.

"So a man may be a witch without knowing it?" he said. "He may act quite innocently in the sun-world and yet harm his neighbour in the moon-world."

"That is true."

"So there is no way in which I can prove to Gaur that I am not a witch, if I may be one without knowing it."

"None."

Dyal rose and came to the table. Morris stopped the machine, wound the tape back a little and showed him that it was now blank. Dyal nodded and prepared to leave.

"It must happen often in the marshes," said Morris, "men being accused of witchcraft when they do not know whether they are witches or not. What happens then?"

"They ask the ducks."

"Oh?"

Dyal shook his head, unsmiling, and left with no formalities at all.

3

It must have been Anne who had persuaded the Sultan not to appoint Dinah Minister of Education—he was quite capable of doing so, even in a matter which with another part of his mind he took seriously. So the slow process of giving him a name in Dinah's language took place in the zoo, every morning, at a time which was thoroughly inconvenient to everyone but himself. It also meant that Morris had no way of avoiding putting Dinah into the cage with the other chimps for at least one half of the morning, and that meant that he had to spend long periods at the observation window. At first he had tried introducing her when the chimps had had their morning's excitement over the sudden harvest of fresh fruit and green leaves that came down the chutes or appeared on the two branches that could still be relied on to extrude bananas. But Sparrow, who had quickly recovered his dominance from Rowse, always used the feeding period to prove his authority over the whole group, snatching fruit and displaying aggressively at all the other chimps in turn, even when he was no longer hungry. The arrival after this process of another ape who had not been through it meant that he then focused all his moral thuggery into subduing her. So it turned out better to let her join in the riot and receive only her fair ration of bullying. She hated being taken to the cage, but in fact the experiment was beginning to work with far more success than Morris would have believed possible. It had taken her about three sessions to learn not to challenge a male—even placid old Cecil—about anything. The first time she had received a real buffet she had shot off to a corner jabbing her bunched fingers together—her usual sign for "hurt". But quite soon she learnt to peel off the invisible gown and mortar-board as soon as she entered the cage and work by instinct. She had always kept the facial responses of a wild monkey, and after a week of integration she was making the gestures of submission and appeasement in a manner indistinguishable from the others. This enabled her to sort out her own place in the hierarchy; there were two slightly older female adolescents in the group, the Deneke sisters, whom she discovered she could dominate individually but not if they ganged up on her; together they built up a precarious relationship, running to each other for grooming sessions when they needed comfort. Dinah was wary now in her relationship with the mature chimps, though she occasionally pestered Murdoch to let her play with the baby; but apart from Sparrow, whom she feared and detested, she seemed well on the way to accepting them all, and they her. Morris thought that in another week or so it would become safe to leave her in the cage most of the time, unguarded. From a scientific point of view this was an exciting step forward. Emotionally it was shipwreck.

On the morning of the murders Morris took Dinah to the zoo as soon as he had breakfasted; it was the day for cleaning out the cages of the big carnivores, and he did not yet care to risk the new slaves doing this unsupervised. Though no one else in the palace would have even shrugged if a slave had got himself mauled, Morris was anxious to keep them. Bin Zair had found them less than a week after his zoo-inspection. They were Sulubba and not negroes, and already very good at their work. Jillad was a dark little man with a very narrow face and hollow cheeks, but intelligent eyes; Maj was large, fat and silent. When Morris had asked how they came to be slaves Jillad had grinned and said that his parents had been slaves before him. Maj had scowled and said nothing. Morris was beginning to think he ought to get Jillad to put some of his life-story on tape, as it must have been unusual; Sulubba, the mysterious desert people who are said to be descended from camp-followers of the crusaders, captured after Christian defeats, are despised by the Arabs but have recognised rights, so it was unusual for them to be slaves; nor were hereditary slaves often sold.

Morris was pleased to find them already in the lower gallery in front of the cages, waiting beside a big pile of fresh-cut young reeds. Dinah pretended to be frightened of them and jumped into his arms. Morris exchanged the traditional greetings.

"The Sultan will be here in two hours," he said. "We must have everything finished and tidy before then. That is far more reeds than we will need."

They shrugged and laughed. Then Morris watched while Jillad coaxed the polar bear into the corner of its cage with a lump of raw camel-meat, allowing Maj to lower the special grille that penned the big beast there. Jillad then renewed the filter chemicals, working quickly and accurately under Morris's eye though he had only once been shown how to do it. Maj raked the stale bedding out of the den, scooped the coarse dung into a bucket and went to fetch fresh reeds.

Immediately there was uproar, wild chattering from Dinah and cursing from Maj. Morris turned to see that Dinah was playing king of the castle on the pile of reeds, and when Maj came for an armful had snatched the other end of his bundle and pulled it to bits, scattering it round the passage. Maj, quick-tempered, lashed out at her with his foot and caught her in the ribs. Jillad

83

laughed. Dinah backed away, chattering, but when Morris came to collect her gathered courage to mock the aggressive slave.

"She is mischievous but not wicked," said Morris. "It is better to be her friend."

Maj only shrugged again and began sullenly to sweep the reeds together and pile them back on to the canvas. Morris loosed Dinah, who went scampering off down towards the chimps' cage, almost as though she thought them better company than humans. But she stopped before she reached them and returned to roam in aimless rushes, like a hairy spider, around the working men, jeering at Maj who rushed to guard his reeds whenever she came near them.

Soon she became enough of a nuisance for Morris to leave the two slaves to get on with the work while he took her further down the corridor for some language practice. He fetched a box of objects from his office and settled down at a point where the slaves could call to him if they needed help or advice. The session went badly, with Dinah refusing to pay attention from the very beginning, and throwing the objects about, deliberately scattering the symbols, and looking down the corridor to jeer from time to time at Maj. Then, quite suddenly, her mood changed and she plucked a little at Morris's shirt buttons which was one of her ways of demanding affection. He cradled her in his arms and gently teased the fur on her ribs. She wriggled slightly and prodded her fingers together, looking into his eyes. He picked out three of the scattered symbols.

yellow circle:	query
white square:	Dinah
purple circle with hole:	hurt

She left his arms and studied the symbols apathetically. All of a sudden she became animated, chattered at Maj where he was working by the cheetah's cage, found a black square and rearranged the symbols.

black square:	person other than Morris, Dinah or Sultan
purple circle with hole:	hurt
white square:	Dinah

84

Morris clicked sympathetically and made her sit still while he felt carefully along her ribs. Nothing seemed to be broken, but the shock of being hit by a human was for some reason greater than her reactions to Sparrow's bullying. Perhaps she was instinctually conditioned to her role as a female chimpanzee, among chimpanzees, whereas her relationship with mankind was an entirely learnt set of responses, a flimsy network that once broken could not repair itself by natural growth, but would have to be carefully re-knitted by some outside agent. Morris decided that he would have to speak to the slaves about their treatment of Dinah. It was the sort of job he hated, being conscious of how likely he was to make a mess of it, and simply put their backs up. But he was determined to try to keep them. They were jewels. Jillad, in particular, was a good example of the weird interweaving of civilisations in the desert—a man competent to cope with a fairly sophisticated gadget like the water-filter, and still a slave, because his father had been one.

They worked fast, too, now that Dinah was no longer distracting them. They were just finishing clearing the litter out of the chimpanzee grove when the special signal that heralded the Sultan fluted faintly down from the zoo doors.

"Finish and go," said Morris. "You have worked well."

Maj smiled and bowed, a portly salute with something of the absurd dignity that invests an orang.

"I will leave the reeds," he said. "They are tidy, Lord. You will not let your ape touch them?"

"Good," said Morris, and hurried away. Dinah loped beside him.

"Ah, there you are, old fellow," said the Sultan. "You'll be glad to learn I'm becoming quite scientific in my old age. I've brought a control group. I thought we might play hide-and-seek for a change."

Anne, leaning on the Sultan's arm, laughed. Today she was wearing an extraordinary get-up; basically it was riding-kit— glossy brown boots, white kid breeches moulded tight to buttock and thigh, taut blouse—but over this she wore a scarlet silk cloak ankle length and buckled at the throat. She also carried a little

85

silver-handled hunting-crop, and looked altogether as though she were starring in a camp re-make of *The Sheikh*.

"A control group?" he said, gaping at her. "You've got some funny ideas about control."

The Sultan chose to be not amused, an act he did very well. He waved an impatient hand towards where Dyal and Gaur stood, a little further along the upper gallery.

"It struck me that Dinah might simply be using my symbol for any big man who happened not to be Dyal," he said.

"Oh, I don't think so," said Morris. "You've got to remember that it's natural for her to think in terms of any group having a dominant male. Sparrow's that down there. You're it up here. In fact I get the impression that she's fascinated by you, but she's scared of you too."

"You have a peculiar line in flattery, Morris."

"Oh, come off it. I'm just telling you Dinah knows perfectly well who you are, and there's no chance of her muddling you up with anyone else."

"Good, good. Now, this game. My idea is that a couple of us hide and Dinah is told which one to find. You've got a symbol for find, haven't you?"

"I suppose so."

"'I suppose so!' Morris, in some ways you're a lout. Just because it's not your own idea, you go out of your way to make it sound impractical."

This was a perfectly fair criticism, and in fact the game went beautifully. Dinah coped with commands such as "Dinah: find: man: big: new sentence: Dinah: find: negative: Sultan." As soon as she discovered that there were grapes for her at the end of each hunt if she got it right she applied her wits to the task. When it was Gaur's turn to be the one discovered he needed some cajoling.

"Come thou," said Dyal, "it is not a witch finding. There is no duck, no poison."

"What's the trouble?" said Anne, in English.

"He's got it into his head that I'm a witch and Dinah is my familiar."

"How sweet," said Anne, smiling at the young savage. He rolled his eyes, clutched his amulet and went. The Sultan looked at her

86

sidelong but said nothing before he too moved heavily out of sight. Morris counted his fifty, spelt out the message for Dinah and let her go. She scampered off, chuckling. He looked up to see Anne standing face to face with the gorilla, imitating its grimace.

"It doesn't suit you," he said.

She understood before he did what he really meant, and ran a calm hand down her ribs and over her hip.

"There's a law of diminishing returns," she said. "When my grandfather was getting on, he used to complain that my grandmother was cheating him over his curries—he couldn't taste them any more, because he must have burnt his taste-buds pretty well clean off with trying."

"That looks a fairly strong curry," said Morris.

She shrugged.

"The fantasies of male domination . . . oh hell. Time I got out of here."

She swung back and stared at the gorilla.

"Get stuffed," she whispered.

But in fact, Morris thought, she was living the fantasy with every bit as much gusto as the Sultan, and even had enough spare sexual drive to flash bright glances towards poor Gaur. Perhaps she got a kick out of the risk; or perhaps she only wanted to spice up the Sultan's curry with the sharp tang of jealousy. Mercifully it was none of his business. He turned to watch through the window where Cecil was examining with intense interest the incipient sexual swelling on Starkie's rump.

When the hide-and-seek was over the usual shooting-match began; Dinah ate her last grapes with slow absorption and then Morris took her down to the cage. He came back to find that the Sultan's tortuous processes of revenge were in action; if your mistress flirts with a handsome young man, what more natural than to humiliate him in her presence, fondling as you do so, before his eyes, the forbidden flesh. The Sultan was speaking in slow Arabic.

"Let the boy guard the door for a while," he said. "Let him learn his duties. It is not good for the young to have no work to do, eh, my dear?"

The last three words were in English, but they would have

sounded insulting in any language. Dyal was visibly put out—startled more than angry—and led Gaur away with a puzzled expression. The Sultan laughed.

"May I borrow your office for a bit, old boy?" he said.

"Make yourself at home," said Morris.

He began to load oranges and cabbage into the chutes, and then he and Dyal watched in silence for twenty minutes while the chimpanzees had their lunch-time threshabout. For one who was not emotionally involved it was amusing to watch. Dyal laughed aloud—a deep and strangely solemn sound—several times. Morris watched Dinah work a sort of three-card trick on Sparrow, confusing him for the moment with a piece of orange-peel while she scuffled a real orange under the fresh bedding and then allowed herself to be harried round the grove until Sparrow forgot his grievance and she could retire, whimpering, to the reeds and eat the orange under cover of her sulks. Yes, Sparrow was thick all right, but so were they all by comparison with Dinah. Dinah was civilised. No. Westernised? Urbanised? Humanised?

On the other hand, comparing her appearance with what she had looked like when she had first joined the group in the cage, weeks ago—why, it had been the morning the hijacked jet had landed—she had lost some of her gloss. Her coat was less shiny and her air less detached. She had the scuffed, used look of the other chimps, though she was still set apart. Thus must the emigré aristos in Boston have looked, cobbling and laundering for a living but still set apart from those who had never known Versailles. Even so, Sparrow and Co were making a monkey of her. Morris could not regard it as a change for the better. He watched the riot with gloom.

This feeling was little alleviated by the arrival of bin Zair, after a shout from Gaur and an answer from Dyal. The Prime Minister came strutting along the black-and-white tiles with a wad of tattered documents under his arms, and though it was a relief not to have to watch him crawl, Morris could only see his arrival as a further knot in the tangled noon. It was to get away from encounters such as this, dammit, that he had come to Q'Kut at all. That and the money.

Bin Zair thrust his wad of papers at Morris without explanation. It looked like a file on financial matters, but it had been clearly dropped and regathered without sorting.

"His Majesty is where?" asked bin Zair, with no formal greetings at all.

"In my office, alone, with the Frankish woman."

Morris had seen Arabs express emotion before, but he had never actually seen a beard torn. Now it happened—at least when bin Zair finished his frenzied wrenching several strands of grey hair came away in his fingers.

"What is this?" said Morris, tapping the file.

"Yes, that is urgent also. It is the accounts for the animals before you came. This year his majesty has demanded a budget, with comparative tables of previous expenditure. He has ordered it by next week! My clerks will do the additions, but the file is disordered and I cannot trust them to know what is relevant. Allah! Allah! That he should be wantoning at such a time!"

Allah was mighty that day. At least, at the sound of his name the office door clicked. Morris switched the camera on and moved hurriedly down the corridor to the corner. The flood of anger hit him like a beam of light. Their faces were set. The Sultan's eyes were cold as stones, and Anne, though flushed and dishevelled, did not now look like a prince's plaything but more like she had done that first day on the aeroplane wing. Whatever they had borrowed the office for, it hadn't been a bit of idyll. Both of them looked at Morris as though he had been caught peeping through the keyhole.

"Bin Zair is here," he muttered. "He's in a considerable flap."

"Who would be a monarch?" said the Sultan. "My dear, you had better not let him see you in that rig. He has high standards."

"Oh, God!" snapped Anne.

"He's in the top gallery, is he Morris? Well you'd better go along the lower one, my dear. Go straight to the women's quarters. That's an order. I'll come and see you there."

She opened her mouth but said nothing, then swung away and strode down the short passage with the red cloak streaming behind her. She was moving so rapidly that it seemed to stay in sight long after she herself had vanished round the corner. Morris turned into his office but he had hardly laid the papers on his desk when he heard the Sultan call. He went out into the corner to find bin Zair and the Sultan standing at the top of the steps into the upper gallery.

"Come here a moment, will you, old boy?" said the Sultan. But when Morris reached the top step it was bin Zair who spoke, in a low voice, in Arabic.

"Lord Morris," he said, "will you go softly to the doors and there tell the young slave who guards them that he is to let no man enter, for any reason. You speak his tongue and can make your meaning clear."

"Dyal could do it," said the Sultan. "Morris is not a messenger boy."

Bin Zair raised his head to the ceiling, as if in prayer. In fact for the moment he looked like a model for St Anthony at the height of his temptations.

"It's all right—I'll go," said Morris.

Round the corner, in the upper gallery, he found Dyal leaning by the observation window, still watching the chimps with large affability. Morris nodded to him and hurried on, to find Gaur in a markedly contrasting state. The young man was just outside the main doors, posed like a sentry but groaning aloud, and with a face so contorted with grief and passion that even the two deaf-and-dumb eunuchs had stopped their touching-game and were looking at him pop-eyed. Morris gave his message quickly and hurried away. He had no desire to witness the fresh out-pourings of torment that would probably begin when Anne, going the long way round, reached the lobby. Thank heavens I've missed out on all that, he thought, almost scampering past the point where the Sultan, bin Zair and Dyal were already involved in what seemed to be a council of state. Little bin Zair was talking in a low, urgent voice, while the two large men looked down at him in silence. As Morris came into earshot bin Zair stopped speaking, but began again as soon as he had rounded the corner into the short passage that led down to the office. Morris was so anxious not to overhear anything, not to become involved, that he almost fell down the flight of steps.

Deliberately he opened and closed the door with a rattle and a bang, and scuttered to his desk, reaching for the pile of papers bin Zair had brought. He was already reading the top one when a splash of unfamiliar scarlet caught the edge of his vision.

"I hope I'm not in your way," said Anne, meekly.

"Good God! You're mad!"

"In one sense, yes. But he's mad all along the line."

"You must go. Really. Please. He might . . ."

"OK, OK."

"And quietly. He's only just up there round the corner. You'll just have to hope no one's looking through the window into the chimp-cage."

"So long. Thanks for everything."

She slipped out. As the door opened and closed the deep note of Dyal's voice reached down to him. Very uneasily he settled to the papers, not even looking up when the Sultan came down the steps and along the passage outside his door, on the way to the lower gallery. His angry voice was punctuated by bin Zair's deprecating squeaks. Most of the documents turned out to be a mixture from two separate files, the first concerning a lengthy wrangle about who ought to pay for a pair of cheetahs that had been delivered dead after what had evidently been a journey of careless cruelty through the hands of half-a-dozen airlines, and the second consisting of correspondence with the court of a neighbouring Sultan, one of whose sons on a visit to Q'Kut had been foolish enough to lose his left arm between the bars of a lion-cage. Presumably the blood-money was a zoo expense. With these were a number of loose sheets, not apparently consecutive, on which a variety of clerks seemed to have made random attempts to detail more ordinary zoo expenses. The noise of some kind of rumpus in the chimpanzee grove came faintly to him. Normally he would have rushed out to see that Dinah was all right, but now he merely sighed and went on with the papers. He hadn't even reached the bottom of the pile when somebody scratched at the door.

"What is it?" he called.

Bin Zair entered, looking very wild.

"Be welcome," said Morris.

"May I rest here?" said bin Zair. "The Sultan is much enraged. He struck his servant. Did you hear?"

Indeed the old man's headcloth was askew and he seemed to have been having another go at his beard. He settled shakily on to the tatty sofa.

"I heard nothing. Shall I make coffee?"

"No, no. His rage is not with me, his faithful old servant. It is with the treacherous marshmen. Children of dogs!"

"What has happened?"

"They have spoken with the oil company. With the company's help they will send a delegation to the United Nations, declaring themselves an independent people."

"But how . . ."

"They have done this thing through the Sultan's own body-guard, Dyal."

"No!"

"It is true, Morris. And they have done worse. They are thieves and serpents. They have planned . . ."

He was interrupted. He had left the door open when he came, and so Morris heard clearly the sudden whoof of a spring-gun, a raucous cry, and then slightly nearer the sound of another gun. Still quivering bin Zair struggled to his feet as another inarticulate shout rang out, drowned in turn by an extraordinary clamour among the chimpanzees. Morris was first out of the door. Something very violent must be happening in the cage, he thought, for both Dyal and Sultan to loose off, especially when their minds were full of this stupid oil business. But when he rounded the corner he saw that the Sultan was lying flat on his back against the mesh of the grove. He hesitated. Bin Zair scuttled past him. The noise in the cage was appalling. Morris looked and saw Dinah scampering round the cage pursued by an infuriated Sparrow who struck or kicked at her continually. She must have heard the click of the latch, for she rushed towards the door, shot through and crouched whimpering on the floor of the gallery while Morris re-latched the door and Sparrow raged inside. One of the hypodermic darts lay glistening on the floor of the cage.

Morris shook his head and turned to where bin Zair was kneeling beside his master's body. A curious orange flush suffused the Sultan's cheeks. He was breathing heavily through his nose, but his lips were smiling. Bin Zair stood up as Morris knelt to feel for the pulse, which was slow and erratic.

"Does he live?" said bin Zair.

"Yes. But he's not well. Get help—Dyal and Gaur."

"Who has done this thing?"

"Nobody. It looks like a heart-attack. You told me he was much enraged."

"Yet he fired a shot. Look, the gun is beneath him."

Morris dragged it out by the barrel. It wasn't the practice-gun and it was now unloaded.

"For God's sake," said Morris, "go to my office. Ring for the Sultan's doctor."

Bin Zair didn't move. Morris looked up and for the first time noticed that the inspection window on the other side of the cage was open. Of course—there had been two shots.

"Dyal!" he yelled. "Dyal!"

There was no answer. Suddenly bin Zair made up his mind and ran off round the corner, lifting the skirts of his robe like a woman. Morris stayed where he was, uncertain what to do. The pattern of the Sultan's heart-beats was very alarming. Dinah appeared at his side, still whimpering and prodding the tips of her fingers together. Morris reached out with his free hand to touch her shoulder reassuringly but she bent forward over the Sultan's body, peering into the sick-hued face as if she could read signs there. Her "hurt" gesture, which she had continued making without thinking about it, suddenly became more urgent and meaningful.

"Yes," said Morris, "he's hurt too."

"Lord Morris," squeaked bin Zair. "Come hither. Look!"

His face pale and frenzied, leaned through the inspection window. Dammit, thought Morris, I bet he hasn't phoned that doctor yet. But he rose, picked up Dinah and ran round to the upper gallery. He found bin Zair bending over another inert body, that of Dyal. A second hypodermic dart projected from the black flesh of the bodyguard's neck; it looked as though it might have struck deep into the big vein that runs by the collar-bone. The face was contorted from its normal calm to a snarl almost like that of the stuffed gorilla, and a dribble of dark saliva ran down from the corner of the wrenched mouth.

"Who has done this thing?" cried bin Zair.

"It looks like an accident," said Morris. "Dyal shot at one of the apes; and the Sultan perhaps in sport, shot at Dyal. The drug in the dart only makes a man sleep, but the Sultan has had a heart-attack."

"Sleep!" cried bin Zair. "He is dead!"

Morris knelt. He could find no pulse at all. The lungs seemed not to move either.

"God take vengeance!" squealed bin Zair.

"Look, for heaven's sake go and telephone for that doctor. A few minutes can make all the difference in a heart-attack."

Bin Zair didn't move. Impatiently Morris jumped up and strode back to the office with Dinah a pace behind him, whimpering to be carried; she seemed to have sensed his mood of fear and fret and sheer irritation at being involved in these dramas. The telephone exchange was having one of its capricious days; after half-a-dozen futile attempts to dial the doctor (feverishly copied by Dinah on her toy telephone) he found himself in contact with the Captain of the Guard.

"Thank God," he said. "This is Morris . . . and may your sons all flourish . . . please, this is urgent . . . yes. The Sultan has become very ill in the zoo. I cannot make the doctor hear. Will you send a good man to him at once? At once, or the Sultan will surely die. Be quick! And captain, bring men up here, and a stretcher—two stretchers . . . good."

He banged the receiver down, looked unhappily round the office as if longing for some excuse to stay there, then moved slowly out and along to the lower gallery, with Dinah still at his side, still whimpering.

The Sultan lay just as he had before, breathing heavily and even peacefully, but with the flesh of his face so strange a colour that it looked as though he had been appallingly bruised three days ago. His hands were the same hue. His pulse was rapid and feeble, but every few seconds would produce a single appallingly heavy beat, like a hammer blow. When Morris had been there a couple of minutes bin Zair came round the corner with a dart in his hand.

"What news?" said Morris.

"The news is good," said bin Zair automatically. Morris stared until he realised that he had embarked, unintentionally, on one of the traditional desert greetings which always evokes the same answer, come plague, come famine, come slaughter of brothers.

"Look," said bin Zair, thrusting the dart in front of his face. Morris took it. It was one of the new pattern, unblunted by repeated shots at the gorilla. Its needle was black with blood.

94

No, no blood was ever as black as that, nor glistened so, as molasses glistens. Morris swallowed several times.

"Do you think that's poison?" he said.

"I think so. And this dart I pulled from the slave's neck. Listen, Morris. When I left the upper gallery to talk privately with the Sultan, the slave gave my master the gun he was carrying My master took it without thought. Now, I believe that when left him the slave fired at my master and my master fired back at the slave. Perhaps one of your apes took the dart, and there it is now in the cage."

"But why on earth . . .?"

"I do not know, except that the marsh-people had turned against my master."

"Even so, it won't work," said Morris. "The poison doesn't make you sleep—it needs the drug in the dart to do that; and the other gun only had an empty practice dart in it."

"How many guns are there, Morris?"

"Three. The practice-gun, the one we keep loaded, and a spare."

"Where is the third?"

"In my office. Come and see."

But the cupboard in the office was empty and three new darts were missing from the drawer below. They found the practice-gun at once, tucked in behind the stuffed gorilla. The one by Dyal's body was the spare.

"Oh, God," said Morris. "Where's that bloody doctor?"

Impatiently he walked towards the main doors. Bin Zair scurried on one side of him and Dinah on the other.

"We must question the guards," said bin Zair. "If no one entered the zoo and no one left, and you and I were together, then it is plain reason that they must have killed each other."

"I don't know. You say the Sultan was very angry. Perhaps he killed Dyal in a rage and then had a heart-attack."

"I have seen men die with heart-attacks, but never with their skin of such a colour. And whence came the poison."

"Oh God! I don't know. Let's see whether Gaur heard anything."

The short passage to the zoo doors was empty. In the lobby beyond them stood Gaur alone. The lights of the lift-panel winked in descending order.

"What man descended in the box?" said Morris in the language of the marsh.

"No man, lord," said Gaur, spreading his palms to show emptiness. And of course it was perfectly likely that the lift was plying between lower floors without ever having reached this level.

"Since I spoke with thee who has come and gone?"

"Only the white woman I love, lord."

"How long since?"

(Yes, Anne had been standing by the gun-cupboard when he'd looked up from his desk and seen her. That damned silly cloak could easily have hidden a gun.)

"Thou didst go and she came. All that as long since as it takes a man to milk a buffalo with a four-month calf."

(Ten minutes? Quarter of an hour? Too long ago, anyway.)

"He says nobody came or went," said Morris in Arabic.

"He is a marshman also. He is fresh from the marshes. That poison does not keep its strength many weeks, they say."

"Well at any rate he won't be lying about whether anyone else has been here. The ninth clan don't lie."

"All men lie, Morris. Who comes now?"

The lights blinked again as the lift ascended. Its doors rattled open and out flooded a pack of rifle-brandishing guards, sweeping with them the puffy little Arab whose main task hitherto had been to mix the Sultan's hangover-cures. Morris took Dinah back to his office and listened to the shouts of rage and cries of astonishment. The Captain of the Guard came to ask for keys, saying that bin Zair had ordered a complete search of the zoo for lurking assassins.

"I'll have to come too," said Morris. "You won't be able to search the bear's cage or the lion's without my help."

"We had intended to shoot them," said the Captain. "What use are they, now my master is dying?"

Morris picked up the keys without answering. The Sultan's body had gone, but as they passed the chimpanzee grove Morris's eye was caught by the second dart. That might be evidence, he realised.

"Wait," he said and unfastened the door. Dinah scampered away, whimpering, no doubt thinking that she was about to be shut in with the lower classes again. The apes, who were in a very nervous state, backed away into corners as he walked across the cage. Only Sparrow didn't move. Sparrow sat against one of the concrete tree-trunks with his face drawn into the full rictus of dominance-display. Morris, as he bent for the dart, kept an eye on him in case of a sudden charge. It took him several seconds to realise that Sparrow was dead. He had been poisoned too.

Four

1

ONLY RARELY HAD the Sultan's deep identification with the Arabs of the desert come to the surface. He had spent most of his time in the whimsical luxury of his palaces, and when Morris was present had revelled in the role of English eccentric; but in essential matters his reactions had been those of the bedu. The palace was where it was partly because of his feudal duties to the marshmen, but largely to satisfy his love of the big sands. He had refused to send Hadiq, or any of his other sons, abroad for their education, saying that they must first understand where they belonged. This beduism had not been a merely intellectual attitude; his favourite sport had been hawking, and he preferred to do this from the back of a camel, sometimes riding several days into the desert and while there regarding the heat, foul water, hardship and pain as normal and endurable. He used to refer to these trips as his health-cures, a way of losing a few stone, but they had been more to him than that.

For these reasons he had been much more admired and respected by the Arabs themselves than were many other little Sheikhs and Sultans. Even so Morris was astonished by how quickly the news of his death spread. Overnight men seemed to seep out of the desert; the dunes along the marsh were pimpled with their tents and the shore-line noisy with their camels; on any flat patch a couple of Mercedes stood twinkling in the sunlight. Three hundred rifles had been loosed off into the air as the old Dakota bumbled down the runway, up, and south with the Sultan's body to the traditional family burial grounds. By next day the number of tents was doubled, and when Morris went to the Council meeting he had to push through crowded lobbies where groups of men stood around shouting at the tops of their voices.

There was a stack of weapons at the entrance to the Council Chamber, and as well as the usual pair of scimitar-toting slaves a young man with a cleft chin, carrying a modern sub-machine-gun.

"What are you?" he shouted at Morris without any greeting. "The war is an Arab matter. We don't want any outsiders."

"Oh," said Morris, rather relieved. "In that case . . . Is Akuli bin Zair within? Since he asked me to come, I must tell him that . . ."

"Bin Zair!" said the man. "Enter. I did not know."

About twenty Arabs sat in a circle in front of the throne. There were several gaps, which gradually filled. Hadiq sat on a low stool beside the empty throne, looking ill and tired, having flown down to the burial last night, mourned all night and returned that morning. He smiled palely at Morris, who settled on to a cushion beside a fat sheikh called Umburak, with whom he had once gone hawking along the marsh shore. Looking round the circle Morris saw that the three or four other Arabs he knew were all important men; so, presumably, were the strangers. The conversation was restrained and desultory, mostly concerning the dead Sultan's virtues and especially his generosity. Every now and then somebody would curse the marshmen.

The last gaps filled. Coffee came slowly round—Morris was served about fifth, surprisingly high in the pecking-order. At last Hadiq stood up.

"You are welcome, friends of my father," he whispered. "But I am sick with grief, so bin Zair, who was my father's right hand, will speak for me."

Bin Zair's voice seemed scarcely stronger, but he was perfectly audible and less squeaky than usual. He made a more formal welcome, naming each of the assembly in turn; then he spoke simply of his love for his dead master, and said how long he had served him and his father before him, and that he could not eat nor sleep until his death was avenged; and then he turned politely to a dark little man, an almost legendary camel-raider called Fuad, and asked how this should be done.

Fuad leaped to his feet, pulled a piece of chewing-gum out of his mouth, stuck it behind his ear and began cursing. It was a peculiar performance, ugly but not very impressive, though he spoke at the top of his voice and his mouth frothed and his eyes bulged and shone with a pathological intensity. His speech contained almost no logical argument, no indicative sentences. It reminded Morris of the hoarse bellowings of an old-style trades union agitator trying to whip an apathetic strike meeting into action.

But it had its effect. Soon half a dozen men were on their feet, including the young man with the cleft chin, who appeared to have forgotten to leave his gun outside. They shouted too. Morris noticed that Umburak and some of the other men seemed totally unmoved by this uproar; they treated it as if the speakers were having a fit of coughing, and waited politely for it to end. But Hadiq was standing by the throne, waving his arms, trying to say something, without effect. Bin Zair leaned over and tugged gently at his robe. Hadiq sat down. Bin Zair waited a few seconds then rose and made a sign to the coffee-man, who came strutting into the middle of the circle, knelt down and began to pound his pestle into the mortar. The shouting stopped at once.

"Go away, fool," said bin Zair. "We have only just drunk coffee."

The man picked up his tools and went.

"Friends," said bin Zair, "the Sultan has something to say."

"The marshmen are on my face," stammered Hadiq, "as they were on my father's . . ."

"What!" said someone. "They killed your father and you will take them on your face?"

Fuad's party shouted agreement.

"It is true there is a certain old treaty," began bin Zair.

"Broken, broken," yelled Fuad. "Death to the treaty-breakers!"

"Let us be told about this treaty," said Umburak. "Let us also be told in what manner the Sultan died, that we may judge whether the treaty is indeed broken."

"Good," said bin Zair. "The treaty is not written, because the marshmen do not write. But they tell it every year at a feast when the floods go, always in the same words. I have heard it many times, and Lord Morris here has a tape of it. It is a peace treaty, ending the fighting between the marshmen and the Sultans, whereby they the marshmen acknowledge the Sultans as owners of the marshes and feudal overlords, and agree to pay a token tribute each year, and the Sultans agree not to harry the marshmen nor send their men into the marshes. There are indeed words about how the treaty ends, but they are very difficult and I do not understand them. Lord Morris?"

Morris put his head in his hands and thought of the clay-masked boys chanting in this place only a fortnight ago. The passage was in fact much less obscure than most of the cryptic utterances that made up the Bond of Na!ar.

"Yes," he said, "it means something like this. The veins of us two are nets of poison. The poison binds our veins into one net. It binds son to son, a strong net. It does not rot. The floods come and go, and still the net binds son to son. The net becomes hard, being old poison. When new poison flows in new veins, but is the same poison in the same veins, then is the Bond broken."

"It is all a lot of camel's wind," grumbled somebody.

"I ought to explain," said Morris, "that the poison the marshmen use on their spears does harden with age. It has to be renewed about once a fortnight. But I have always taken those last lines to mean that the Bond will last for ever, because the alternative is impossible."

"Yet lo, it has happened," said bin Zair. "The thing was done as closely to those verses as the bodyguard could achieve. Now I will continue to tell what I know. On the very morning of the murders a man came to me from the marshes. It is part of my office to know what is happening among the savages, so I have always shown favours to certain savages who brought me news, and this man came with a story that the marshmen were preparing to betray their lord. He said that the Sultan's bodyguard, this Dyal, had learnt that the Sultan was preparing to prospect for oil in the marshes, and that the marshmen, to keep the oil, had declared themselves an independent nation and were going to send a delegation to the United Nations. At once I took this news to my master . . ."

There was now some agitation in the old man's manner as he recounted his doings that morning, his insistence that the Sultan should talk to him out of earshot of Dyal, and the Sultan's rage at the story. There were cries of disgust from the Arabs when he told how they had found poison on the darts; even the placid Umburak muttered angrily. Occasionally he turned to Morris for confirmation, and at the end called to him to explain the deliberate imitation of the story in the Testament of Na!ar and the relevance of the lines Morris had translated earlier. Troubled and stumbling, Morris did so.

"And has the Lord Morris more to tell?" he squeaked at the end.

"Well, yes. Two days ago I talked to the bodyguard, Dyal about the possibility that the Sultan might wish to drill in the marshes. He said he did not believe this was possible, but that if it happened then the treaty would be broken, and the marshmen would fight, and he would fight on their side. Certainly this seems to bear out what bin Zair has told us . . ."

"Kill them! Kill them all!" shrieked Fuad.

He seemed to have the meeting on his side. They voted with their lungs, raucously. Morris sat tugging at his lip and wondering what he could safely do to prevent his irreplaceable research material being bombed and burnt into oblivion. He was fairly sure that bin Zair had the facts roughly right, on the surface, but he was equally sure that it wasn't really like that—OK, two men had killed each other, horribly, but what conceivable chain of reasoning could turn that into the cause for a massacre of a whole race, a whole culture? Morris was almost nerving himself to object—to object and be over-ruled—when his eye was caught by a movement in the uproar where there had been no movement before. The new Sultan, Hadiq, rose slowly from his throne and held his arms high.

Arabs of the desert do not respect Sultans as such, much, so it must have been some residual awe for the dead man that brought the meeting to silence.

"I say it is impossible," said Hadiq. "Morris, friend of my father, tell them that it is impossible. Tell them that Dyal cannot have killed my father, nor my father him."

Well, it was an opening. Unwillingly Morris took it.

"Certainly two days ago I would have said it was impossible," he said. "I would have wagered all the money I have against it, yes, even after I talked to Dyal. And still, despite what bin Zair and I have said, I see two difficulties, and also a third matter.

102

First, we must suppose that Dyal had planned this killing before-hand; there was not time or opportunity that morning for him to take the extra gun and hide it and poison the darts, and so on. Therefore he had time to consider his plan. Yet we are to suppose that he poisoned the dart with which the Sultan was to shoot at him. He chose this death. Is that probable?"

The point about poisoning was a strong one, but was lost when Fuad shouted that the marshmen were wild animals, and who could understand their minds? Morris did not sit down.

"Secondly," he said, "my darts do not work immediately unless they pierce a vein. Who remembers the day when the hijacked aeroplane landed? On that day the Sultan boasted about two shots he had fired, the second hitting a small window of the aeroplane at several hundred yards, and the first with one of my dart-guns hitting the leg-vein of a chimpanzee in the cage. Both these were very fine shots, but the shots that killed the Sultan and Dyal were finer still—over twice the distance at which the chim-panzee had been shot, and through wire mesh, and remember that the second shot was fired in haste."

This argument, which Morris thought equally strong, made very little impression, producing only a series of anecdotes about incredibly fluky shots over great distances. Morris stayed stand-ing.

"Lord Morris has a third thing to say," said bin Zair, deftly choosing an instant of silence to break the flow.

"Yes," said Morris. "The Sultan and Dyal were not the only people much enraged that day. There was a Frankish woman there, whom the Sultan had taken to be one of his women; he would not let her go. When I came to my office after the arrival of bin Zair, I found her closing my gun-cupboard. Later I dis-covered it was empty. And there was also another marshman, a young man who was mad for love of this woman. Now, when bin Zair and I went to the lift-shaft we found only the young marsh-man there, but we could see by the lights that the lift was descend-ing . . ."

"Yet the slave told us it was empty," squeaked bin Zair. "And you yourself have said, Morris, that the ninth clan do not lie."

"He said no *man* was in it," said Morris. "Now it is possible that the lift was empty and merely descending because someone had called it from below. But it is also possible that the woman waited and persuaded Gaur to help her shoot the Sultan and Dyal, she to escape and he for love."

"Whence came the poison?" said bin Zair. "Such a killing, as you say, would not be a thing forethought of."

"The marshman was freshly come from the marshes," said Morris. "If each of these approached close to one who trusted them, then they could shoot the dart easily into a vein."

"It is not possible," said Hadiq, speaking full-voice for the first time. "It is not possible that Dyal should slay my father. Nor is it possible that Gaur should slay either of them."

Bin Zair nodded, sucking his cheeks in and out, while the rest of the Council disputed this point. When silence settled he spoke.

"Yes," he said, "your tale might be true, Lord Morris, though I do not think any man here would wager on it. In the same way it might be true that you or I did the killings."

"You *and* I," said Morris. "If we had been in league, we could have done it, though to what profit I do not know."

"This is all politicians' talk," shouted Fuad. "Everyone knows that the old marshman killed the Sultan so that the marshmen should take the profit from the oil which belongs to us Arabs. I say . . ."

Somebody was tugging at his sleeve, but he went on shouting, lashing himself into fresh fervours of rage. Morris was glad, in a way, to have this motive for the Arab interest in the case out into the open. He was even more glad not to have Fuad on his side in the discussion. Once again it was bin Zair who brought the meeting to order, though Morris didn't notice him doing it. All that happened was that while Fuad was still bellowing away four slaves appeared, carrying a cine projector and a collapsible screen, which they proceeded to erect regardless of the storm of words. By the time they had finished even Fuad was seated again, and waiting in polite silence.

The Council Chamber having no outside windows, it was a simple matter to dim the factitious sun behind the stained glass, though it then felt strange to sit in the expectant dark knowing that a few yards further off a real sun still beat downright upon the dunes.

104

"Lord Morris has forgotten," squeaked bin Zair, "that he kept a camera trained upon the apes. Now we may see something. Allah, it is badly developed!"

Certainly there was something wrong, but it was never easy in Q'Kut to trace a technological fault to its origin. This film looked as though it had been over-exposed, so that the tree-trunks and the loafing chimps were all dark silhouettes against the background glare from the windows. For several minutes the chimps had the show to themselves and made nothing of it, lying around in undramatic heaps, reaching with lazy limbs for odd bits of left-over orange peel or vacantly fondling each other. Dinah must have been in one of the corners where the lens didn't reach. Morris saw Sparrow lurch over to Starkie and give her a random buffet. One of the Arabs commented in the dark that he was just like some other Arab. Everyone laughed. Then, very suddenly, two figures strolled into view on the far side of the cage and stood talking. The small one, by his beard, was unmistakably bin Zair, and the large one, by his robes and figure, the Sultan. For a while they stood silhouetted against the glaring windows. The Sultan held one of the spring-guns cradled on his arm. Bin Zair talked to him with rising energy, hoicking at his beard, gesticulating like an actor. The Sultan seemed to answer once or twice, but suddenly he took a pace forward and struck bin Zair with his free hand, so that the old man almost fell; instead he turned his staggering into a sort of bow and backed slowly out of the picture. The Sultan, with the gun dangling now from his left hand, turned his back on the camera and gazed across the desert. All at once he staggered, as though struck; he swung round, aimed his gun almost at the camera and fired, and in the next instant collapsed against the bars. A chimpanzee (Rowse?) was ambling over to look at him when with a whirr and a click the film ended. The slaves turned the lights on and cleared the projector and screen away.

"Thus was the Sultan shot," said an old Arab. "Shot in the back. Just so does a man stagger as the bullet strikes. I have seen it over my own sights."

A general murmur of agreement rose. Those who had not personally shot enemies in the back, presumably ashamed to make their innocence public, joined in the grunts of assent. But

105

something in Rowse's gawky movements in the last few frames had caused Morris's mind to make a forgotten connection. His suggestions so far had been not exactly frivolous, but at least academic, an attempt to sow enough doubt in these stony minds to divert them from immediate war. Now he saw a perfectly serious possibility—something which (if you knew the people concerned) was actually more probable than bin Zair's hypothesis.

"There is yet another way in which the deaths might have come about," he said. "This young man, Gaur, as the Sultan Hadiq will witness, was in deadly fear of my apes, thinking them demons. Now, we kept three spring-guns, one for use, one for practice and one spare. Only one was necessary, but as you know the Sultan loved guns. Now, is it not possible that the young man, hoping to kill some of the apes, put poison on the darts that were kept for use? And Dyal and the Sultan shot each other half in sport?"

"It is much more possible that he killed for love," said someone. "A young man will do anything for love. Do you remember, Umburak, how your cousin . . ."

It was a long story of sex and violence and the breaking of sacred obligations to host and kin. Apparently all the Arabs knew it already, for they occasionally corrected the speaker about some detail. But they listened to it right through, without impatience.

"Yes," said Umburak, when the story was over, "a young man will do anything when he is mad for love."

"And an old one too," said a jeering voice.

This must have been an insult too close to home, for at once a dignified old man on the far side of the circle, who had hitherto remained completely silent, was standing up, shouting at the speaker, with his hand on his dagger. Several others joined in. A chain reaction of accusation began, spreading from the old man's lusts back to a hideous desert feud which had begun a generation ago when the Hadahm had poisoned a well belonging to the Amahra. Most of those present seemed still to owe allegiance to one side or other in the quarrel, and for several minutes it looked as though blood might be shed over it again. But bin Zair and the young man with the cleft chin and one or two others rushed about the riot, pushing angry men apart and coaxing them

106

back on to their cushions. Bin Zair sent for coffee again, and at the sound of the thudding pestle the last of the tumult died.

The silence still bristled. Before the coffee was made a man in Fuad's party stood up again.

"This Lord Morris," he said in an angry voice, "talks like a politician. I ask you why? Now he has told us three or four stories of how the Sultan might have died. They are children's stories, and we are men. But he keeps the guns in his room and he speaks the filthy language of the marshmen. All we men know truly that the marshman shot the Sultan for the oil, but this Lord Morris tries to hide the truth with words and stories. Why? Does it not show that he and the marshmen plotted together to kill the Sultan?"

Morris was astonished, but not afraid because it was impossible for him to take the idea seriously; it took him some time to realise that it was not impossible for others, a point brought strongly home when he looked up from trying to gather his wits amid the uproar and found that the young man with the cleft chin was dancing in front of him but somehow keeping his gun-barrel pointing steadily at Morris's chest.

How do you rebut a charge like that? Morris looked desperately round, caught Hadiq's eye and saw him say something to bin Zair, who rose unsteadily to his feet again and with a quavering old hand plucked the gun away from the young man. It was a remarkably deft, accurate movement, in fact. Bin Zair pointed, and the young man went back to his place. Silence fell as the coffee-man began his tedious ministrations.

"Let Lord Morris be served first," said Hadiq loudly.

"This young marshman and the Frankish woman," said Umburak, "have they been questioned?"

There was a stir of interest, perhaps because the verb was one which included the possibility of torture.

"Gaur is gone," said Hadiq, after a pause. "He came to me the day my father died. He had not learnt to speak more than a little Arabic. He said 'Your father. My father.' He put his hands to the collar of his robe and tore it from top to bottom. He wept. I have not seen him since. I think he has gone back to the marshes."

"Let him be sent for," said someone. Several people with better local knowledge explained the folly of this remark.

"There is still the woman, then," said Umburak.

"I am told," squeaked bin Zair, "that in the full heat of that afternoon a naked marshman came to the boathouses, leading a veiled woman. He came from the palace. He took the boat-guard's gun from him and stunned him with his fist. When the guard woke a canoe had been taken."

There was a brief murmur of discussion, not very interested, and then Fuad was on his feet again, shouting "What does it matter? The old savage killed the Sultan. The young savage killed the Sultan. Morris helped or he did not. However it be, the killing was done by one of these devils from the marshes. Let them be punished. Let them be driven out. We do not want them in our land!"

"I have heard that when men drained the marshes above Basra much good land was exposed," said the supposedly leche-rous elder.

These two speeches brought the meeting to its full fervour. The notion of war, combined with the idea of fertile land (which then would be eroded to desert in a generation by bad husbandry) seemed to stir almost every Arab soul. Even the impassive Umburak was on his feet, shouting, and it took Morris some time to realise that he was dissenting from the motion.

"Fools! Fools! Fools!" he was shouting.

Nobody paid any attention. He looked round, ignored Morris, strode out of the circle, picked up a heavy alabaster spittoon, lifted it, carried it into the middle of the circle and slammed it down upon the mosaic floor. The effect was remarkable; there must have been some flaw or stress in the bowl, for the pedestal shot clean through it and it crashed to the floor and broke, spilling out date stones and tangerine peel and chewing-gum, all mixed with the gub of ancient hawkings. The silence after the crash was beautiful.

"You are fools," said Umburak. "How will you fight against the marshmen? This is no camel-raid. How will you go among the reeds, where your enemies know every winding and hide in every patch of cover with their poisoned spears? One scratch and a man dies. Lo, the Sultan and the slave died with the prick of a poisoned needle. You have guns, but you have only six hundred fighting men. They have eight thousand, and I, with my

108

own eyes, have seen a marshman spear a small pig at thirty paces. I tell you, it is not a camel-raid."

This was not a popular speech.

"We will not fight them in the marshes, then," said the young man with the cleft chin. "The Sultan has two aeroplanes. Let him buy bombs and napalm and thus drive these demons out of the reeds on to the sands, where we can deal with them."

"I will not do it," shouted Hadiq. "By God, I tell you I will not do it. I tell you the treaty is not broken. We do not know it to be broken. It may be that Gaur killed for love. It may also be that some other man came to the zoo and tricked him—he did not know our ways. Shall I now hunt like animals the people my father loved and protected? By God I tell you I will not."

"Had the Sultan no braver sons?" shouted Fuad. A ripple of shock ran round the circle, but Morris sensed that the question was merely premature. In a few days it could be asked openly, and the suggestion made that Hadiq was reluctant to attack the marshmen because by their help he had come to his inheritance. He rose, very pale, but suddenly looking remarkably like his father.

"Hear me," squeaked bin Zair. "Umburak speaks well. Fuad speaks impertinent folly. You cannot fight the marshmen at once. Thought must be taken. Preparations must be made. Therefore there is time to make further enquiries. Let a man go into the marshes to seek out Gaur and this woman, and bring them here."

"He will be speared before he has paddled a mile," said Umburak. "It is their custom."

"Let him go under the hand of Na'ar," said bin Zair (who like all Arabs was quite unable to pronounce the !) "They will not harm him then."

"Who will go?" said someone.

"Let Lord Morris go," said bin Zair.

"No! For God's sake!" said Morris.

"He speaks their language and knows some of their customs," said bin Zair, as though Morris had not spoken.

"But . . . but . . ." said Morris.

Bin Zair rose and with a tiny jerk of his head indicated that he wanted to talk to Morris in private. They moved off together until they could whisper in the corner below the frilly gallery where the women sat for the feasts.

"It is well that you are reluctant," said bin Zair. "Thus they cannot say that you are running away to your friends."

"Running away?"

"I know Arabs, Lord Morris. They have come here to fight, and now they must wait. In two days, three days, they will look for other sport. They will remember the words of Kadhil, that it was you who planned the murders . . ."

"Why on earth should I?"

"The oil, Lord, the oil. The smell of it makes Arabs mad, and so they believe it must make other men."

"I see."

"You will be safe in the marshes."

"But what about the zoo? Those two damned slaves have disappeared. What about . . ."

"Oh, that happens always. Slaves hide at the death of their lord. He was killed in the zoo, so the zoo slaves hide, lest they be tortured. I will find you fresh slaves, and by my beard I will see that they do their work. You will go?"

"Oh, hell!"

"Lord, if you do not go, I cannot answer for your life."

"Oh, I suppose so."

"Good. I will suggest to His Majesty that you are appointed Minister for Native Affairs. Thus you will have authority."

That's great, thought Morris, turning sweaty with fear back towards the sinisterly silent ring of Arabs. Absolutely great. If only Mum could know. My son, the Minister for Native Affairs. Great.

2

A conscript into the noble army of martyrs has trouble deciding what to pack. Morris was not exactly a hypochondriac, in that he was seldom ill and when he was took as little medicine as possible; this was not heartiness, but a perpetual vague fear that some really ugly ailment was waiting to get him, and that if he was lavish with drugs for minor ills they would have lost their potency when the big bug pounced. So even in England he kept a well-stocked medicine-cupboard, and had come to Q'Kut with half a chemist's shop; and that had been supplemented by such things as antibiotics for sick bears and eye-lotions for panthers. He had plenty to choose from against the swarming horrors of the marsh.

Dinah flounced round, thrilled with sensed excitement. He had given himself various excuses for deciding to take her along—there was no one to look after her in the palace; he couldn't leave her unguarded in the chimpanzee grove without risking traumatic troubles that might undo weeks of work; she might amuse or impress the marshmen—but he really knew he was taking her for company. He was afraid to go alone. She was his teddy-bear, to share with him the witch-riddled dark. The malaria season was not yet at its height, but he had been giving them both Paludrine since the floods began to recede. He packed her sedatives, so that if she became a real nuisance he could take the bounce out of her, but he thought the heat of the marshes would do that anyway.

When he had packed the medicines, clothes, mosquito net, compass, torch, rag books, fruit, favourite toys and so on there was still a couple of hours before it would be tolerably cool. He hoped to find a guide in the early dusk when, according to Kwan, there was always a lot of movement in the marshes as the buffalo were brought back to the villages. Meanwhile, to distract Dinah from her physical fidgets and him from his mental ones, he got out the plastic counters. Almost the first that spilled out into the lid of the wallet was the black square with the gold hand.

He picked it up, stared at it and put it to one side. But Dinah leaned over and with a long arm snatched it back. She too stared at it for a while, panted a little and then prodded her fingers together. It was always exciting when she actually showed she wished to communicate, rather than merely demonstrating like a star pupil that she was able to, so Morris picked out the purple circle with the hole in the centre. Unhesitatingly she placed it to the right of the other:

> black square with gold hand: Sultan
> purple circle with hole: hurt/be hurt

111

Morris snapped his fingers encouragingly, made a quick note and then fished out more tokens. He already had quite a bit of evidence about Dinah's memory processes, but this mostly concerned matters which she had learnt by repetition. There was not much about single events that had made enough impression to stay firm in her mind. She had evidently been impressed by the death of the Sultan; it would be interesting to see whether this—a purely external event though involving a major figure in Dinah's own mythology—could be linked in any way with her attack on Sparrow, Sparrow's retaliation, or Sparrow's death—things, one would have thought, much more deeply impressive to her mind. Morris picked out five more nouns, spread them on one side of the table, added the Sultan's own symbol and left the single verb lying where it was. Dinah hesitated, picked up her own square and studied the remaining symbols for anything that might mean eat or food. If she had been human she would have shrugged her shoulders to acknowledge the expected disappointment; her own way of doing this was a little grunt and a hunching of her back before she returned to making a sentence that involved the single verb "hurt".

She brought the Sultan's token back to the centre of the table and formed the same sentence as before, but she seemed dissatisfied with it and without any encouragement from Morris returned to the remaining nouns. She almost did what he expected first go; her fingers hesitated over the yellow square "nameless object" which in this case would surely have been the dart, and then they hovered over the black square which might have meant Sparrow. But when she returned to sniff at the two symbols already chosen she seemed to make up her mind:

black square:	person other than Dinah, Morris, or Sultan
purple circle with hole:	hurt
black square with gold hand:	Sultan

She chattered at Morris, and looked with her brown, round eyes into his face, seeking what? Confirmation? Approval of her cleverness? Morris astonished her by rewarding her with a whole bunch of grapes, and while she ate them in her nest he sat quite still, pulling his lip and thinking.

A chimpanzee can communicate. A chimpanzee can be mistaken as to the facts it communicates. Can a chimpanzee lie? With the surface of his mind Morris began to sketch out a possible series of experiments to investigate this problem, but the work did not satisfy his deeper mind, which in fits and starts insisted on rearranging the events of the last few days into a different pattern. He had already been naturally nervous about the journey into the marshes. Now he was very frightened indeed.

3

Morris and Hadiq stood by the boat-sheds under two brollies and looked at the grey reaches of water and the brown stands of reed. The retreating flood had left a long band of mud along the shore. where, hidden in slimy burrows, the lungfish were beginning to croak their painful evening dirge; no scientist, as far as Morris knew, had ever investigated this particular species; he himself believed that the noise was no sort of chant or mating-song, but simply a by-product of the process of breathing; you could hear how it hurt.

"God protect you, Morris," said Hadiq in a worried voice.

"I'll be OK, I expect," said Morris in English.

With a sigh he put Dinah on the ground. He had rubbed her all over with insect-repellant—a process she took for an exotic form of grooming and adored—so that she now had the tousled appearance of a dog after a bath. He too reeked of citrus.

"What must I do, Morris?" said Hadiq suddenly.

"Do? Do?" Morris felt impatient of any idea of action. There were enough activists already in Q'Kut. But with another sigh he took the brolly from the hand of the reluctant brolly-slave and walked with Hadiq along the shore. Dinah stayed where she was in the shade of the other brolly.

"Do as little as you can," he said. "Protect yourself. Talk with the Shaikhah, your mother. Take your father's guns and give them to the eunuchs from the marsh."

"Why do you say this? Is my mother in danger?"

"Long ago your father and I were friends at Oxford. He left suddenly to return here, and for many years we did not meet,

113

though we sent each other letters. Then he came to London and sent for me, and we dined together and he drank a lot of wine ..."

"So have many good men."

"He had a strong head, but that night his tongue ran away. He told me why he had left Oxford. Being the son of the then Shaikhah, he was also your grandfather's heir, but your grandmother had borne three daughters before him, so there were two sons older than him, by other wives. These two sons poisoned your grandfather, but then quarrelled as to who should rule; there were several factions among the Arabs, but the marshmen knew who was the true Sultan; when your father returned Kwan and Dyal armed the eunuchs, and with their help your father captured both brothers. He told me they took a long time to drown. Now many of these people ..." Morris nodded towards the tents of the Arabs "... remember that your father became Sultan over the bodies of your uncles."

"So I am an Arab but I must not trust the Arabs. I must trust the marshmen, though a marshman killed my father—or so they say."

"I believe they say wrong. Anyway, my advice is that you arm the eunuchs, trust no one else, and move as slowly as you are able. I shall be back with news in very few days. If you must take action, talk first with bin Zair."

They turned and walked slowly back towards the boat-sheds, to the ugly noise of the lungfish adapting themselves over thousands of generations to live in an altered world.

Five

1

IT WAS STRANGE how the reed-beds rustled. There was no wind, and the feathery plumes at the top of the stems stayed still against the hazy sky, as though they were posing for a woodcut. But down at water-level the fibrous leaves stirred and hissed. Morris had done a little canoeing in Europe in a featherweight modern derivative of the kayak, propelled by a double-ended paddle. The craft he was now learning to control was twice the size and ten times the weight, a marshman's canoe made of reeds, several layers thick, tarred, and shaped into graceful upward curves at prow and stern. He had to kneel to paddle, driving the blade upright along by the fat thwart; the whole boat was slightly curved in plan, so that gliding through the water it naturally moved in a slow arc to the right; this was counteracted by the tendency of the paddle-stroke to push the prow to the left—a cunning arrangement, the result of centuries of sophistication of design, but awkward for a beginner. The kneeling position was also peculiarly tiring for the hams.

Morris tired quickly. He had been concerned to drive the canoe as fast as possible into the cover of the reed-beds, because it now seemed to him possible that one of the factions of Arabs might wish his mission to fail, and try to achieve this by setting a marksman somewhere along the shore to pick him off; the awkward sploshings of his paddle and his own panting and cursing had been the loudest sounds in the marsh. He rested and these noises and the thud of his heart slowly quietened enough for him to hear only the plop of drops from the end of his paddle lying across the thwarts. Dinah, destroyed with heat, slept in the centre of the boat by the provisions.

When he started paddling again he found that the knack of boat-control had suddenly come to him; it was now that he first noticed the rustling. It sounded as though some large, lithe thing—not a pig, not a man, but perhaps a snake or crocodile— were moving parallel to his course through the reeds, but peer as he might he could see nothing. The channel he was in branched, unsignposted. He took the wider branch. There was nothing to show that he was not paddling into a blind alley, an inextricable mudbank, an ambush. But the ambush had been sprung before his coming.

Rounding the next bend he came at once on a corpse. It lay face up among the reeds, naked, the corpse of a portly brown man, almost submerged but buoyed by the reed-roots. As Morris drew alongside two columns of flies rose into humming clouds above the two wounds, one a sharp gash in the throat and the other where the genitals had been hacked off. Morris rested his paddle to look and wonder but the curve of the keel began to swing him in to the reeds, so he dug the blade in and paddled on. There was nothing he could do. The body was that of his own zoo-slave, Maj. He was glad Dinah hadn't seen it.

He felt very sick and cold, though the swamp heat hung round him like butter-muslin. From time to time he glanced up at the little beehive-shaped box that swayed from the end of a bamboo pole stuck through two special rings set in the upcurving prow. The box was made of woven reeds, covered with red clay, patterned with cheap blue glass beads and polished. In one or two places the clay had cracked away. It seemed a very dubious protection.

Even so, the next time Morris rested he cupped his hands round his mouth and called.

"People, I come from the heir of Nillum under the hand of Na!ar. By the Bond I call you. Send me a guide."

He was so nervous of the silence and strangeness that his cry was a croak. He told himself he was a fool and shouted again, loud enough this time to wake Dinah, who whimpered feebly at him then curled up in the bottom of the boat as though it were her own nest. Nothing else happened. Next time he paddled on

116

he discovered the cause of the sinister rustling—he was doing it himself. The slight ripple of his wake was enough to disturb the limp lower leaves without making the stiff spears quiver at all. Reason is king, he thought. To connect cause with effect is to drive out fear. But then the realisation that that was not a sentence you could translate into marsh-language—not even an idea you could express—brought fear seeping back.

He stopped and called for a guide several more times. Dinah became livelier as the air cooled, but her natural sense of balance kept the boat trimmed as she moved about. Once, in what seemed to Morris perfect stillness, she snorted angrily at a stand of reeds and something there began to move—a solid, animate body. Without waiting to see whether it was man or boar Morris paddled rapidly on. Night came fast, between one rest and the next. The dews condensed, and the half moon that had begun as an aureoled haze changed to a hard-edged object. Dinah lay in the bows and watched its reflection gliding through the water.

Moonlight is deceptive. Daylight, even the drear haze that imbrued the marshes all day, comes from all directions and gives things distance and dimension; but moonlight comes from one place only. Things exist or not, as it strikes them. The silvery reed-plumes existed but were useless; a glistening patch of clear water existed, but was passed in ten strokes; everything else was black and indecipherable; there was no variation in its blackness either—any bit of it might be a buffalo, or a mudbank, or mere shadow. The only sure way of making progress was to drive towards whatever glistened.

Following this principle Morris finally stuck. The channel he was in opened quite suddenly into a sort of lake, almost a hundred yards across and twice that from end to end. The sensible thing would have been to work round the edge, looking for another exit, but in sheer relief from the claustrophobia of the reed-channels he started to paddle straight across it. After about twenty strokes he ran into a mild resistance, and without thinking paddled more strongly to get through it. In another twenty strokes he was stuck. Dipping his hand overboard he found that just below the glistening surface of the water lay a great mesh of weed. Paddling didn't seem to move him an inch, backward or forward, so he shrugged in the dark, then clicked to Dinah who came humping aft for supper. Into her last banana he prodded a sleeping-pill which she swallowed without noticing. Then he groomed her for a while until she dropped contentedly asleep.

He called once more to the unanswering dark, carefully unrolled the mosquito net down the length of the boat and finally slid under it. He lay on his back looking up through the mesh at the stars and thought of Maj, lying in almost the same position, dead and mutilated. The bloody fool, he thought. Or perhaps they hadn't told him about the marshmen.

2

A drip woke him. The dew had condensed on the net in tiny beads, which had slowly joined to each other and runnelled down folds until a minute reservoir had collected and forced a thin, chill stream into his left ear. He woke, and was wide awake at once, knowing where he was and why. With a slow movement he edged away from the drip, then raised both hands above his head to roll back the netting. The droplets had made it opaque, but when he exposed the first clear pearly triangle by the sternpost he knew that it was dawn and would soon be sunrise.

He rolled a little more, then lay still. Something was moving on the water, and a faint, strange muttering filled the air. Deciding that he could not lie there indefinitely he rolled the net back as far as his knees and sat up, very gingerly and ready to duck.

The moment his head appeared above the thwart the muttering became a clamour of voices. Deliberately he re-enacted the role of a man waking from deep sleep; he yawned, stretched, rubbed his eyes and looked around. In front of him lay the lake, lightly disturbed by glistening sleek shapes, one of which shifted and became a buffalo, hook-horned and bearded with the weed it was eating. A whole raft of this weed lay between him and the animals. He was, in fact, stuck about twenty feet into the raft and in the clear water behind him lay a ring of boats, each of which held two naked black men—one kneeling with the paddle in the stern and the other standing amidships with his spear-thrower poised. As he turned to them the gabble stilled. He looked and saw the tense, poised bodies, so practised in their art

118

that the boats did not rock a millimetre; he saw the glistening black stuff on the little flint spear-heads; he knew how Maj had died.

"I come under the hand of Na!ar," he said. "Do you greet me with spears?"

The nearest warrior hesitated, then lowered his spear-thrower. He took the spear carefully out of it and slid a little sheath over the poisoned tip. The others were starting to do the same when their stances changed, and their faces also. Morris felt his own boat rock wildly. He looked over his shoulder and saw that Dinah, woken by his voice, was struggling to free herself from the mosquito netting. He clicked his fingers loudly, then rolled his end of the net rapidly towards the threshing figure; she must have seen his knees for she dropped flat and allowed him to drag the rest of the net clear before rising, panting with fear, and rushing into his arms.

When Morris, holding her, turned carefully to renew negotiations with his rescuers they were gone. Only the reeds swayed.

"People," he called, "I come from the heir of Nillum. I am a good-comer. Do not fear me."

He would have liked to add that they mustn't be afraid of Dinah, either, but the language had the wrong mesh to trap that thought; fear is a relationship between A and B, to be expressed by a full root then extended by syllables nominating the poles of the relationship, the whole then modified by various consonantal transfers to the placatory imperative; but the language, for all its richness, contained no word for chimpanzee, nor for any of the more general terms all the way up to "animal"; the only nominal extenders carrying the thought of "unknown living creature" were always applied to the horrors of the moon-world; while to incorporate Dinah's name in the phrase would have turned it into a piece of formal boasting, used normally as a step in the ritual of declaring a blood-feud. Morris swallowed twice, watching the motionless reeds, thinking feverishly of relationships which would not land him in claiming anything that a marshman would think impossible.

"We come under the hand of Na!ar," he called at last. "My woman is also a good-comer."

Well, Dinah, he thought. Now we're married. Don't worry—

I'll divorce you as soon as we're out of this bloody marsh. He gave her a couple of oranges to seal the bargain.

Suddenly the reeds rattled again and a single canoe slid out; in its centre, as before, stood a man with his spear-thrower poised. Before Morris could cry out the arm shot over, and the dart was standing stiff in the thwart, a foot from his right hand. It took him time to see that a cord trailed from it across the weeds.

He called his thanks and fastened the cord, which appeared to be made of human hair, round the upcurving stern. The man shouted and hauled. His canoe was anchored to something in the reeds so that, with Morris using his paddle to thrust the weeds down where they gathered in skeins under the stern-post, the trapped boat was gradually drawn clear. More canoes slid from the reeds, but still nobody answered any of Morris's remarks; only when the little fleet began towing him down the channel did they utter a sound; a man in one of the leading boats started a paddle-chant, which was a rhythmic list of the virtues of a certain she-buffalo interwoven with a punning counterpoint about the vices of the singer's mother-in-law. The song ran from boat to boat, each man answering the next with a fresh line; some lines seemed to be new, for they raised laughter and catcalls, but when Morris looked about him for the minimal comfort of cheerful faces he saw that every man in the fleet kept his head turned well away from him.

They came, quite soon, to a low mound rising out of the water. Nothing grew on it, but its whole surface was covered with a random pattern of cattle-pens and tunnel-shaped reed huts. As soon as Morris's keel grounded he started to rise, but sat heavily back as a dozen men seized the rope and hauled the canoe well clear of the water. Even so when he stepped on to the land he found he was ankle-deep in slime. He picked Dinah up, and with his free hand lifted the pole from the rings, so that he could carry the hand of Na!ar above him, like a chinese lantern, still shedding its mysterious protection around him. The men formed into two straggly groups on either side of him and together they all walked up the hill, moving in such a fashion that Morris walked in nobody's footsteps and nobody in his.

The hut at the very top of the mound was larger than the others, though not so much that Morris could have stood upright in it. Before its opening two mats had been unrolled and on one of these sat a man, grey headed and wizened and as black as a prune. He was tiny for the most part, with limbs like sticks and hands that were almost transparent; the exception was his left leg which was so swollen with the activities of some parasitic worm that the flesh had completely enveloped the foot and the whole limb looked like a black plastic bag filled with jelly.

Morris walked past him, between the mats, and slid the pole into the spear-rings by the hut entrance, then returned and sat on the other mat with Dinah on his lap. He groomed her carefully, to keep her placid. It was difficult quite to judge how far to conform to what he knew of the customs of the marsh; he did not want to offend anyone, but nor did he wish them to think of him as subject to those customs. At any rate he must keep silence until the old man spoke.

He watched two small boys further down the slope training a buffalo calf; one of them skipped backwards in front of it, dancing and calling its name and clicking his fingers; the other walked behind it with a bamboo pole and when the calf tried to veer away from the dancing boy he clipped it sharply on the side of its head to straighten it up; thus, when the calf was grown the boy or his father would be able to call it to the milking floor by dancing, singing and clicking his fingers in front of it. Kwan had told Morris about this, but it was not the same thing as seeing it happen.

Canoes slid out across the water; most of the men were returning to the buffalo pastures. Because of the haze Morris could not see the lake where he had been trapped; still less could he see the palace perched on its hill, though he believed he was looking in the right direction. The world was a mile wide, walled with the warm steam. Two women came up from the boats carrying his belongings and set them at the edge of his mat without a word. Five minutes later a girl brought a bowl of buffalo milk up the hill; she looked about twelve years old, but either she was pregnant or disease had shaped her like that. These three women sat down a little out of earshot; a fourth arrived from behind the hut with a bundle of reed; they settled down to split the canes and pound them with two flat stones.

121

Suddenly the old man picked up the bowl of milk and drank three big gulps, then passed it to Morris, who managed to do the same, despite its harshly acid flavour. Dinah reached up a long arm and put a finger in the bowl and then into her mouth. She spat. The old man's face changed, but not interpretably.

"Of what clan is this stranger," he said.

"My clan is Brit. My woman's clan is Tchim. My outer name is Wesley Naboth Morris. For speaking it is Morch. My woman speaks no words. No words are spoken to her."

"Wah!"

"What is this place?"

"It is Alaurgan-Alaurgad. The chief elder of it is one Qab, of the water-snake clan, who sits on this mat."

"May Qab enjoy many clean wives."

Qab waved a deprecatory hand to where the squalid quartet of women worked at their task in the moist dust. Morris thought he had made a good start; Alaurgan-Alaurgad was not mentioned in many of the songs, but it had an important role in the Testament of Na!ar, for it was on this dull mound that the hero, pricking his own spear-hand to let the blood fall on this soil, had sworn his oath that he would not drink milk again until he had killed Nillum ibn Nillum. Now that hand had come back; it hung above the hut of the chief elder. Morris thought it a good omen, but he wished that the people of Alaurgan-Alaurgad seemed less remote.

Dinah became restless, so Morris let go of her; there was no point in putting her on her leash, as soon she would become prostrate with the increasing heat of the morning; meanwhile it would do her no harm to rove around a bit. There did not seem to be much mischief she could do on Alaurgan-Alaurgad. She scampered round the space in front of the hut, noticed Qab's wives and bustled over to see what they were doing. They rose, flustered, with little shrieks of alarm. She picked up one of the stones and banged it on the other in the way she had seen them doing, then tried to copy their activities with the reeds but made a mess of it; so she scattered their work around in frustration and came back to Morris. Her eye was caught by the pattern on the mat; she settled down and started to tease at it with her forefinger. The women picked up their reeds and moved to a new

122

place; one of them went and fetched two fresh stones. They left the ones Dinah had touched lying where they were.

"It is not a woman," said Qab suddenly. "It is a moon-world creature. The women know it."

Women, of course, were the experts in the detection of witches.

"You speak some truth," said Morris. "Dinah is not a woman. She is not a moon-world creature. She is, as it were, the cousin's cousin of a dog."

"It is not a dog," said Qab, examining Dinah critically. At that moment she became bored with the mat and noticed the hamper of fruit lying beside it. She was at the fastenings in a flash, and Morris had to hold the lid shut to prevent her rifling it. Furiously she flung herself in a circle round the mats, rushed over to frighten Qab's wives, came back to see whether that had had any effect and at last jumped chattering to the ridge of Qab's hut, where she sat grimacing at the steaming landscape. Well, she's out of mischief up there, thought Morris, and turned patiently to his host.

"Qab," he said. "You hear me speak the words of your people. Kwan of the ninth clan taught me these words. They are not the words of my people and perhaps my tongue will stumble. When I speak unacceptable words, do not think that it is my own soul speaking . . ."

"You propose to tell me lies," said Qab.

"No, no."

"Speak then acceptable words. Do not tell me again that your creature is a dog. Morch, you came to our pastures in the night. You slept in the middle of Tek's Lesser pond. We heard you calling in the dark. You rose unharmed in the dawn. The witches are your friends."

Despite the lack of cause-and-effect constructions in the language it was possible to put together a fairly damning case by producing a series of short, unconnected sentences, or single-word accretions, as Qab had done. Morris half-rose until he could reach the roll at the furthest end of his bundles; he opened it and spread it out until Qab could see the ultra-fine mesh of the mosquito net.

"We slept beneath this cloth," he said. "See how small are the holes. Not even the cleverest witch can pass through."

Qab fingered the net with his fleshless hands, fine as a lemur's.

"Wah!" he said. There was a longish pause before he restarted the conversation. Morris sat looking at him; this was not what he had expected, after the archaic nobility of Kwan, the civilised calm of Dyal, the raw dignity of Gaur. This little man carried none of that weight. He did not even seem cunning, let alone clever. In another context he might have been an old peasant sitting on his doorstep, being approached by a stranger with some slightly unorthodox request and simply thinking how to make money out of the visit.

"Thou comest," he said at last, "under that hand."

He used the same archaic second person that Gaur had once used.

"True," said Morris. "The descendant of Nillum sent me. He requires the aid of the people."

"Qab has heard that the Bond is broken."

"Morch has not heard that story."

"Qab has heard this: a warrior of the ninth clan lived in the hut of the descendant of Nillum. The descendant of Nillum slew him with a poisoned dart."

Curiously, this was the sort of conversation to which the language was well adapted. Qab had used a form implying that the Sultan was still alive.

"A poisoned dart slew Dyal, of the ninth clan," said Morris. "At the same hour a poisoned dart slew the descendant of Nillum."

"Who saw this fight?"

"No man, perhaps. I heard shouts. They used not weapons but practice-darts."

(There was a word for these, as every male child was presented with a practice-dart and spear-thrower on being initiated into his first age-set.)

"Qab," said Morris, "a man hunting his enemy will smear his dart-tip with poison. Will he also smear the dart-tip of his enemy with poison?"

"Riddles are for children and witches."

"I do not speak riddles. The place of the fight was the hut of Dinah and her family. A warrior stood at the door, guarding it. This warrior was Gaur, of the ninth clan. He was new come to the place, and did not know our ... our tracks. He greatly feared the kin of Dinah. On certain days Dyal and the descendant of Nillum threw practice-darts at the kin of Dinah, for sport. Did Gaur smear the darts with poison, hoping to slay some of the kin of Dinah?"

"No man of the sun-world knows the mind of another."

"True. Now this Gaur has come to the marshes again. I wish to ask him this. I wish also to ask him what people passed the door where he stood guard. Will you send for Gaur?"

"Ho! I must send for a warrior of the ninth clan when he has taken a new woman into the reeds! Who hunts the boar with a feather?"

"He is under the Bond."

"The Bond is broken."

"That is not known. When Gaur has spoken it will be known."

"Morch, this is an old tale. The blood-guilt is on the man that throws the spear. Another man has poisoned it. The thrower does not know. But the blood-guilt is his—every child knows that. It is in many songs."

It was interesting that Qab knew that Gaur had brought Anne with him; it also accounted for Qab's many hints that Morris was really a creature of the moon-world—the story of his witch-craft would have reached the marshes before him. But it was no help in the frustrating task of presenting a logical argument to a stupid and secretive old man in a language solely designed for making an elaborate and detailed picture of the surface appear-ance of things and actions.

"These two dead men were brothers," said Morris. Dyal had used the word in Arabic which means blood-brother.

"Yes," said Qab; it was the minor affirmative, a convenient grunt which agrees with a proposition only provisionally.

"I have heard songs in which brother fought with brother. Always they used unpoisoned spears."

"Morch, you tell me lies. These are lies a child would know. A man who fights his brother does not use a practice-dart. He uses a new spear, never before tried. He does not put poison on it nor say spells over it. How should a man begin to kill his brother with a practice-dart?"

Morris opened his mouth to answer, but the very shape of

125

Qab's question defeated him. It wasn't simply that the ugly little savage had restated Morris's case as though it were a clinching rebuttal of that case; also his modification of the relation-root of killing which made the action incomplete—"begin to" was a very blurry translation—this showed how impossible it was going to be to *prove* a case to the marshmen by any logical chain of argument. It was as close as Qab could think to the idea of purpose and motive, and at the same time impossibly far from them.

A little to the left of where they sat, but almost down at the greasy edge of the water, two boys were practising with their throwing-sticks, those stunted clubs with which the marshmen stalked small game. The art, Kwan had said, was to throw them with the wrist only, not moving any other joint, so that the duck or water-lizard or whatever it might be was not scared by too much movement. The boys stood like little wizened statues, aiming at the horns of a buffalo-skull in the mud in front of them; Morris couldn't see the flick of the black hands in front of the black bellies, but the throwing-sticks didn't seem to miss at all. They struck the horns with a light clunk, sharply, in a steady flow, until the boys walked forward to pick them up. There seemed to be no connection between thrower and stick and target. Qab's method of argument was like that—one sharp little isolated fact after another, related each to each only by his speaking them. Morris tried again.

"I do not tell lies," he said. "I tell you things that are difficult to say with your words. Let us talk of another matter. I will tell you what the Arabs say."

"You are an Arab, Morch."

"No."

"You are white, like them."

Morris had been, during his time in Q'Kut, so subconsciously aware of his status as a white man among brown men, that it was a shock to realise that to people as black as the marshmen they were all equally pale strangers.

"I live with the Arabs, but I am not an Arab."

"You are certainly not of the people."

"True."

Qab nodded. Morris saw that in his mind only two types of

126

man inhabited the sun-world. Anyone else came from the other place. He ploughed on.

"The Arabs also say that the Bond is broken. They say that Dyal poisoned the darts. They say it is the manner of the marshmen's hunting, but then the descendant of Nillum took the dart from his body and threw it back, as in the Testament of Na!ar, poisoning Dyal also. They say the beginning of the fight was this: there are great riches in the marshes . . ."

"The buffalo give good milk this year, it is true."

"They do not seek to take your buffalo. Again, it is hard to say in your words. But first they will take the water. There will be no more floods."

Qab frowned at Morris, then turned to stare at the grey, unruffled water that interlaced the brown reed-banks.

"They say that Dyal killed the descendant of Nillum," said Morris, "He did not wish that the Arabs should come among the marshes. They say the Bond is now broken, and they will take vengeance. They will make war, saying it is for vengeance, but in their hearts they desire your land."

"The Bond is broken. We may go among the Arabs and slay and steal."

"I say the Bond is not broken. I say the new descendant of Nillum sent me here. I say he asks your help. He must show the Arabs that the blood-feud is foolish. Gaur must tell the true story of the killing. I seek for Gaur, coming to you under that hand."

Morris had spoken with emphatic oratory and now gestured, without looking round, to where the box swung on the pole. The possibility of war had made Qab listen with real interest, and his eyes followed the gesture. At once his face changed. His hand was clapped in horror to his forehead and his mouth breathed soundless syllables. Morris swung round.

Dinah had been very quiet, presumably already listless with heat. Not so—she had been, for who knows how long, squatting on the roof-tree solving the problem of how to reach the box. At the moment of Morris's gesture she must have worked it out, twisting the pole in its rings until the curve of it brought the box above her head. Morris leaped to his feet and grabbed the pole in the same moment that she grabbed the box. He hoicked up, she down; something gave and he was overbalancing with the pole waving

127

while she was scampering to the other end of the roof to examine her trophy.

He opened his fruit-box and took out a banana, then hurried to the other end of the hut and clicked his fingers at her. She looked up. He showed her the banana. She put the box to her ear and shook it. Silently Morris cursed her intelligence—she would prefer to win a reward by solving a problem than win one by being good. He hadn't much time, for she was experienced in closed-box problems and would soon spot that there was no lid or catch to this one, but that it was woven all in one piece, and then her strong, dark hands would tear it apart in seconds. The moment she was absorbed in her problem he swung the pole along the roof and knocked her off the end.

She fell, twisting like a gymnast, landing fully-balanced on her feet, still grasping the box. He grabbed at it. She wrenched from the other side. The ancient wickerwork collapsed and out of its ruins tumbled a pale shape. Morris had just time to see that it was the bones of a hand, wired together with copper, before she had pounced and was scampering away to the next hut, leaping for the roof and settling down to examine her trophy. As he raced across with the banana in one hand and the pole in the other she wrenched a finger from the hand and put it in her mouth.

One chew and she was in a tantrum, the hysteric indignation of those who have been cheated by themselves. No banana—only dry bones. She spat the finger out, rose to her feet and tore the hand apart, throwing the bones to and fro round the hut, screeching with disappointment. Morris scuttered about picking the bones up and stuffing them into his shirt pocket. The wrist-bone landed in the corner of a buffalo-pen, six inches deep in slime, and by the time he had probed it clear Dinah was back on top of the original hut, smugly eating the banana he had dropped.

He knelt on his mat and took the bones out of his pocket, arranging them loosely in their proper pattern; but being no anatomist he found himself with three unlikely oddments left over, which he was only able to place by the position of the broken wires. When at last he looked up he saw that another man had joined them, younger than Qab, small and sturdy. This man held a spear in the stabbing position with its serrated flint tip two feet from Morris's neck and glistening with black unguent.

"I will mend the hand," whispered Morris. "See, I have all the bones."

"The Bond is broken. So the hand is broken," said Qab. "This is sure. A witch comes to Alaurgan-Alaurgad, where Na!ar swore his oath. He brings a creature who breaks the hand. He dances before this creature, clicking his fingers like a child training a buffalo calf."

The third person was not chosen because Qab wished to state his case dispassionately, but because there is a class of beings to whom no wise man will speak direct.

"I am not a witch," said Morris. "Dinah is not a creature of the moon-world. I do not command her. Would I come here thus, by day, when there are warriors in Alaurgan-Alaurgad, with spears to kill me?"

"Ho," said Qab. "The witch came in the dark, but the good mimulus-weed, which sinks by night, deceived him with the appearance of clear water. A witch lives in the moon-world, as one may see from the colour of this witch's skin. To send a witch back to the moon-world he must be killed in the sun-world. A child knows this. Witches are very stupid, being dazzled by light, in the sun-world. Strike, Fau."

Morris looked bleakly round. About fifty men and women had come from somewhere and stood in a half-circle to watch him die. Dinah tossed her banana-skin down from the roof. It fell with a flap on the mat. Fau lowered his spear.

"The men of my age-set say 'Let us take him to Gal-Gal'," he said.

"Strike," said Qab.

"His words are perhaps true."

"He tells many lies. A child would know them. He is so stupid with sunlight."

"I slay him here, now. Then the other clans say 'Was this a witch? Who is Qab to declare the Bond to be broken? When did the water-snake become wise?' There will be many buffaloes to pay, Qab."

"Strike, Fau."

"Let us take him to Gal-Gal. Then the duck clan will not say

'When did the water-snake learn the smell of a witch?' They cannot then demand buffaloes. You are an old fool, Qab, and soon you will die. Your sons have taken all your buffaloes. You are like spear-poison which is seven and seven days old. Yes, soon you will die. But my age-set is full of strength, and we say 'Let us take one calf to the duck clan now. Let us not pay seven sevens calves next flood.'"

Qab relaxed and scratched his crotch.

"Can the witch make my leg clean?" he asked the steaming air.

"I am not a witch," said Morris shakily. "I do not heal wounds nor drive out blackwater spirits. I only carry a message from the descendant of Nulum. But let us go to Gal-Gal. Let Gaur be sent for also."

"Ho!" said Qab. "Will Fau carry such a message to the ninth clan? Ho!"

"I will give Fau a sign to take to Gaur's new woman," said Morris. "He will come."

Qab looked suddenly impressed. He shouted to his wives, who came shrinkingly over, eased his leg on to a sort of sledge and prepared to drag him into the hut. He stopped them with a snarl.

"Dniy," he shouted, "thou has a daughter who will die soon. The witches have touched her, so this witch can harm her no more. Give her to him for a wife, and my sister's son will pay thee a third of the next calf of his lame mottled cow."

A fat little man with a twisted leg strutted grinning from the ring. Hell, thought Morris, but he was in no position to give any more offence to the people of Alaurgan-Alaurgad, so he drew a sliver of reed from the mat, made it into a loop and tied the ends together. Dniy lowered his spear and Morris put the loop over the sheathed point.

"Good," said Qab. "The witch's hut is that where Tek died."

His wives dragged him into the hut. The ring of watchers melted away, except for a man who squatted down a few yards off to make dung. Morris's second wife (counting Dinah as the first) was a little black girl with a festering sore on her left shoulder. She came alone, very timidly, up to the mat in front of Qab's hut and grovelled in the dirt in front of him. She wore a blue-bead amulet round her neck, and a blue-bead belt, and the loop of reed round her right wrist.

"How many years have you?" asked Morris.

"Seven, Lord," she whispered into the dirt.

The marshmen could count, but usually didn't bother. Seven meant any lowish number.

"What is thine outer name?"

"My lord has not yet told me."

Morris thought, for the first time for years, of his own mother, longing for a friendly girl instead of her cold, clever, stodgy son. She used to make long, Barrie-ish fantasies about this other child she would never see. When Morris had sorted through the house after her death he had found a shelf of picture books with the same name written in each of them.

"Thine outer name is Margaret Lucy Morris," he said. "For speaking it is Peggy."

"I am Peggy," she said, pronouncing the word exactly as he had done. "I am Margaret Lucy Morris." She got that right too. She looked up. Her eyes were glazed with fright.

"Little Pegling," he said, lacing his speech with all the friendly diminutives he could think of. "You are welcome. See, this is Dinah. She sleeps when the sun is hot. Her home is a big tree. She is a little naughtikins. She likes to be touched, very gently, thus."

He showed her how to groom Dinah's coat, and in doing so found a disgusting great tick, fat with blood. Peggy laughed when he squashed it and soon came to help. Then he gave her a banana, which she ate with grave doubt. She became afraid again when he insisted on dressing her sore with antibiotic ointment, but endured his touch. After all, if he had taken her down to the water and drowned her like a kitten, she would have thought that perfectly proper, and wouldn't have resisted. About noon she showed him to their hut, sideways and down from Qab's, but well above the flood-line. There was an old mat there which she unrolled for him, before going back to make the first of many journeys down with his belongings. She was shocked to find that he had no weapons, but wouldn't let him carry anything else, except Dinah.

While she was staggering to and fro Fau came to his hut with the armature of a modern electric motor, presumably looted from the hijacked plane.

"To-morrow I seek Gaur," he said. "The stranger will give me a safe sign for the new woman."

"Come this evening," said Morris. "When do we go to Gal-Gal?"

"On the third day. Let not the stranger fear that Qab will poison him. My age-set will not permit it. There is good sport on Gal-Gal."

Worrying though it was to be still in the third person, it was also a relief to feel that one could eat and drink with nothing more to fear than the swarming ailments of the marsh. Morris thanked Fau and settled down to unpick the wire from the armature.

It was early evening before he had the hand assembled. Peggy was fanning a stinking little fire of dried dung right in the entrance of the hut. He would have liked to tell her to make it elsewhere, but this was her first day's housekeeping, and he could see that every other hut on Alaurgan-Alaurgad was being similarly treated.

"Peggy," he said. "I will need a basket for this, before I go to Gal-Gal."

"I will ask my mother's sister. She makes our baskets."

"Good."

Morris laid the completed hand on the mat. Struck by its size he spread out his own beside it, and found that his fingers did not reach as far as the last knuckles. That was curious. He had always envisaged Na!ar, despite the emphasis in the Testament on the hero's size and strength, as another little wizened marsh man; but he must have been almost a giant. Like Dyal, like Kwan, like Gaur.

"Dost thou know any of the ninth clan?" he asked.

"My lord need not fear. I am not beautiful enough for a ninth-clan warrior to steal me."

Morris laughed, waking Dinah at last.

"Who are their fathers?" he said.

"Their father is Na!ar," she said. "He was big. They are big."

"Where does Na!ar live?"

"Does my lord not know? Why, he lives in the body of the descendant of Nillum. He takes eight wives, one from each clan, and he begets on them warriors. Thus does Na!ar still fight for the people."

Dinah stretched, scratched and looked around her. Morris offered her an orange, and while she was eating it she noticed Peggy, shrinking a little away from the edge of the mat, on which she would not have dreamed of setting foot. Dinah looked at Morris with puzzled limpid eyes. He clicked with his fingers encouragingly.

"Be still," he said, as she moved carefully over to inspect Peggy at two-inch range. She noticed the weeping sore on the black shoulder and immediately made a funny cooing noise and prodded her fingers together.

"Dinah is sad thou art hurt," said Morris.

"My lord must not see the place," said Peggy, with a curious huffiness, like a teenage girl whose boy-friend has drawn attention to a pimple on her chin; then she was distracted by Dinah's vacuum-like kiss. In a minute they were sharing a second orange, putting it pig by pig into each other's mouths. In ten they were starting down to the shore, where the slow cattle were plunging home through the soupy lake while their warrior-masters danced, clicked and sang on the shore.

"Keep fast hold of her hand," called Morris. "She has fewer years than thou."

With something that was almost a lightening of heart he watched them move towards the melee; Peggy ought to have been carrying a toy bucket and spade, and beyond them should have stretched the sandy levels of low tide and beyond that still the lightly curling wavelets of a holiday sea. He thought with detached interest about what Peggy had told him, and knitted it in with what Dyal had once said about the problem of finding women when first he came out of the marshes. It explained, far better than any amount of buffalo-milk, the persisting size of the warriors of the ninth clan. It explained Dyal's unservile relationship with the Sultan, and Gaur's last words to Prince Hadiq. It also explained why it was almost impossible that either Gaur or Dyal had deliberately killed the Sultan.

Once there had been two races in Q'Kut, in that lost Saturnian age when the dunes had been green. Neither race had been Arab. There had been a big-boned, dominant people, and a race of scrawny near-slaves. Then the Arabs had come, and the big people had fought them, and the last of these, the hero Na!ar,

133

had died fighting. Then those first Arabs, seeing the impregnability of the marshes, had reached a status quo with the little people by adapting their relationship with the extinct big men. There was no guessing quite how much had been changed, but the way it worked now was this: in each generation wives were sent from the palace to the marshes; these wives were the Sultan's but were "lent" by him to his bodyguard—an arrangement which would have seemed shocking to most Arabs, and so was not widely known, though Morris felt he ought to have guessed that his fastidious friend would not have found it easy to beget children on women who reeked of rancid milk; after a while the children of these wives went back to the marshes, where the sons became the ninth clan; the largest and strongest was then chosen to be bodyguard to the next Sultan, and thus the system bred for continuing size; the prohibition on marriages in the ninth clan kept the genetic lines reasonably clear, though Morris didn't like to think what happened to such babies as *were* born . . .

So Dyal had been Gaur's father, and Kwan Dyal's—their real fathers, that is; but in their own eyes the father to whom they owed their duty as sons had been the Sultans, and when Dyal had called the Sultan "my brother" he had not been using a figure of speech. Among Arabs sons have murdered fathers and brothers brothers through all their blood-veined history, but Morris could not remember a single reference in any of the marsh-people's songs to parricide, and fratricide was governed by the Rules of Cricket, as described by Qab.

Morris was wondering whether Hadiq had known this (and hence insisted so strongly that neither Gaur nor Dyal had killed his father) when his two wives came trailing up from the shore, with Peggy carrying a bowl of buffalo-milk in one hand and Dinah wearing the blue-bead belt over her left eye, like a tipsy coronet. Several happy children followed them, shrieking ruderies.

Night fell. The function of the filthy fires became apparent, as their smoke drifted through the tunnel-shaped huts and cleared the malarial mosquitoes away. Morris showed Peggy how to make a nest of reeds for Dinah; then he dressed the sore on her shoulder again.

"That will soon be well, Pegling," he said.

"My lord, do not call me little-names. I am a woman. I wear a blue belt. My mother's sister put it on me."

He sighed. He was exhausted with last night's efforts and to-day's drama. She too was swaying and red-eyed, in the yellow flicker of the reed rushlight that burnt in the corner of the hut.

"Among thy clans thou art a woman," he said. "Among mine thou art a child."

"I will never be a woman," she whined. "I will never smear myself with sour milk. In three days they will take us to Gal-Gal, and they will spear thee for a witch, and drown thy wives."

Morris was too tired to feel the shock just then.

"Perhaps I am not a witch," he said. "Or perhaps it is a good life in the other world. Where wilt thou sleep? Shall I make thee a nest like Dinah's?"

She smiled, somehow, and without a word went to Dinah's nest and crawled in beside her. Dinah adjusted her limbs without waking. By the time Morris had constructed a tent of mosquito netting over the pair of them they were fast asleep, fast entangled.

He sat down and wrote a careful note to Anne, most of which was taken up with an explanation for someone who couldn't read phonetics of how to pronounce in the language of the marsh the formal summons "Thy blood-brother calls thee to Gal-Gal."

Six

1

MORRIS WAS NOT at all prepared for Gal-Gal, when the fleet came to it in the middle of the third morning. It was a holy place, mentioned in many songs, often with modifiers which meant "of a dark, reddish hue" and "stony", so he had envisaged it as another great mound among the reed-beds, like a blob of Devonshire, red clay and small stones.

Gal-Gal came out of the mists almost between stroke and stroke of the paddles, looming like a fortress. It was one vast slab of red rock, striated from end to end, and terraced over the ages by the rub of the river. Some movement of the continents had tilted it so that the layers ran five degrees from the horizontal and its flat top sloped up to a sort of prow about sixty feet above the water. The clefts and ledges along its side were fuzzy with stunted growths, mostly a strange succulent shrub whose branches projected at gawky angles, carrying little fat blue-green leaves and hanging bunches of wizened brown berries. There was a slow current here which kept a wide reach clear of reed and mimulus; down this the fleet swept.

Morris was being towed. Nobody would come in the canoe with him and Dinah, except Peggy, and he wasn't given a paddle. He had been passed from village to village all the previous day, some of them on mounds like Alaurgan-Alaurgad, others consisting of huts built on rafts of reeds which were added to as they sank or as the floods rose. At each village most of his escort had returned home and only a few token warriors and elders continued with him. At the last one they had picked up a number of women and small girls.

"Perhaps you will find a friend," he had said to Peggy, as he had watched a group of these scramble shrilling into a large canoe.

"Lord, they are of the duck clan," she had answered with surprise and something like disgust.

The suppuration of her sore had gone and the skin was creeping across it. He had spent much of his time telling her European stories, Snow White and Oedipus and Beauty and the Beast; in exchange she had sung him, reluctantly at first, some of the women's songs, which men are not supposed to hear. The words were slightly different from man-talk and the songs disappointing, very repetitive and often meaningless, but with haunting, wailing melodies. Her small voice went unnoticed in the general clamour of the fleet's progress. At the moment Morris was being towed by two canoes of the heron clan, who had some sort of ancient antipathy to the men of the watersnake clan which was expressed in a ritual of jeering, a series of grotesque similes wherein the herons taunted the watersnakes for their big stomachs and the watersnakes taunted the herons for their small penises. Kwan had once said something about one of these clans always taking its wives from the other, but Morris couldn't remember the details. The men of the two clans took the ritual seriously, snarling at each insult and putting real venom into their replies, but the other clans shouted with laughter. They seemed to be in no particular awe of Gal-Gal, for the racket continued as they jostled for landing places and began to swarm like baboons up the red rock.

Morris waited till his canoe was safely moored, then he settled Dinah, prostrate with heat, on to his left hip and with his right hand picked the pole out of its rings. The raw new box swung above his head with the ancient bones inside it.

"Bring food," he said to Peggy.

"Lord, no food is eaten on Gal-Gal."

"Bring water then," he said crossly, "or I shall die thirsting."

He stepped ashore and watched as she filled the water-bottles from the river and dropped a couple of Campden tablets in each. He had not told her what the tablets were for, nor had he told her a magical fable about them. He had simply forbidden her to give him water without them or to drink it herself. She was an obedient little doll.

Ages ago someone had cut good steps up the side of Gal-Gal.

137

A worn flight of them rose to the left of the landing-place but ended in vacancy where a section of rock had fallen sheer away. The marshmen ignored them and scrambled up anyhow; there seemed to be several easiest-ways-up, such as boys find in a good climbing-tree. Morris, burdened with Dinah and the pole, chose to follow a crude sort of litter on which lay a man so deformed and bloated that he seemed like a piece of abstract soft sculpture. Three wives and a son carried this litter, going a long way round to find the most convenient path from terrace to terrace. At one such point they caught up with an old woman one side of whose body was completely withered, so that leg and arm were like dead branches. As she scrabbled to haul herself up a three-foot step the young male litter-carrier reached out with his foot and kicked her to one side, so that she fell clumsily and lay twitching. Without looking at her the four of them hoisted the litter over the obstacle and scrambled on. Mysteriously, it was at that moment that Morris's tolerance of the marsh-people broke.

He didn't do anything visible. He simply changed his mind. No doubt ever since he had found Maj's body he had been building up to this decision, but now, as he helped the beldame to her foot (taking care only to touch sound flesh in case the withering was infectious) he found himself saying the hell with them. The Arabs have got them right. A conceivable alternative future for mankind, phooey. They are a dead end, a waste product, excrement. The language is an accident, and might still turn out to be a tool of minor importance for psycholinguistic research, but what was its point beyond that? Perhaps it wasn't even as astonishing as Morris thought it—cold natures tend to find weird outlets for their romantic drives.

The old woman stared at him for a moment with dark, unreadable eyes, but said nothing. He picked Dinah up and using the pole as an alpenstock climbed on. The heat off the rock struck back with a steady, dull intensity. Sweat streamed all down him. His gasps seemed to fetch in nothing breathable and his heart slammed erratically. He reached the top on the verge of heat-stroke and stood there, gulping and blinking.

Slowly the red blur left his vision and the thudding blood became quiet; he took a waterflask from Peggy and poured some over his neck and chest, then he told her to spread a mat on a

138

bare patch of rock and lowered Dinah on to it. There was no shade, but the noon haze veiled the sun. One was steamed, not roasted.

"What happens now?" he said.

"I do not know, my lord. Only the women of the duck clan come to Gal-Gal. The men of the other clans do not speak about it."

He looked at her with strange exasperation. She was one of them too, or would be, one day, if she survived today—a cheerful drowner of strangers, a passer-on of repellent diseases and obscene cruelties. On the other hand Dinah liked her.

"Rest." He said. "Drink if you are thirsty."

Of course he should have tried to escape with her. They might have been safe, sneaking away through the witch-protected dark. She might have known the way. But he had become obsessed with his mission, and the need to talk to Gaur, even on Gal-Gal.

In fact nothing much happened for a long time, except that more and more people arrived. The top of the rock was not a clean slope as it had seemed from the water; it was more like a slightly cupped hand, lowest at the wrist and rising to the finger-tips; about in the centre of where the heart-line would have run was a large, rectangular slab of a different sort of stone, and below this lay a natural arena, forty feet across, where nobody walked. Morris watched the new arrivals, many of them crippled or deformed, but all wearing rather more beads and ornaments than had seemed normal on Alaurgan-Alaurgad. Several men wo.e, not as covering but as decoration, strips of cloth which he recognised by the pattern as being upholstery from the crashed plane; many wore waist-belts from which dangled dark little rubbery blobs which seemed to have no aesthetic value at all, but only when a young man strutted by wearing a belt of magnetic tape from which hung two similar objects, but paler and not yet fully shrunk, did Morris realise that he was looking at the genitals of defeated enemies. This young man had killed Arabs not long ago. Maj. Jillad? Where had he got the tape?

Morris was distracted from this problem by the arrival of the other hand of Nillum, carried up with no ceremony at all by a middle-aged man with a grossly distended stomach, who waddled over with it to a group of warriors, leaned on the pole and stood chatting like a farmer at a cattle-market. Everybody was behaving like that—like, in fact, guests at the reception after a large wedding, greeting and gossiping in noisy groups. Nobody looked at Morris at all, and after a while he left his wives in each other's care and started to wander about.

The stone object turned out to be man-made, a thing like a giant's coffin, lidded with three enormous shaped blocks of grey sandstone. Along its sides ran a series of blobs and lumps that might once have been a bas relief but were now uninterpretable with age. Morris was not surprised. There had been the broken steps below, and out in the desert there were stone-lined wells of great depth, an achievement beyond any known technology of the Arabs who had lived there in historical times. It was curious to realise that even the primeval-seeming marshmen had been preceded by a different people, but in itself the stone thing was like so many other stone things, apparently interesting but really boring.

A faint wind stirred, creating the illusion of coolness. Something seemed to be happening up at the far end of the platform, though nobody near Morris paid any attention to it. Lethargically, almost like a tourist at a village festival, he strolled towards it.

Close to the cliffs at the highest point of the rock a group of women sat on the ground with a number of gourd bowls between them. Two other women and a girl no older than Peggy knelt in the middle of the circle being made up for the ceremony. The pots contained pigments, a greyish white, a muddy orange, indigo and olive. The bodies had been painted white all over and white paint had been rubbed into the hair which had then been teased out into spikes. By the time Morris arrived the white had dried on the first woman and she was now being painted with herringbone stripes of the other colours; the pattern ignored natural contours, marching over breast and buttock like a Roman road. The old woman with the withered arm and leg sat just outside the circle, swaying like a drunk and singing in a monotonous wheeze, words which Morris didn't know, though the inflections and modifications were of the same type as in marsh speech—he imagined this was a secret language, used only for magical chants. The whole process seemed dingy and banal. The painting was crude and the result ugly but not frightening—scarcely even striking.

140

His attention, such as it was, was distracted by a group of men coming up to the circle with a curious tangle of wickerwork and plaited reed ropes. Roughly they picked the old woman, still chanting, off the ground and carried her to the edge of the cliff; for a moment he thought they were about to throw her over, but they lashed her into the wickerwork, settled a bowl in her lap and lowered her over the edge with the ropes. She seemed to be in a sort of trance all the while, and her dreary chant came faintly up to Morris's ears from below. Crane as he might he couldn't see what she was at down there, though the men moved the ropes along about twenty feet of cliff. He gave up and looked out across the marshes.

Far down the reach of the main river a long canoe nosed out of the reeds, paddled by at least six men. They seemed to have a white passenger, but it was too far off to be sure before the canoe's prow swung towards Gal-Gal and the foremost oarsmen hid the rest.

When the old woman was hauled back the pot in her lap was half full of little orange berries. The men carried her back to the circle of women, one of whom took the pot and another washed the old woman's good hand in what appeared to be urine. A small girl appeared carrying a wicker basket out of which she took a bedraggled brown duck. It was a pitiful thing. The girl held it under one arm and with her free hand forced its head back and its beak open. A woman used two bits of reed like chopsticks to drop one of the berries down its throat then poured a little water on top. The girl put the duck down in the middle of the circle, where it stood in a dazed fashion, flapping one wing with feeble strokes. The other wing had been broken. The women who were doing the make-up stopped their task to watch. The old woman came out of her trance and fell silent. The babble of men's voices surged on in the background, but here was a little island of stillness, in the middle of which the duck fell dead. Morris almost believed he could hear a slight thump as it hit the rock. Suddenly all the women looked at him for the first time. He hadn't thought they'd noticed his presence, but now they stared at him with a single, black, inquisitive glance. The little girl who was being painted laughed aloud.

At first Morris thought that the trial was over, that he had

141

been found guilty, that the other preparations were all for some ritual to do with his slow death. He swallowed dryness, became dizzy and managed to sit down without actually falling. The dizziness left him but the fear remained, mingled with growing disappointment and resentfulness. If one was to be speared, or poisoned, or drowned inchmeal, one was at least entitled to expect that the moment of decision should be less hugger-mugger. One didn't wish to seem egotistical, but one would appreciate it if the smelly little savages who had brought one to this place to die would stop gossiping about buffaloes for a few seconds and turn round and watch one's fate. And surely they could have spared a less seedy duck to die with one.

Slowly he realised that he had misread the incident, and that the women had only been checking the quality of the poison berries. He stood up and saw that somebody else was watching him, a group of five young men, black and naked, the shortest of them almost twice as tall as the average marshman. The family likeness in three of them was so strong that he couldn't decide which was Gaur, and when he waved a friendly hand they all five turned away.

Dinah was still asleep, but Peggy had news.

"Lord, men of the ninth clan came."

"I saw them."

"They brought a woman, white as thou."

"I do not see her."

Peggy led him to the edge of the rock and pointed. A single long canoe was moored in the middle of the channel.

"She hid," said Peggy with a giggle. "She was ashamed when the men shouted."

2

The ceremony proper didn't begin until that curious quarter-hour when the whole marsh air turned to a glowing, coppery fog. It was like being inside a sunset cloud. At this time, Peggy said, witches are weakest, caught between world and world.

Proceedings began with an argument about seating arrangements. The dry-dung fires had been lit to drift their acid smoke around the rock-top, and the whole crowd had gathered, jostling,

142

round the arena; but there was a certain orderliness in their behaviour for the first time that day; the men seemed to have grouped themselves into their seven clans, above each of which a resin-soaked torch of reeds flared and fumed. The women of the duck clan sat on the ground opposite the stone object, which was now decorated with a rope of shells of fresh-water mussels, and several small unmeaningful bits and bobs. Dinah had woken and Peggy had taken her down to the canoe and given her fruit. Now Morris led his wives, holding each one by the hand, towards the arena. Two clans bustled aside to clear a path for him, but began to mutter and grumble when he stopped level with their front rank and signed to Dinah to sit down. An old man with a weeping pink mess where his left eye should have been half-turned to him, and without looking at him directly said "The witches stand beside the house of spirits."

"There is no witch," Morris answered, even more loudly than he had intended.*

A puzzled mutter ran round the arena. The old man opened his mouth to speak again, but changed his mind and merely pointed. Dinah looked up and snickered at him.

"There is no witch," said Morris again. He'd had plenty of time to wonder how he would face his accusation, but had not expected it to come so early. His previous attempts to argue about his supposed crime with Gaur, Dyal and Qab had, he now saw, foundered on a property of the marsh language, whereby the negative relation carried certain positive implications, so that to say "I am not a witch" had been to admit the possibility that he might be. Earlier Morris had been bound by his own feeling that the language and culture were sacrosanct, but now he didn't care how many strands of that intricate old network he broke as he threshed to escape.

* To those to whom it seems ridiculous to find a footnote dangling from a moment of high drama, I apologise for my lack of art. Briefly, Morris had constructed a phoneme-group which was grammatically (and therefore to marshmen logically) impossible, but at the same time was perfectly clear in its meaning. He said " khu//ralçutlangHo"—"khu//-" negative relation-root "-r-" euphony insert "-al-" nominal qualifier ending, inapplicable to relation-roots, "-çu-" positive-identity relation-root, "-tlangHo" nominal qualifier of witchcraft. A rough English equivalent might be "Notness is witch."

Curiously it was the children who first grasped what he was actually saying. He heard Peggy gasp, and at the same moment the child in her skin of paint began to whine. What, no witch, when she had spent eight hours putting her make-up on? The men on either side of Morris drew back still further, as if embarrassed by this faux pas. The old woman stopped her snivelling chant and listened while one of the other women whispered in her ear. She muttered what must have been an order, for as she snivelled on the women huddled together, active at something in their midst, whispering brief phrases. In an extra-ordinarily short time one of them stood up and walked slowly round the edge of the arena to the stone object, against which she set (with an action that reminded Morris strangely of the Queen laying wreaths at the Cenotaph) three crude mommets. They were identical, made of reed and cloth, without arms or legs. Only the narrowed neck between the round head and the long body made them human at all, but human they undoubtedly were—Dinah, Morris and Peggy, ready to stand trial for witchcraft.

The little orchestra of women struck up the overture on quite different instruments from the ones Morris had heard at the flood-going feasts; these were two long, thin drums, reed pipes and clay groaners. The old woman also groaned and began to shiver or rather to shudder. She sat to one side of the orchestra, and on the other knelt the two painted women and the painted girl, each with a little pot in front of her. The noise from the orchestra was a weird, continuous wheeze, unpatterned, as though a wild-life recording enthusiast had put his microphone against the stomach of some big beast with indigestion. The arena was an ellipse, with the orchestra at one end and the House of the Spirits, the stone object, at the other; all round the perimeter the black crowd jostled for position, but no one interfered with Morris's view; they left a clear three feet all round him, like filings repelled by the pole of his presence. This was nothing to do with the hand of Nalar dangling above his head—at least the fat man who carried the other hand was given only so much room as the bulge of his stomach cleared for him.

Suddenly the old woman's shuddering came to a climax. Her withered limbs shook in the still air with a life of their own. She cried aloud a single word of her secret language—a command by the sound of it—then rigor gripped her. She toppled sideways and lay still.

Nobody paid any attention to her, because on her cry the two painted women jumped to their feet and began to dance; each held her pot in her left hand and used the right hand as a lid as she hopped round the arena in short, galvanic leaps, both feet together as if tied by a rope. They hopped in opposite directions, and the first to pass Dinah had the most extraordinary effect on her; she rushed away from the arena to the end of her leash, and when she could get no further she had what looked like an epileptic fit on the ground, writhing and sobbing. Morris moved back and knelt beside her, trying to calm her with his touch. Peggy came and squatted on the other side of her, frowning in the dusky light.

"Dinah is eaten with a spirit, Lord."

"No. She was frightened by the dancing woman."

"It is the spirit T!u who dances."

"Peggikins, it is a woman covered in white paint."

He regretted his words the moment he had said them—if the child was going to be killed, it would be easier for her if she accepted the whole grisly mummery as something true and real. He lifted Dinah, panting and whimpering, and carried her back to the arena, where she lay still with her head buried in his shoulder. Peggy took his free hand unasked.

The two women by now had reached the very centre of the arena and were standing back to back, jigging up and down; the noise of the orchestra seemed to change, but not in any meaningful way; the women jigged round until they faced each other and began to hop backwards; as soon as they were far enough apart to do so they bent almost double and, still hopping, started to take the contents from their pots and dribble them down on to the rock. It was a process that reminded Morris of something— yes, a gardener sowing seed along the line of a drill—but the women moved not in straight lines but in two outward moving spirals like the arms of a nebula, leaving their trail of whatever it was behind them, bent double, hopping all the time. It must have been killingly exhausting, but they kept it up for twenty minutes until they reached their place by the orchestra.

The music changed again. The women put their pots down

and picked up the child, who held her own pot cradled in her white arms; they carried her to the middle of the arena where they left her kneeling. The orchestra stopped playing and the child opened her mouth and sang a thin and tuneless chant in the secret language, rocking her body to and fro with the pot huddled against her chest. The chant was short, but she repeated and repeated it until Morris could discern the grammatical form under the meaningless words. In English it might have gone:

> The —— comes to ——
> It ——s into the ——
> It ——s this and that
> It ——s to and fro
> Ai!
> It ——s the ——.

While she was singing it for the fifth or sixth time, watched in total silence by the hitherto restless crowd, a flood of fear washed suddenly into Morris, filling every creek of his being, as strong and uncontrollable as nausea. His tongue seemed to stick to his palate; it made a sucking noise as he wrenched it away with his throat-muscles and clung back as soon as he relaxed. He shut his eyes and bowed his head, filled with furry darkness. Only the touch of Dinah's head against his cheek meant anything other than this gulping dread, which wasn't even dread of pain and death, but was as though a vast invisible bird had nestled down on to the rock, covering him with its stifling feathers of fear. He loosed Peggy's hand and teased the back of Dinah's head, unconsciously at first but slowly gathering out of her a vague comfort that enabled him at last to look up again and face his trial. As he did so the girl broke off her chant in mid syllable.

She stiffened. Her head went back. Her mouth was open and her eyes stared. One drum beat, very slowly. The girl rose to her feet as though the sound jerked her upwards and with a strange mannish gait started to strut round the arena. At one drum-beat she thrust her hand into the pot; at the next she drew it out; at the third she tossed whatever she was holding out across the arena. She moved widdershins round the outside of the circle, throwing with her left hand towards the middle something that fell with a light rattle on to the rock. Again it was a motion like seed-sowing, but this time that of a Victorian sower broadcasting his wheat-seed across a field. The crowd on either side of Morris seemed to shrink back a little when she was throwing in their direction, and then to relax again when the danger was past; but in fact all the little projectiles fell well short—it must have been a very practised performance, for all that the girl moved like a creature controlled by powers outside her.

By now it was almost dark. The girl did two circuits and stopped near the orchestra. The stiffness went out of her. She dropped the empty pot with a crash and at the same moment looked down at her left hand and started to wail, a real child in real pain. Two women ran out of the shadows and pulled her down beside a larger bowl, where they sponged at the paint on her arm, using bits of cloth on the end of reeds; the arm itself seemed to be twisting about as if there were no bones in it, but they were careful not to touch it with anything except their cloths. The wailing diminished, but Morris in his daze of fear, though he shut his eyes, seemed to see the arm grow monstrous, a snake with fingers at the end, or the leafless limb of a dead tree. He realised that once the old woman with the withered side might have been just such a girl, tossing out poisoned seed at a witch-finding, wailing as the poison penetrated the thick paint and began to bite like fire into the young flesh, starting the process that would one day wither the whole side . . .

But when he looked up he saw that two men were standing over the inert form of the old woman, prodding her with the butt end of their spears. A mild hum of talk had broken out, such as civilised people produce between items at a concert. He shifted Dinah to his other hip and as he did so let her see that the white leaping things that had given her the horrors had vanished from the arena. She chattered a little and blew in his ear, then wriggled to be put down; so he settled her at his feet, fixed her leash and stood on it, so that she could only move a couple of feet; contentedly she began to fasten and unfasten the buckle of his sandals.

One of the painted women came back into the arena wearing on her feet two thick little reed mats which prevented her soles from touching the poison-seed; she carried half a dozen flat dishes which she placed at various points in the arena; then she

fetched a big gourd and poured water out of it into the bowls—
all this without any ceremony, as though she were preparing a
meal in her own hut. Then she went back to the shadows.

At last the old woman stirred, groaning. The men who had
been prodding her stood back and watched as she rolled on to
her stomach and pushed herself with her good hand into a sitting
posture. She called out, quite strongly, in the secret language, and
a cry answered from the dark. A woman brought a closed wicker
basket and put it in front of her. She shuddered again and sang a
short, fierce invocation in the secret language, waving her good
hand to and fro over the basket. The woman with the mats on
her feet then carried it to the exact centre of the arena, where she
lowered a flap in its side and retreated. Total silence fell again.
The night was now dark, and the mists beginning to clear from
the dull moon; the seven torches burnt yellowish-orange, with
sudden spurts of green; the ring of jet-black bodies seemed to
absorb most of the little light they gave. Morris peered at the
meaningless basket.

Something moved at the opening and immediately the orchestra
struck up a series of quavering hoots and whistles, backed by a
dull pattering on the drums. Hesitantly the duck stepped out into
the open.

It was quite a presentable creature, something like a female
mallard but larger. Its wing, as far as Morris could see, was not
broken but lashed to its side. Once out in the wavering torchlight
it lost its shyness, cocked its head a little sideways and peered
about, then darted forward and scooped up a few seeds from the
rock. The marshmen sighed. The old woman craned forward,
her little eyes glistening in the flames. The duck, with absurd
confidence, began to follow one of the spiralling trails of seed,
but suddenly darted aside for a drink of water from the nearest
dish. When it had drunk, raising its head to the moon to swallow
each sip, it wandered about until it hit on another trail of seed,
which it again began to follow round the spiral. Morris had
another of his attacks of sick fear. Dry-mouthed and gulping he
tried to work out where the girl had thrown the seed from her pot.
In his mind's eye he could see her white, ghastly figure, with its
drab aureole, strutting round the arena. He could envisage the
jerky arc of her sowing-arm. But he couldn't calculate where the

148

seeds might have fallen—more towards the outside than the inside, he thought.

Slowly the watchers became more intent. The bird, after various meanderings, was now pecking among the seeds which had fallen over to Morris's right, not quite where the three mommets sat, but uncomfortably close to them—supposing the oracle was worked by mere proximity—part of the terror was the meaninglessness of the whole procedure—if he had known what the duck's movements meant, and how they could be read, he'd have had fixed points to pin his fears on, to reduce them to rational order, to master them, even. But . . . why, I haven't even been accused of anything, he thought. Let alone given a chance to answer. The hell with them!

For the moment resentment overcame his fear, and he peered with hot eyes at the duck filling its crop with gusto, pausing only for sips at the water-dishes. The savages followed its progress with a sort of aware concentration which also infuriated him. They knew what was happening, goddammit.

"Oh, get on with it," he whispered. "For Christ's sake get on with it!"

Almost as his lips moved the bird's actions altered. It darted towards a bowl of water, missed and performed its gulp and swallow in dry air. The whole crowd hissed with indrawn breath. The old woman cried aloud. The orchestra began to make as much noise as its instruments would permit, but this was immediately drowned by the shouts of the audience, everybody bellowing at the top of their lungs. He felt a movement at his side and glanced down to see Peggy skipping with excitement and whooping too. The bird was now straight in front of the mommets, staggering around, gulping and swallowing at nothing. It almost fell but recovered, and with a wild flapping of its free wing darted in an arc towards Morris himself, collided with one of the water-dishes, swung away and crashed headlong into the side of the basket in the centre of the arena. The basket fell on its side and rolled away. The bird also fell, on to its back. Its feet paddled at air for a moment and its free wing flapped twice. And then it was dead, as stiff as if it had dropped frozen out of the sky.

The shouting died only slowly. Two women with brooms of

reed swept a path to the duck's body, and two others picked the old woman up and carried her there. One of the painted women brought dry reeds, and the other a flaming rush-light to light them. The old woman pulled some feathers out of the duck and threw them on the flames, watching intently as they curled and stank and became ash. One of the painted women knelt beside her and with a sliver of flint slit open the duck's belly by the vent and teased the entrails out. While the old women smelt and fingered them the crowd talked, in a relaxed but expert way, about the trial. Morris caught fragments from the two nearer clans . . . Wah, that was a brave duck . . . the spirits are strong . . . Tchinai finds the trail hard to read . . . do you remember that she-witch from the garfish clan . . . in my father's day they caught fierce witches . . . the duck found death close by the House of Spirits . . . No, by the centre . . . it is a hard trail . . . but wah, it was a brave duck . . .

Soon he was yawning. The tension that should have been there was gone out of him, replaced by a dreary sense of uselessness and moral exhaustion. Apathetically he squatted down and teased Dinah's fur for a while, and then played which-hand with her. Peggy sat and watched the game, but kept glancing at the arena, where the two women with brooms were now meticulously sweeping the whole surface, scooping up the little heaps of seed they made on to flat leaves and throwing them on to the fire, where they stank with a new and strangely chemical smell. Three of the torches had burnt out and were not re-lit. Time passed.

At last there was a fresh stirring of interest. Morris stood and saw the old woman being lifted to her feet. The clans surged forward to surround her, a jostling mob of which Morris wanted no part, so he stayed where he was. Not long now, he told himself. Soon be over. Probably won't hurt at all.

Suddenly a roar of angry voices broke out round the old woman. A thin man disentangled himself and rushed at Morris with his spear raised and its poison-tip unsheathed; but he was slowed by some deformity of his leg and as Morris cringed another man caught up with him and snatched the spear from behind; it was the second man who actually threw the weapon, not at Morris but out into the dark, over the cliff; he was Fau.

"Nearly thou art dead, Morch," he shouted cheerfully and

swung round to face the rush, his own spear raised. The crowd surged down towards them, but not in any kind of organised charge—far more like a mass of bellicose drinkers being thrown out of a pub on Saturday night, each man intent on his argument with his neighbour—but as far as Morris could see in the swaying light of the remaining torches none of the poisoned spear-heads were unsheathed.

Dinah leaped to his arms. He hefted her round and snatched up Peggy with his free arm, thus leaving himself quite unable to ward off from the three of them any shaft or blow. Yelling, the marshmen flowed about him absorbed in their impenetrable quarrel, shouting ancient insults from clan to clan and from age-set to age-set while Dinah and Peggy sobbed with fear against his shoulders. It seemed to him that amid the human mess there were people actually trying to defend him, or at least to argue his case, while there were others attempting to get at him. The presence of his defenders was more useful than anything they actually did, because nobody could aim with any accuracy in the melee, and a weapon that missed him was certain to hit a marshman and start one of those complicated feuds that run from generation to generation and end in an epic when everybody is dead.

So the battle raged in Homeric confusion around the bizarre standard of the hand of Na!ar. There seemed to be no conceivable resolution. But suddenly out of the dark came a sinister rescue.

It began to his left, but he didn't notice it until the quality of the shouting to that side changed, and by then the wedge of ninth-clan warriors had almost reached him; the new cries came from the men whom Gaur and his brothers were simply picking up and tossing to either side. A black hand reached out and grasped the elbow that held Dinah. He almost let go of Peggy as he was snatched out of the scrum, like a handbag from a bargain-counter, and carried bodily across the top of the rock, wives and all.

They put him down at the cliff edge, and thankfully he lowered Dinah and Peggy, though he expected that he himself would be instantly tossed into the dark waters.

"Flee," said Gaur. "Friend of my brother, show my brothers thy boat. Go."

One of the huge men picked Peggy up. Another took Morris by the arm. They went down the rock face like falling stones. The boats bounced and wallowed as they jumped in, but before Morris had settled they were cutting out across the glistening water towards the single long canoe.

"Wai," wailed Peggy, "I am stolen. I am stolen."

"Yes, and I will roast thee for my supper," said one of the big men. Another bellowed with laughter.

Behind them Gal-Gal was tumult still, filling the night with screams of vengeance and shouts of triumph and, on a different register, what sounded like the hysterical laughter of the women of the duck clan. The canoe bumped alongside the larger boat.

"Oh, Christ," said Anne in a dismal voice. "I've been eaten alive by mosquitoes."

She didn't sound as though she expected anyone to understand, and gasped when Morris answered.

"I've got some Camoquin somewhere," he said.

Before they had finished transferring his stores Gaur and the last three warriors slid alongside.

"Wah!" said one of them, "that was a brave duck!"

For all their size they barely rocked the long canoe as they took their places. Someone gave an order that was no more than a grunt. The paddles dug in, all together. The grunt came again, marking the stroke, and again and again as they shot down the main reach, leaving clamorous Gal-Gal behind so rapidly that before Morris had recovered from his first shivering-fit of relaxing terror it had diminished from looming cliffs to a vague hull-like blackness beneath the moon, a stone ark, stranded in the floods with its cargo of the alternative future.

"Where are we going, sons of Na!ar?" he whispered.

"Gaur has an island," said someone.

"Protect us from the things of the moon-world, witch, until we get there," said someone else.

"What the bloody hell's been going on?" said Anne.

"Am I not then stolen?" said Peggy, with a ridiculous hint of disappointment in her voice.

"God knows," said Morris in English.

The rhythm of the grunts altered. The stroke side paddles lifted all together, poised, dripped silver driplets, lunged backwards against the water. With a gurgle and rustle the canoe swung through a sharp arc and up a narrow little channel between two bare mudbanks. Well rowed Balliol, thought Morris. Well rowed Balliol.

3

"I've been a bloody fool," said Anne.

"I could lend you my spare shirt and trousers," said Morris.

"Oh, I've got a pile of perfectly good clothes, but Mr Muscles won't let me wear them. For God's sake, I'm not even allowed to sit on one of those bloody stupid mats. I have to kneel here, like this."

"I'm sorry," said Morris.

He meant it in more ways than one. He would have preferred to see her clothed. To a man with a low sex-drive the Q'Kuti culture had been a curious release from vague guilts. Even in respectable Bristol Morris had been continually nudged by little reminders that he was some distance off from the admired male norm of modern British life, though that was obviously no more a real norm than the stringy girls in the glossies are, in the true sense, models of British womanhood—still, in England Morris had felt *got at*, whereas in Q'Kut the sex-obsessed Arabs actually seemed to admire his capacity for continence. Now, with this girl kneeling naked in the dust beside him, however unbecomingly mottled with mosquito bites, he was being got at again. He knew quite well what she expected him to be thinking, and if she'd known how wrong she was she would have thought even less of him.

But he was actually sorry for her too. She was not merely physically naked. Further down the slope of Gaur's island Dinah and Peggy were playing peep-bo round a hut. They were naked too, in the sense of being without clothes; but they were not stripped down to the bare soul, as Anne was, the thing itself, unaccommodated woman. She had even lost all her roles so far that she had allowed the flat diphthongs of some northern city to reappear in the voice that had once told him that Mummy would have thought vets were beneath them. She had become like a creature in a cage in an old-fashioned zoo, something totally uncivilised.

153

"Have you learnt any of the language?" he said.

"You know what I'm like. I can't even begin. Can you make him let me go? Where the hell is he, anyway?"

"Gaur? He went back to Gal-Gal to try and buy something I saw one of the men wearing."

"You never told me what the hell was happening up there, while I was being eaten."

"I didn't really understand it all myself. I was being tried for being a witch. They give a poison to a duck and watch how it dies, and one of the women of the duck clan reads the signs. That went on most of the day—the preparations and the actual trial, I mean—and then right at the end there was a row over what the witch-finder's verdict was. You see, a lot of people had come to Gal-Gal with various diseases. The theory seems to be that when you send a witch back to the moon-world with luck he drags along with him some of the moon-world creatures that have been causing people's limbs to swell up or drop off or go septic, so there were a crowd of people there who wanted to see me die—in fact to stand as close as possible to me while I was dying..."

"It sounds a bit like Lourdes."

"Ung?"

"OK, I've never been there—but I *was* a nun for a few weeks, once."

Morris stared at the brown wall of reeds that ringed the prison-island, all set with poison-stakes through which only Gaur and his brothers knew the paths. He thought that a civilisation that allows you to become anything also allows you to become nothing. In other cultures you have to be what you are.

"Anyway," he said, "the witch-finder decided I was a witch, but not the sort who ought to be killed. Don't ask me why. Gaur didn't give a very coherent explanation—he didn't think it was interesting. The explanation, I mean. It was just a fact, like all the other facts in the marsh. Besides, the idea of mutually coherent superstitions is peculiarly western—I mean the idea that if two beliefs are logically incompatible one of them must be wrong... but the upshot was that the sick men wanted to kill me and the others—who'd only come for the fun—fought them off, and then Gaur pulled me out of the ruckus. It's no use

154

asking for any more explanations. The language doesn't run to providing the questions, let alone the answers."

"And you're going to let it go on that way? You aren't going to do anything to bring the poor bastards up to date?"

"I don't know. Anyway, I think I've done it already."

"What do you mean?"

"Well ... oh, I don't know ... we've kept talking about this thing ... the Bond of Na!ar ... as if it were almost something like a belt, or a strap—just a single bond on its own. But really, well, I expect you've seen how the camel-drivers secure an awkward load with an extraordinary criss-cross of lashings which doesn't look as if it would ever hold anything, but it does its job for ninety miles and at the end the camel kneels down and the driver undoes one knot and pulls at one rope and the whole network just ... well ... shrivels off the load? I think the Bond's like that. Or rather it's part of a network like that, only much more complicated. And it's starting to come undone anyway. The language is an image of the culture, an enormous web of relationships. It can adjust to little changes, births and deaths and diseases and bad floods, by allowing for an adjustment of relationships. If you take the cross-threads out of a spider-web the spider can scuttle across and repair them—but there are two or three threads—the ones it spun to carry the web in the first place—which it can't repair. Cut one of them and the web collapses. And now the marsh culture is starting to unravel in two places. I made a hole in the language last night, and whoever killed the Sultan was trying to slice through the main girder-thread. The marsh-people can't repair the damage because they don't think in terms of cause and effect."

"Who did kill Bruce?"

It took Morris a moment to remember that that was her name for the Sultan. He pulled at his lip and watched Peggy teaching Dinah to play the strange and sinister girl-children's game of the marshes, which looked like an elaborate version of mud-pies but was in fact a ritual to prevent the ghosts of one's eventual husband's female ancestors from sucking one's own spirit away when one slept in the corner of his hut where once they too had slept. Peggy was very much senior partner now. Beyond them the brown wall of reeds hid the water, and above them the white

155

mists hid the sky. There were women who had been brought to this place by the ninth clan warriors and never since that day seen anything else. That could be Anne's fate, too, and who could say whether she did or didn't deserve it?

"Tell me what happened that last day in the zoo," he said. "You and the Sultan went to my office. I think you quarrelled. Bin Zair turned up. The Sultan sent you away. I went to the main doors to tell Gaur not to let anyone in. When I got back to my office you were still there. Can you fill in the gaps?"

"What the hell's it got to do with you?"

"I need to know."

"You can bloody well . . . oh, forget it. I'll tell you if you'll get me out of here."

"I'll try."

"OK. Done. Well Bruce took me to your office to screw me, but I wouldn't let him. He'd spotted Mr Muscles making eyes at me, and he just wanted to show everyone I belonged to him. I wasn't having any. I said I was through with him unless he promised to let me go. He was furious. I mean, we'd had this sort of row before—he liked being stood up to for a bit provided he got his way in the end—but that morning he wanted it then and there. I was seething too. When he sent me away, I stopped as soon as I was round the corner, before I reached the chimp cage, and went back to look for one of your pop-guns. I just wanted to loose off at the fat slob. But the cupboard was empty."

"Did you look at the darts?"

"No."

"I see. Then you left the office and walked along in front of the cages. I heard the Sultan come past about half a minute after you'd gone. I didn't think you'd had time to get out of sight."

"I didn't. I was about opposite the polar bear when I heard their voices. I turned and waved."

"Was he carrying one of the guns?"

"I didn't notice. He turned his back on me, so I left. OK?"

"And then?"

"What do you mean?"

"Well, you reached the lobby. How many people were there? Did anything else happen?"

"Look at me."

156

He did so. The very process of talking to him had changed her, given her a layer of confidence. There was even a hint of malicious sexuality in her glance.

"Have you talked to Mr Muscles?" she said.

He nodded.

"And now you're just being sticky-minded, wanting it all over again?"

"I want to know what happened," he said crossly. "Look, when we'd found the bodies bin Zair and I rushed along to the lobby. Gaur was there and no one else. The lift was going down, and Gaur said that nobody was in it. No, wait a bit, he said that no man was in it. I want to be able to prove that nobody except you, Gaur, bin Zair or me killed them. Or some combination of us."

"Unless they killed each other."

"I don't think that's possible."

"If you say so. Really, that makes it in my interest that there should have been someone else in the lift."

"I doubt it. Arabs will kill pretty well on suspicion. You ought to know that. Especially if it's a woman."

"Uh-huh. Well, I suppose so. What happened was this. I was still seething when I got to the zoo doors, and there was Mr Muscles seething too. He looked at me, and half reached out his hands. I've never seen anyone look so miserable . . . no, that's not true—I have in the camps. What I mean is I've never seen anyone look like that for love. And I thought the hell with Bruce—why not? So I smiled at him and took his hands. He wanted to have it there and then, but I could see he was frightened of Bruce. He went out and shooed the eunuchs away, and as soon as the lift came back he dragged me in, took it down half a floor and pressed the emergency stop. I was surprised how quick he'd caught on about lifts."

"He'd learnt that from Dinah, I expect."

"Oh. Well, we didn't have much time, but he was pretty good for a beginner."

"You took the hell of a risk. If the Sultan . . ."

"I was so bloody furious that I'd have done it in front of him, given the chance. Anyway Mr Muscles knew just enough Arabic for me to be able to arrange that he'd take me away, into the

157

marsh. My idea was that he'd take me right across and I could get to the oil-rigs and hitch a lift out from there somehow. But that wasn't his idea at all—it turned out he's only *got* one idea."

Morris grunted. Her account of the morning of the murders tied in closely with Gaur's, though considerably less like *The Song of Solomon* in tone. He'd known it would. The ninth clan do not lie—though no doubt under the new dispensation they would soon learn.

"What are you going to do?" she said.

He sighed and picked at the tasselled edge of the mat. It had been woven by the eel clan, he thought—that intricate knotting was their trade-mark. There was no way of telling whether it had been made one year ago or a hundred.

"I don't have to do anything," he said. "It'll just happen. It'll all come undone. In ten years' time rich nits will be able to pay two thousand quid to take a safari trip out here. They'll have outboard motors on the canoes."

"About me!" she snapped. "What are you going to do?"

"Oh, sorry. Well . . ."

He called to Peggy, who immediately stopped her game and came soberly up the slope, leaving Dinah to slap in a random fashion at the graves of ghosts.

"Dost thou remember, Peggy, the song of Anintu?"

"Anintu the warrior? I can sing that song."

"Sing that song."

Peggy knelt by the mat, interlaced her fingers behind her head and sang a reedy repetitive chant. Dinah sidled up and tried to copy the pose. Morris translated in a whisper, about the warrior-woman in that lost age when the desert had born grass, who had fought feuds, owned buffalo, even married wives—though she had also taken lovers and had children.

"But I want to get out of here," said Anne, whiningly, when the song was over and Dinah had dragged Peggy back to the mud-pies.

"It'd be a start. If he accepted the idea you wouldn't be his belonging any more. You could come and go as you wanted—though he wouldn't be under any obligation to lend you his canoe or show you the waterways . . . I don't know . . . I think he might

158

even welcome the idea. I suppose it depends whether he thought you'd . . . I mean whether you'd still . . ."

"How mealy-mouthed can you get, Morris? I'll keep him happy."

Trapped by her altered tone he turned and stared at her. The change was extraordinary. In an instant she had grown into the role, and was sporting invisible uniform. The Emperor's new uniform. He had seen her hold her head at just that angle before, once, when she had stood on the tilted wing of the airliner with a gun at her hip.

Gloomily Morris turned back to the reeds, thinking here we go again, the whole stupid circle of mindless action beginning once more. There's only one real hero in this story, and he's dead almost at the start—the Jap pilot who brought the plane down out of the bucketing thermals on to an inadequate runway with an assassin sitting beside him holding an unpinned grenade.

"I hope that lad brings back some decent gen," said Anne in a bored voice. "Then we can get weaving."

Probably she always overdid it at first, hamming her part until she had settled in to it. But she had an instinct for survival—even that weird false note in the car, when she had described the builder of the palace as absolutely giddy bonkers, had been a precise echo of the Sultan's taste.

The invisible sun climbed higher. Heat and humidity swelled unrelenting. When Morris rose from the mat to try to create a faint breeze by strolling slowly round the camp, he saw that all the area where he had been sitting was dark with his sweat. As he walked it gathered like dew on the hems of his shorts and squelched inside his plimsolls. Dinah crept whimpering into the hut and collapsed. Anne slept frowning and Peggy smiling. Two stolen women who belonged to Gaur's brothers sat cross-legged by another hut, chewing the roots of a particular bamboo and spitting their chewings into a pot to become the basis of the bitter fermented milk-drink which seemed to be the warriors' staple diet. The warriors were with Gaur, or herding buffalo. There were no children, not because the ninth clan were an infertile cross-breed, like mules, but because ninth-clan children were an anomaly in the system, and so had to be adopted into other clans at birth, or if that failed, drowned. Morris wondered what Anne was

159

doing to prevent pregnancy—whatever it was it could not last for ever. The fate of that unbegotten, hypothetical half-caste child decided him to do his best for her when Gaur came home.

An hour later the long prow nosed out of the reeds. Black and massive, four warriors strode up the slope like emergent water-gods. Gaur was noticeably the largest and most magnificent, the leader, though two of the others were older than him. In the palace his dignity had been withdrawn and silent, but here he swaggered up the slope, radiating arrogance and kingship.

"Where is my woman?" he said, tossing a tangle of magnetic tape down on to the mat.

"This woman came to Q'Kut with a dart-thrower in her hand," said Morris. "Her comrades were slain, but she came with thirty captives, she alone."

"Ho!" said Gaur.

"Among her people she is a warrior. Chiefs fear her. I have seen her speak with the Sultan as if she were a man of his age-set. She is a woman like Anintu in the song. But now I find her before thy hut, without clothes or weapons, forbidden to use a mat, as if she were one of those."

Morris gestured angrily at the two women by the other hut, crouched in the mud beside their owners. Anne timed her entry well. She had rifled Morris's kit for a khaki shirt and shorts, and she was wearing the bandolier and gun which Gaur had carried in the palace. Somehow she managed not to look ridiculous. She stood smiling at Gaur and held out her hands to him. His glance flashed sideways to where his brothers sat drinking their milk-mess, and then down to Morris and back to Anne. He laughed aloud and took her hands.

"Ho!" he said again. "We are in need of warriors. I must avenge my fathers with the deaths of many Arabs, but the people are afraid of new things and will not come. You did not need to talk of Anintu, Morris. This is a time of new things."

It was astonishing to Morris how far Gaur was prepared to contort the language to express these ideas—but of course, he was still very young. Magnificent though his physique might be, the cartilege of his mind had not yet hardened into bone.

"Perhaps there will be no killing," said Morris. "We must go to the palace and talk with thy brother; the Arabs will try to kill us first. When it is known how thy fathers died, then we can consider killing. Can we go to the palace this dusk?"

"We go at dawn," said Gaur, and that was that. He looked at Anne and then around the muddy mound of his home.

"Ho, there are many people in this place," he said. Before Morris could translate Anne had taken Gaur's hand and given him a little pull towards the canoe. Together they scampered down the slope like a couple of undergraduates running across the Meadows towards a punt on the Isis. Morris watched the prow vanish into the reeds and then began to unravel the magnetic tape. Gaur had even managed to recover the reel, though the human trophies had luckily been retained by their owner. Quite soon Peggy woke, saw that he was doing what looked like woman's work and came and took it from him, nimble-fingered. Dinah slept on, smashed with heat, but the careful rewinding of tape on to its spool would not have been one of her accomplishments.

Let's pray there's something useful on it, thought Morris. That's all.

Seven

1

THERE WAS A MOMENT when the water between the reeds and the shore lay like black glass reflecting the paling sky and the last few stars and the ridiculous palace, turned the right way up; then another moment when the surface became smeared; and then it seemed to smoke, breathing out a layer of greasy mist which would rise and hang all day over the marsh, shielding it from the torturing sun. When the layer of mist was four feet thick Gaur grunted once, the paddles dug in and the two canoes hissed out of the reeds towards the landing stages.

They had spent the night in a village of the water-vole clan, because it was only a mile from the shore-line. Gaur and his brothers had simply descended on the village like rooks on a seed-bed, demanding food and sleeping-mats without any kind of payment. Three of them had gone scouting along the shore in the dusk; they had found the nibbled remains of the body of another Arab—presumably Jillad—and also two places where men had lain hidden, waiting, as if for somebody to return from the marsh. During the night Morris had twice heard distant shots, but they might have meant anything, as Arabs are as likely to loose off their guns at a feast as at a fight.

They caught the boat-guard snoring on the silk cushions of the Sultan's never-used launch. He was fully dressed, with an ancient rifle across his lap. "Do not kill him," Morris had whispered, knowing that matters were already sufficiently precarious without the additional problem of blood-feuds with the cousins of boat-guards. Gaur had nodded and become part of the black water in the boat-shed. The guard woke with a wet black hand round his mouth and a wet arm pinning him to the shiny thwart. Morris stepped gingerly into the rocking launch.

"Salaam Alaikum," he whispered. "If you cry out you die. Let the man speak, Gaur."

"Who is it?" said the man.

"I am Morris. I know you. We have been hawking many times along the marsh edges. You have shown us good sport."

Before the man could reply Anne came quietly into the shed.

"There's one tent about thirty yards away," she said. "And there's a newish truck just behind the sheds. The rest of the camp's further off—I can hear them beginning to wake up."

"Fine," said Morris. "Gaur, thy brothers must leave now, before the sun comes. Peggy, hold Dinah fast. Anne, you'd better keep watch for a bit—I'm going to try to persuade this chap to drive us up to the palace. Now, my friend, is that your tent behind the sheds?"

"It is my brother's."

"And is that your fine truck?"

"It is the Sultan's."

"How long have you served the Sultan?"

"Seventeen years."

"You are a faithful man, and should be rewarded. If I ask him, he will give it you."

In the half light Morris could see the man's eyes widen. He was a dark little middle-aged Arab with a puckered scar along his left cheek, the result of wild shooting in a pig-hunt. He probably already regarded the truck as virtually his own property, but if it were formally given to him he could then with honour loot something else from his patron.

"But first I must reach the Sultan, who is my friend," said Morris. "I think there are men in the camp who might try to kill me."

The man thought for a few seconds.

"I am your friend also," he said. "Let me sit up. I will drive you to the palace. I will take you on my face and my brother will give us clothes to hide who you are."

"The Sultan will reward him also," said Morris. "What is the news?"

"The news is good," said the man automatically. "They are all fools," he added with that dismissive sideways movement of his hand, so typical of Arab talk. "They say they will fight the marshmen because they killed the Sultan, the two servants of bin Zair, and you also. I thought you were a spirit, Morris—for that reason alone I was afraid. But already they are quarrelling about who shall have the oil-rights and in what proportions. They have bought aeroplanes and bombs and napalm, but the pilots have looked at the marshes and say they cannot fly over them in the day because of the mists—and how else can they fight with the marshmen? They do not know marshmen as I do, who have been the Sultan's boatman for seventeen years."

To trust him or not to trust him?

"We are on thy face, then?" said Morris. "I and the marshman and our women?"

"Have I not said so?" said the boat-guard. "Good, I will wake my brother and bring clothes—for how many?"

To trust him.

Waiting for his return Morris reflected that it was strange that one should be able to rely on the abstract notion of being on a man's face with as much confidence as if it had been a physical phenomenon—not with absolute certainty but, say, about as much as one would rely on a car starting, and far more than on a phone call getting through.

One could even rely on the brother, despite his obvious fear of Gaur and dislike of the whole business. Half an hour later they drove without hurry through the waking camp. Anne sat in the front seat, heavily veiled, with Dinah even more heavily veiled in her lap. Gaur, Peggy and Morris sat in the back, the two men robed like bedu and with Morris perched on a pile of tent-hangings with the guard's rifle across his knees. Morris shouted anonymous greetings to any waking Arab in ear-shot. Perhaps the whole charade was unnecessary. It was difficult to connect the pastoral-seeming tents with murder, as the Arabs stirred to the dawn hour which was one of the two tolerable ones in the Q'Kuti day. Here and there Morris could see men at their prayers, with their mats spread beside gleaming limousines. As the lorry climbed the hill the steam above the marshes seemed to climb too, continuing to veil distances which one would have thought a higher viewpoint would bring in sight. Gal-Gal was somewhere there, in that mess.

The truck stopped under the enormous overhang of the upper floors. Morris climbed down, stiff from five nights on bare damp ground; he looked at the glass, self-opening doors, beside which a sabre-carrying slave, not a eunuch, lounged. Morris remembered his face—he was one of the regulars, a sardonic, spoilt gang who owed all their allegiance to the Sultan and tended to despise free Arabs. That was hopeful. Morris stripped his robes off, said to Anne "Count twenty, then come straight to the lift," and strolled towards the doors in shirtsleeves and shorts. The slave gaped at him.

"I am no spirit," said Morris. "I bring good news for the Sultan. Let my friends pass."

The doors hissed apart as he trod on the mat. Inside the entrance hall two other slaves were playing draughts on the floor. Four strange Arabs were talking round a low coffee-table with rifles at their side, and a handsome young man with a cleft chin was asleep on a divan. Morris remembered him as the man who had waved a gun at him in the Council Chamber. Ah, well.

The lift was already waiting, open. Morris moved over as unobtrusively as he could and put his foot against the bottom of its door. The glass hissed apart again and the rest of his party came quickly in—but not smoothly. It was Dinah, as usual, who betrayed them. He had forgotten to tell Anne to carry her, and she was scuttling along on all fours, chattering angrily as she stumbled among her cloying robes. One of the slaves looked up from his game and shouted with laughter and surprise. The Arabs in the corner broke into clamour. The young man on the divan woke, shouted and reached for his gun, but by then the lift doors were closing. Peggy screamed with terror as the sudden acceleration sucked at her bowels. Gaur laughed. Dinah, delighted to be back in a world where there were control buttons to play with, leaped towards them, stumbled over her robes again and chattered with anger. Morris picked her up. His palms were sweaty, and his whole skin seemed to be tingling with the effects of unused andrenalin. It was not a sensation he enjoyed, not because it was in itself unpleasant but because it reminded him, like one of his rare bouts of sexual energy, that given a different history he would have been a different person.

The moment the doors opened he flicked the Emergency Stop switch down, then changed his mind and reversed it. The minute's possible delay was not worth the admission that he had anything to fear. For the same reason he forced himself not to run to his rooms, but the moment he was in them he dumped Dinah, snatched at the telephone and dialled.

"Salaam Alaikum. Do I speak to bin Zair? I trust you had finished your prayers. Yes, I am not dead... You are most kind... I have the young bodyguard and the Frankish woman... No... Ah, I was told of two Arabs found in the marshes, who by signs showed that they wished to cross to the sand on the far side, so the marshmen guided them; perhaps they were Maj and Jillad. I shall be sorry if they have gone. They were good zoo-men. When does the Council meet? Good, I will come and bring the young bodyguard so that he may be questioned. Wait. There is another matter which I do not know whether I should raise at the Council. I seek your advice. I have spoken with many marshmen, and I believe that if they were approached by a man with proper authority, such as yourself, they would welcome the company into the marshes to explore for oil... oh, I do not think it would be dangerous if I were there... yes, it is good news, but I do not know how welcome it will be to some of the Council... then perhaps I had better not speak of it... but meanwhile nothing must be done to alienate the marshmen... of course, you know these Arabs better than I... I will leave all that to you... are you there? Hello, hello... Good. That is all. Farewell."

Rather pleased with himself Morris put the receiver down. The last bit of bustle he had heard might well have been the man with the cleft chin arriving for fresh orders. He dialled again. The connection did not sound good, but no one expects a place like Q'Kut to run to a particularly refined system of wire-tapping. A voice he didn't recognise answered, claiming to be the Sultan's Secretary and claiming that the Sultan was in conference. The man spoke with the blasé effrontery of any official who does not even hope to be believed. Morris put the phone down, pulled his lip and thought.

"I think we're OK for the moment," he said to Anne. "But the Council meeting may be tricky. Do you think you could bear to put that veil back on and go to the women's quarters—Gaur had better go with you so that you aren't spotted sneaking around unguarded, and he'll get you past the eunuchs if there's any trouble. I want you to find the Shaikhah."

"Bruce's first wife? She and I don't click."

"So I hear. You'll have to make it up, that's all. The point is I want some fire-power hidden up in the gallery. Before I left I suggested to Hadiq that he might try to arm the eunuchs—see what you can do—slide a bit of veil through the screen if you've brought it off—don't show yourselves or make any noise until I give a signal—I'll clap my hands. I don't want any shooting, only the threat, so if you can manage it you'd better see that the guns aren't loaded. OK?"

"Sure," she said. He explained to Gaur what he wanted, then got his tape-recorder out and wound the strange spool on to it, spinning it through at top speed to find a couple of breaks where it would need splicing. He had just switched the gadget to "Play" when he heard Dinah whimper. He looked up.

She had managed to wriggle out of her clothes and was standing in the middle of the floor, peering at Peggy. Peggy stood quite still, with her dark eyes staring wide and a curious blue-grey tinge to her skin, as though all the blood had drained from behind the blackness.

"Art thou ill, little Peggikins?" he said.

No answer. Her eyes didn't even flicker towards him. As he crossed the floor he smelt the reek of fresh urine. Her skin was weirdly cold and clammy. He picked her up and carried her into his bedroom, where he stripped off the soiled robes and laid the black, chill body in his bed. She was breathing, and he found her pulse, heavy and slow. Shock, he thought as he piled the blankets on her. Cultural bloody shock—much as a chimpanzee must feel when it is whisked from the living jungle to a concrete grove. He piled several more blankets on her and turned the thermostat of the air-conditioner up to a hideous ninety degrees. Dinah

167

leaned solicitously forward from the other side of the bed and with gentle fingers plucked at Peggy's straight, coarse hair. All of a sudden her pose changed and the fur along her shoulders bristled. But she had only heard the noise a second before Morris as it swelled to its full clamour. He rushed back into his living-room to turn the volume down, and found Gaur there, staring pop-eyed at the tape-recorder. Morris stood listening, made a note of where the sounds came, and rewound the tape to the place he wanted.

"There is no ghost in the box," he said, using the same gram-matical contortion that he had before his witch-trial.

Gaur smiled.

"In seven days I have changed seven age-sets," he said.

"Will thy people also change age-sets?"

"Perhaps. What do we do now?"

"We go to the Council; hide throwing-sticks in thy robes. I take thee among men who perhaps wish to kill thee."

"So thou camest to the marshes for me."

Morris shrugged, unable to explain his real motives for under-taking that unpleasant adventure. Peggy, he thought, would sleep for several hours. Dinah he must take with him. He sorted carefully through his wallet of chips to check that it contained all the symbols he might need; then he nestled the tape-recorder into the bottom of a canvas grip and covered it with fruit. Dinah watched both processes shining-eyed, and took his hand eagerly when he clicked to her; but inwardly he was deeply reluctant to involve her in this quarrel, a thing no more concerned with her species than the question whether he was a witch had mattered to the duck on Gal-Gal. Only it *had* mattered. It was the answer that hadn't—the duck would have died either way.

2

The Council began with extreme casualness. The coffee-pestle was already busy when Morris and Gaur reached the anteroom; they could hear the slightly syncopated thud whose rhythm, to the true Arab connoisseur, became somehow incorporated into the taste. Besides the two regular guards in the anteroom there were two heavily-armed strangers, one of whom Morris thought he recognised as having been in the palace entrance earlier that morning. He slouched over and barred the way.

"I am called by Akuli bin Zair to the Council," said Morris mildly. "This man is a witness whom the Council have asked to hear."

"And the ape? Is she also a witness?" snarled one of the strangers.

"A better one than you, bin Duwailah," shouted one of the regular guards, more truly than he knew. It sounded as though there was a certain amount of needle here, but the two strangers refused to give way until the young sheikh with the cleft chin appeared from the hall and cursed them for fools.

"But the slave must leave his weapons," he said.

Morris translated, and smilingly Gaur handed his belt, with its sheathed dagger and holstered revolver, to one of the regular guards.

Deliberately Morris allowed Dinah loose as they entered the hall itself; she had been restless with curiosity ever since she heard the noise of the coffee-pestle, and now she raced across the mosaic floor to investigate, to try the taste of a coffee-bean and spit it out, and then to pout at the dozen sheikhs already assembled. The diversion allowed Morris to settle on an unoccupied patch of cushions, to check the position of the recorder-switch while he pretended to be sorting Dinah's fruit, and finally to run a vague eye round the Council Chamber and see that a dark wisp of veil dangled through the tracery of the women's gallery.

He sighed with relief and snapped his fingers at Dinah, who ran over to see whether he was going to pay proper attention to her.

"Sirs," he said as he took her on his lap, "I ask your pardon for bringing this ape to the council, but she has been much frightened on our journey in the marshes and I cannot leave her alone. She is more valuable than many hawks. The Sultan paid ten thousand dollars a month to keep her in Q'Kut."

After a mutter of astonishment the conversation shifted to the subject of animals and their prices, famous mares and camels, and a long account of how someone's uncle had traded into Somaliland on a rumour of a strain of superb horses and had

169

come back with nothing but a shipload of mules. Where he could, Morris brought in references to their own Sultan's wealth and generosity.

In about ten minutes Hadiq arrived, escorted by bin Zair and the new secretary, a dark-skinned little man who bore a vague resemblance to bin Zair himself, and turned out to be his nephew. Hadiq, looking strained, made a little speech of welcome and thanks for the advice they were about to give him. His eye fell on Morris.

"Hi, Batman, welcome back to the Batcave," he said.

"Hi, wonderboy," said Morris. "Let's go."

But Hadiq rose from his throne and crossed to where Gaur stood, massive and withdrawn, outside the circle of councillors. He took both his hands and greeted him in Arabic. Gaur stumbled through his reply. Several of the Arabs looked furious, and one leaped to his feet, shouting that he owed no allegiance to a Sultan who befriended the murderers of his own father. Three of the younger men jumped up with their hands on their daggers. Morris got ready to clap, long before he had planned to, but bin Zair came scuttling off his stool by the throne, tugging at their arms, squeaking for calm. They settled. Hadiq went back to his throne. Coffee was served, tiny cups offered to each man in strict order of preference. Morris was delighted to see how high he came on the list, but all the same he watched the process carefully; there is a well-known Arab technique whereby the coffee-man secretes poison under his thumbnail and by pouring coffee over it is able to eliminate any selected guest. Morris got his three tiny helpings unthumbed, but even so he was very nervous. This was not his sort of scene at all—it had to go just right, with no opportunities for re-runs and erasures.

Dinah seemed to sense his nerves, but luckily didn't respond by fidgeting around, badgering the coffee-man and mocking the grave sheikhs. Instead she nestled into his lap, still as a sick child, and fingered at his shirt-buttons.

As the junior councillor at last shook the coffee-cup to show he had had enough, bin Zair rose.

"Friends of two Sultans," he said, "you are very welcome once more. And we have good news. Lord Morris is returned safe from the marshes, so we do not have his death to avenge. But we also have bad news. As you know, we have bought aeroplanes and bombs and napalm, but the pilots whom we hired—both good men who have fought in many little wars—say they cannot fly these planes across the marshes. The changes in the air, they say, would break an old aeroplane in pieces. Moreover they say it will be very difficult to find any targets in the haze."

"They simply want more money," said someone. "All mercenaries are the same. Offer them double. The Sultan is very rich."

"They have refused double," said bin Zair. "I think perhaps some fool has told them how the marshmen would treat them if they were forced to land among the reeds."

"Cannot men be found who are not cowards?" shouted Fuad, the hysteric camel-raider, just as if he had maintained the same pitch of frenzy all the time Morris had been away.

Bin Zair smiled and pulled his beard.

"Now," he said, "we who live by the marshes know this. When the floods are fully gone, the reed-beds become very dry, and it is then the custom of the marshmen to burn certain patches. Now, at that time, if we buy hovercraft and mount flame-throwers on them, we could safely burn . . ."

Hadiq was rising to his feet, pale and nervous. But Fuad spoke first.

"How long?" he shouted. "Hovercraft? They will take many weeks to come."

"The reeds will not be fully dry for four months," said bin Zair.

Fuad started to shout again, sensed somehow that the feeling of the meeting was against him and sat down; his Adam's apple jerked about in his throat as though he were actually swallowing bile.

"We cannot wait here for four months," said the young man with the cleft chin.

"In my time I have waited twenty years to take vengeance," said Umburak, placid as ever. While he told the well-known details of two ancient murders, Morris managed to catch Hadiq's eye and make a tiny signal that he wanted to speak. The reminiscent mutterings were still dying away when Hadiq stood up.

"Four days ago I buried my father, whom I loved," he said. "Still I do not know how he was killed. Have you news, Morris?"

171

It didn't sound as though the Council was prepared to devote more than a few seconds to this academic point, but Morris cleared his throat and answered loudly.

"Yes, I have news about that, and also about the oil."

At the marvellous word the whole tone of the meeting changed. There was a brief outburst of muttering and whispering. Morris clapped his hands, as if for silence, and though he didn't dare look he thought he heard a faint rattle of metal on stone, somewhere up in the gallery. In the following hush he fished a tangerine out of his basket and gave it to Dinah to keep her quiet; but she must have sensed his nervousness, for she insisted on huddling into his lap to eat it.

"Yes," he said, "I have spoken with many marshmen, both about the oil and the death of their lord. It was clear to me that they did not know that the oil even existed. It follows from this that bin Zair killed the Sultan."

He spoke the accusation directly at the old man, peering for some sign of guilt or shock, but saw only a slight jerk of the head and widening of the yellow-oozing eyes. The result was that he didn't notice the nephew until he saw a revolver being brandished under his nose. He shrank back. Dinah clutched too tightly for him to free an arm. The nephew was prodding at the safety-catch but his spittle was already reaching its target on the wings of his curses. Then suddenly he reeled back. The revolver rattled to the floor and he lay supine with blood streaming from his temple where Gaur's throwing-stick had struck.

Everybody shouted. Morris pushed Dinah clear and leaped to his feet, shouting too, and pointing to the gallery. A few yelling heads turned, then more. The ensuing silence was ridiculously dramatic.

"Let no man move," panted Morris. He turned from where the six dark muzzles poked through the frivolous white tracery of the screen and knelt by the fallen man. The pulse seemed reasonably strong, and the gash in the forehead not deep, though very productive of blood.

"Let Salim tend to the wound," said Umburak in an arid voice. "We would hear your accusation, Morris. We have known bin Zair many years."

Morris went back to his cushions pulling at his lip. Dinah

scuttled out from behind the throne, crept into his lap and pulled her lip also.

"Let us begin with the film bin Zair showed us," said Morris. "Now, the Frankish woman left my office and passed in front of the cages very shortly before bin Zair and the Sultan also came that way. She says she was still in the gallery when they came, and she turned and waved to them. Yet we watched the film for several minutes before the Sultan and bin Zair appeared, and we did not see the Frankish woman. Nor did Dinah appear in the cage. Moreover you all said that the Sultan staggered like a man shot in the back—would he have staggered so if he had been struck with a sharp dart in the neck?"

There was some disagreement on this point, with evidence adduced from personal experience of shooting men in the back, and (given equal weight) from the elderly westerns nowadays available to any Arab who didn't mind doing two hundred miles across the desert to the nearest drive-in cinema.

"Furthermore," said Morris, "I have taken many films with that camera, but none so bad. What does all this mean? It means that the film was taken in the early morning, when the sun shines from the east. This was done for two reasons—first because nobody would come to the zoo at that hour, and second in order that the bad light would help to hide the fact that the larger figure was not the Sultan but one of the slaves bin Zair had found for the zoo, a man called Maj."

"I am an old man and unused to machines," said bin Zair. "What do I know of films?"

"You told me that you had made a film of a male prostitute who dances among the Hadahm," said Morris.

"True, I have seen it," said somebody.

At this piece of corroborative evidence, however peripheral to the real case, a new note entered the coughs and whispers of the men. One of *them*, and not this dubious Frank, had now cast his tiny stone at old bin Zair.

"There are other matters," said Morris, "which bin Zair both understands and is ignorant of. At the flood-going feast he questioned me about my tape-recorder, and yet I am told he uses such things in his work. And you yourselves will remember that at some moments he cannot understand the marshmen's language,

173

and at others he understands it clearly enough. However, let us return to the film. The big man in the picture may have been Maj, but the little man was undoubtedly bin Zair. Therefore the film must have been made with his help.

"The points are not very strong," said Umburak. "The ape might have been hiding, the light might have been bad, who knows how a man will act when a bullet or dart strikes? And a woman's evidence—a woman who then ran from the palace—it is all frayed rope."

"There is more," said Morris. "Let me continue about these slaves. At the flood-going feast I asked bin Zair for better help in the zoo, and within two days he found me these two men. Now one of these men was a good mechanic and the other was large and stout, like the Sultan. They were Sulubba, and they told me that they were hereditary slaves . . ."

A few grunts of disbelief filled the pause which Morris deliberately left.

"On the morning of the murders," he went on, "they were cleaning the cages and had brought a pile of fresh reeds to make bedding for the animals. They had brought more than was necessary, so when they had finished they left a pile of reeds in the passage near the chimpanzee cage . . ."

"Enough to hide a man?" asked Umburak.

"No," said Morris. "But enough to hide a gun, and some other small object."

He fished more fruit out of the basket for Dinah, and in doing so pressed the "Play" button of the recorder.

"Now before bin Zair came to my room," he said, "I heard a lot of noise from the chimpanzees, noise enough to drown the sound of a quick scuffle and perhaps a shout of anger. When bin Zair came to my room he said he had been struck by the Sultan, and asked whether I had heard anything. I said I had not. We talked for a short time, and then . . ."

He didn't time it quite right. There was a longish pause, during which mutters of doubt and impatience began to gather strength. But suddenly they were drowned by the rushing whoosh of an airgun, a hoarse cry and another whoosh. Morris lifted the recorder out of the basket, ran the tape back to the monkey noises, and played some of them.

The reaction was that of children watching a conjurer, small cries of amazement and even delight, deliquescing into seriousness as each man explained to his neighbour the significance of the sounds. Head after head turned towards bin Zair, who sat stroking his beard but showing no more emotion than a look of scholarly interest. Morris gave him time to answer, but he was too wary for that.

"Whence came the tape?" said a providential straight man.

"I will tell you. It concerns the two slaves of whom I was speaking. When I went at your bidding into the marshes I had travelled less than a mile when I came upon the body of a man floating in the water. He had been killed with a spear-thrust, stripped naked and mutilated. He was Maj."

The news brought only a few cries of rage, and many reminders that the man had not been a true bedu, but a Sulubba.

"Now, later," said Morris, "I went to a ceremony in the marshes, and there I saw a marshman wearing this tape as an ornament from which hung the penises of two pale-skinned men. I made enquiries and found that this marshman had come upon two men lying in wait in the two channels that led from the landing-stages below the palace. They were armed and hiding, as if to ambush a man coming into the marshes. The marshman came from behind and killed them. In the canoe of the smaller man was this tape."

A dour, tall Arab who had not so far spoken coughed for silence.

"I believe I have heard of this pair, under other names," he said. "They were skilled assassins. Certainly if they were thus taken by surprise it proves that the marshmen would have been difficult to fight in the marshes."

The point was argued around for a while, and the true identity of Maj and Jillad discussed, and tales of their earlier, more successful craftsmanship retold.

"And what is the significance of all this?" asked Umburak at last.

"I think bin Zair's whole object was to open up the marshes," said Morris. "He visited the oil wells from time to time, and I think he probably arranged with them, in exchange for a large sum of money, that he would bring about a situation in which it

175

would eventually become possible for the marshes to be drained and exploratory drilling begin. A war between the Arabs and the marshmen would be one way of achieving this. If an Englishman appeared to have been killed by the marsh-people that would help too, and you will all bear witness that it was bin Zair who persuaded me to go into the marshes. On the other hand, if the marshmen killed Maj and Jillad, that would remove two witnesses who might have been troublesome later. He was right in this—I have no doubt that Jillad took the tape in order to blackmail bin Zair later."

"It is a long way round to travel in order to kill a man," said Umburak.

"Yes," said Morris. "But it had to be, because simple killing wasn't the object. The object was to persuade both the Arabs and the marshmen that the Bond was broken, and to do this by seeming to follow as closely as possible the story in the Testament of Naŀar. The Arabs, he was sure, could be persuaded to fight quite easily; but the marshmen had to hear of the Sultan and a warrior of their people killing each other with poisoned spears. This was a complicated effect to achieve, but I believe he had been thinking about it for more than a year. A year ago, just after the flood-going feast, a man called Kwan died, very suddenly; Dyal told me it had happened as if by magic. Dyal was a marsh-man, and to the marshmen the poison they use on their spears is a magical substance. A poisoned spear is sent to the Sultan at the flood-going feast as part of the tribute, and I think it possible that bin Zair was then testing the poison to see if it worked. It did, but as the poison loses its virtue in two or three weeks he had to wait another year.

"Suddenly he became very interested in the zoo, and inspected every detail. I think he had not thought of doing the murders there until he came one morning and saw the Sultan playing with the spring-guns. The marshmen throw their spears with a spear-thrower, so a spring-gun is quite a close parallel. He found two men, who were far too good to be zoo slaves. That morning they came to the zoo early and hid the gun and recorder among the reeds—indeed Maj became very angry when my ape started to throw the reeds about. Then bin Zair came to the zoo with papers for me to work on, so that I had to go to my office. He insisted that the door should be close guarded, so that there was no question of anybody else having done the killing—though he did not then know the Frankish woman was still in the zoo. He told the Sultan some tale which would persuade him to walk down into the lower gallery, and he gave Dyal tobacco to chew with poison in it—something very quick-acting, a cyanide capsule, perhaps. He knew that Dyal would not eat it in the Sultan's presence but that he was very much addicted and would chew it as soon as he could. Bin Zair must have been alarmed to see the Frankish woman still in the zoo, but Dyal was already dead, so he was forced to continue his plan.

"As soon as she was out of sight he started the tape-recorder—perhaps he pretended he had brought the Sultan down there to listen to it—and when the ape-noises began he struck the Sultan with the hypodermic dart. If he struck accurately into that vein the anaesthetic would act in two seconds, and the ape-noises would conceal any shout or scuffle. The poison would take some hours to act—I ought to have noticed that Dyal died quickly and with a contorted face and the Sultan slowly and peacefully. And yet they were supposed to have died of the same poison.

"Then bin Zair came to my office, saying that the Sultan had struck him—to account for any noises I might have heard—and waited for the recording of the two shots. We rushed out and found the Sultan's body, but my ape had taken the dart and used it to attack an enemy ape, who later also died. Then bin Zair ran round to the upper gallery, where he struck Dyal's dead body with another dart, and hid the remainder of the tobacco.

"So died my friend the Sultan. And all at once very many Arabs came from nowhere out of the sands, as though knowing that some such thing was about to happen . . ."

Suddenly there was uproar. Hitherto the Arabs had listened with an intentness that would have been more reassuring if Morris hadn't known how eagerly Arabs will listen to any accusation, however incredible, for the sake of retelling it later round some camp fire. There were hands on belt-daggers, and implausible cries of innocence. Ostentatiously Morris turned his head towards the guns as if ready to give a signal, but the Council calmed itself.

"There was a rumour," said the dour sheikh, "that the marsh-men were planning to attack the palace. Fuad brought the news to my tents . . ."

"And he is bin Zair's father's cousin's wife's brother's grand-son," added someone—a piece of instant desert genealogy that brought grunts of confirmation.

"Fuad told me that if there was war the Arabs could take the marshes and drain them and profit from good fresh land and the oil beneath; therefore, being loyal to my Sultan, I drove across the desert though I had my camels on good grazing."

"But the marshmen knew nothing of any such attack," said Morris. "Whence came this rumour? Furthermore, whence came the bombs and napalm in so few days, with two good aeroplanes and experienced pilots? Such things take time to find, unless a man knows in advance that they will be needed and is friends with an international oil company. Note also that it was bin Zair who persuaded me to go to the marshes at all, after I had begun to suggest doubts about his story; and lo, when I return to the palace it is already known that I am dead . . ."

Morris allowed his voice to tail away. There were a few more loose ends he could have tied in, but he didn't want to muddle his case with complexities. To calm himself he started to pick his way along the fur of Dinah's fore-arm. She cradled herself close to him, crooning slightly. The Arabs evidently recognised the dramatic moment and waited without snivel or cough for bin Zair to begin. He took his time, but at last he sighed an old man's patient sigh.

"Morris has spoken," he said. "Now I must collect my wits. You must understand that I did not come to the Council expecting to hear so mad an accusation. I am surprised that Morris did not add that I flew to the zoo on the back of a winged lion and that these poisons were fetched for me by the djinns at my command. Alas, I am an old man. I loved my master. I served him many years. I crawled many times to his feet. How should I kill him? But lo, you listen like children round their grandmother to this wild tale. And there is no evidence here, save the word of Morris. He says he saw this, he heard this; he brings a tape, which he says he found in such-and-such a place, and there are noises on it. But perhaps he put the noises there himself. He says the marsh-

178

men knew of no plot, but he alone speaks their language—how shall his tale be tested. He says I slew my master. Who saw me do this? No man, says the Lord Morris, this story-teller, and here at least he speaks truth."

This was a strong point. The Arabs, even more than other people, prefer the evidence of the most drunken, short-sighted, corrupt and biassed witness to that of the most coherent net of circumstantial reasoning.

"No man saw you, bin Zair," said Morris. "But my ape did."

"And how shall it bear witness?" cried someone.

"Thus," said Morris, releasing Dinah and spilling the counters into the lid of his wallet.

"Are we all crazed," cried bin Zair, "to listen to such nonsense?"

"We will listen," said Hadiq. "I have seen how this ape makes words. My friends, it is true. Morris will explain."

"Ai!" said a fat sheikh. "Let us at least see, and then we can decide. It will be news to tell, certainly."

Everyone agreed with that. News is a valuable commodity in the desert, and to be present at the beginning of a fresh piece of news—the birth of someone's son, the theft of a camel, a quarrel over grazing, a record bag by a famous hawk—makes a man welcome in many tents.

"Now see," said Morris. "Dinah cannot speak. Her mouth and tongue are not of human shape. She can make a few signs with her hands, as a deaf-and-dumb person does, and when we stood by the body of the Sultan she made a sign to me that the Sultan was hurt, thus."

He prodded the tips of his fingers together and Dinah, looking up from her search among the counters for the blue/white square that meant grapes, copied him with a puzzled air.

"I am a scholar of languages," said Morris. "I came to Q'Kut to study the language of the marshmen. But another part of my study is to see to what extent an ape can learn language. We use these little coloured counters for words. Thus." Morris explained the meaning of each counter as he placed it in position.

white square:	Dinah
orange circle with hole:	get/fetch/find

179

black square:	person
purple rectangle:	(qualifier) big

Dinah sniffed eagerly at the array, looked round the assembly, poked a finger at the qualifier, scampered teasingly round the circle and finished by tugging triumphantly at Gaur's white robe.

"This is childishness," squeaked bin Zair angrily, but he was immediately shouted down by many voices, even those of his own party. What! Interrupt a scene that would fill a hundred evenings with good talk!

Morris clicked to Dinah who came rushing over for her reward; he showed her two small branches of grapes and gave her one which she ate while he explained the next sentence.

yellow circle:	question
white square:	Dinah
white circle:	eat
green/blue square:	banana

He laid the second branch of grapes beside it. Dinah sniffed rapidly, compared the grapes with the noun-square, snickered scornfully and snatched out of Morris's hand the large red circle which meant "No."

She watched Morris with dark, excited eyes as she ate the second lot of grapes, already thrilling to her thrilled audience. He explained a new sentence:

white square:	Dinah
orange circle with hole:	get/fetch/find
black square with gold hand:	Sultan

He could see she was puzzled. She sniffed the message several times, turned the black square over to see if she could thus convert a king to a commoner, chattered a little, pouted, and loped off to inspect the audience. She paused momentarily at the throne, perhaps reminded of scenes where Hadiq had been present with his father; she also hesitated a short time over Gaur, and longer over the old fat sheikh; at last she came to the inert body of bin Zair's nephew and possibly it was that that reminded her. At any rate she came scampering back to Morris, prodding her finger-tips together, and then hunted through the counters for the purple circle with the hole. It didn't take her long to arrange her two-word sentence.

black square with gold hand:	Sultan
purple circle with hole:	hurt/be hurt

A whispering sigh rose from the council as Morris explained the meaning. The hunt was up. Bin Zair's thin, grey hand combed ceaselessly at his beard. Nobody looked at him direct.

Unfortunately Dinah didn't make the next step of her own account, so Morris, rather than lose the momentum of the trial, had to ask her a leading question:

yellow circle:	question
black square:	person
purple circle with hole:	hurt/be hurt
black square with gold hand:	Sultan

Dinah considered the problem with a protruding lower lip, judiciously nodding her head up and down as if to shake her thoughts into a pattern. Morris offered her only the yes and no symbols, placing them equidistant from her; and though she was slow in coming to her conclusion her arm in the end snaked out with no hesitation and snatched up the large green circle. The room released its breath. Morris had intended to explain, if they got this far, that Dinah didn't connect the darts with the act of firing the guns, and that therefore if she said a man had hurt the Sultan that man must actually have struck him, but he sensed that the audience was not in a mood for logic. Even Dinah, when he offered her a few more grapes, seemed more interested in the game than the reward. Perhaps she too felt the human lust for drama, the quickened pulse of the closing hunt. They had already used all the symbols Morris needed for his final question but he held them up again to explain their names and her eyes followed each one to its location in the line of meaning.

181

white square:	Dinah
orange circle with hole:	get/fetch/find
black square:	person
purple circle with hole:	hurt
black square with gold hand:	Sultan

Relative clauses had once been a bugbear. A year ago Morris had been brooding on grammatical devices to obviate them; but suddenly, between session and session, Dinah had sorted the problem out for herself, poking the symbols out of the straight until the two halves of the sentence could be read along different lines. By now there was an established grammatical convention whereby relative sentences went at right-angles, the symbol on the corner (in this case the black square) containing in itself the relative link. Her discovery of this principle had been probably the most exciting moment in Morris's life, both for the logical beauty of it, and for the realisation that there might be no limit to her abilities.

So now he was perfectly confident that she would understand the message; he was less sure that her memory would be up to the task of recognition—after all, he well knew how long it takes a quite intelligent human to learn to distinguish one chimpanzee from another. He watched with real anxiety as she at last nosed up from the symbols and looked round at the hushed Arabs.

Slowly, walking on her knuckles, she sidled across the circle and peered into the face of a man with a green headcloth and a straggly dark wisp of beard. He shrank away; his throat worked as if there was a scream imprisoned there, but Dinah only chattered in a dissatisfied fashion, came back to the message, read it again and started off in a different direction.

Her progress was far from systematic. Sometimes she went straight across the circle and then back to the man she had just inspected; often she would dart back to Morris as if to check that she was doing the right thing; when she did this he gave her a few more grapes, which she ate slowly as she zig-zagged across the bright mosaic floor. The process cannot have lasted more than a few minutes, but suddenly in the middle of it Morris experienced a shuddering shock of recognition—something like the spasm of fierce wakefulness that shakes a man back to this world just before he falls asleep—or as if the lobes of his brain, having been fractionally out of phase, had jerked back to full sympathy. All this had happened before. On Gal-Gal a man had watched his life or death being decided by the erratic movements of an animal, a trained animal, to and fro across an arena ringed by silent, intent spectators. Morris, after his bout of activism, had watched his fate with an apathy close to accidie; and so did bin Zair watch now. The difference was that the duck on Gal-Gal had not yet eaten its poison; whereas Dinah had long been eating hers, day by day, from Morris's own hand, the ancient poison of words.

There must have been something unnoticeable about bin Zair, an inherent camouflage that might have made a marvellous hunter out of him if his life had not been spent on the track of more illusory game. Dinah only spotted him as if by accident, grey and silent on the cushions. Her glance flicked towards him as she was crossing the arena, and away. She continued half a pace on her path, then froze. Very slowly, as if she herself was the hunted creature, her head swung back towards bin Zair, her left hand staying poised in the air for the next pace. She stared at him for one of those unmeasurable times that was probably only half a heartbeat; then she was darting across the floor to him, pulling at his robe, hooting with excitement.

Bin Zair must have been ready for her. Even before the Arabs broke into excited chatter and applause his curved dagger was out and striking. He was old but very quick—Morris's eye only registered when the blow was over that at the tip of the gunmetal blue curve of the blade something sticky and black glistened.

But Dinah was quick too; the blow, aimed at her ribs, caught her glancingly above the wrist as she shied away. She screamed and raced to Morris, flinging herself into his arms and showing him the red, inch-long slash through the dark hair. He clutched at her, dragged the wound to his mouth and sucked. His mouth was full of blood. He spat it out and sucked frenziedly while she struggled. She was very strong but he shifted his grip and managed to hold her, sucking and spitting. In his mind's eye he saw the deft blow again, and remembered how neatly bin Zair had

183

plucked the gun from the hands of the young man at the earlier Council meeting, and confused both movements with something he had not seen, the blow that had struck the Sultan down. His lips were very sore. Bristly little hairs filled his mouth, as when a toothbrush starts to disintegrate. A hand shook him by the shoulder.

"Lord," said Gaur's deep voice, "you cannot suck the poison from the wound . . ."

Morris looked up, dull and hopeless. Dinah wriggled and bucked in his grasp. The dagger floated in front of his face with a drop of blood drying on the surface of the poisonous smear.

"This poison has died," said Gaur. "See."

A black finger-nail pinched at the blacker ooze and broke through. Now Morris could see the inner stickiness under the hardened outer skin. Gaur squeezed and black fresh globules of the stuff were forced through to the surface.

"Now it is alive again," he said, and tossed the weapon away. Probably he had weighed it in his hand while Morris had been sucking at Dinah's arm, for though few Arab daggers are any use for throwing this one flew straight to where bin Zair sat erect on the cushions, silent and waiting judgment. Morris, still in his daze of shock and effort, did not actually see it strike, but he saw bin Zair flinch, recover and with a careful hand draw the dagger from his thigh, leaving a streak of blood on his white robe. Everyone fell silent. With difficulty the old man rose to his feet and looked round the ring of them, bowing his head slightly when he came to Hadiq.

"It was Allah's will," he squeaked. He turned and limped away.

"Shall I pick him off?" called Anne in clear, clipped tones from the gallery.

"No," sighed Morris.

Four hours, he thought. You take four hours to die. That man killed Kwan. He killed my friend Kwan. Now he's dying the same way himself, and what he wanted to happen is going to happen anyway.

Dinah whimpered and he realised he was still holding her with all his strength. He let go. She looked with horror and disbelief at her arm, still puckered and bleeding. To distract her he peeled a banana and gave it to her. She had begun to eat it left-handed without much relish when her whole body stiffened as if with cramp in his arms. Her eyes remained open but the banana slipped from her hand.

"Gaur!" he called in alarm. Gaur strolled over and knelt by his side, feeling Dinah's limbs and forehead.

"That is not the work of poison, Lord," he said judiciously. "A speared man becomes hot, like fire, before he dies, and his joints are loose. Thy creature is cold and stiff."

Morris only grunted and lurched to his feet with Dinah in his arms. He remembered to bow to Hadiq before he turned and staggered wearily away. Before he was through the doors the Council was in full spate again, retelling all these dramas.

3

Up in his rooms Morris laid Dinah in her nest; she whimpered as he persuaded her stiff limbs into the necessary curve, but once she was nestled in her eyes closed and the slow hammer-beat of her pulse began to ease to the normal rhythm of sleep. He covered her with a blanket and slumped into one of the chairs, where he sat sweating and worrying in mazed circles until he realised that he could at least do something about the sweat. Resetting the thermostat reminded him about Peggy.

She was asleep too, but stirred and smiled when he felt her pulse, which seemed normal. She was a resilient little brat, he thought. Perhaps Dinah was only undergoing a sort of shock coma too— it wouldn't be surprising, after everything that had happened to her, but it was a bit uncanny that both of them should suffer the same sort of collapse at the same moment—several times, as his worry and tiredness slipped gear into a kind of feverish doze he had the same recurring vision of the two primitive little females groping through a dark, arched tunnel in opposite directions, brushing against each other as they passed and then groping on to emerge, somehow, in each other's worlds. Fully awake he knew it was more likely that Dinah's collapse was an effect of the poison, and he could only hope that it had lost enough of its virtue for her to survive, but as soon as he half-slept again the same sequence returned.

After about the third or fourth time another creature seemed to be there in the tunnel, scuttling hurriedly from end to end, greyish and wispy, completely ignoring the slow, small figures that might have been Dinah and Peggy; it moved rapidly through the dark but as soon as it reached the twilight zones at the ends it hesitated and scuttled back, unable to emerge into either kind of daylight. It was bin Zair.

Awake again he thought about the old man. A decent old goat, really. Morris discovered that he both liked and respected him, and that the murders were strangely easy to forgive, even Kwan's. Was this the result of that bizarre element of innocence that permeated the appalling cruelties and slaughters which were the sole history of the desert tribes? Or was it simply another symptom of the tepidity of Morris's own nature? Or was it that what bin Zair had done had an inner inevitability, a moral logic, that made other courses of action seem fanciful, mere wishful thinking? The palace stood like a teetotum balanced on its spindle, maintained there only by its own circular momentum—that was Morris's world of high civilisation, to which the Sultan also and even Dinah partly belonged. Beside it lay the apparent mess of the marshes, which was also a balance, a taut and intricate web maintained by its own tensions, Qab's world and Gaur's and Peggy's. But the balance of bin Zair's world had been broken, so that it was inhabited by whirling or scuttling creatures like Anne, or the dead hijackers, or the young man with the cleft chin . . .

Bin Zair would be praying now, if he was still conscious. He wouldn't be thinking about this sort of thing. If he wondered at all about his own compulsions he would think in the language of money and prestige and tribal obligations and watering rights. He would perhaps regret that he had evolved a scheme so crazily complex, but he wouldn't consider its underlying . . . well . . . propriety. It was proper that he should have used a modern hypodermic dart tipped with a primitive poison, proper that his plan should involve films and tapes as well as the swift blow of the killer, proper even that it should take place in a milieu where a supercivilised prince was attempting to recreate the jungle culture of apes . . .

"I have slept, Lord" whispered Peggy from the bedroom door.

"Now my bladder is very full. How may I leave this hut and empty it?"

With a sigh Morris rose and showed her how the lavatory worked. She thought its flush was the finest toy in the world and wasted a lot of water playing with it.

Epilogue

THE APPALLING CLATTER of the rotors slowed, deepened and
flogged into silence. Even with the help of the radio beacon
which Gaur had placed there, Gal-Gal had been hell to find in
the mist; so the noise seemed to have gone on unbearably long
while the helicopter had swung and hesitated, jerking in the
erratic air, and the cabin had seemed to absorb heat into itself
until it became like a lava-bubble floating blindly and stickily
towards a vent.

With a sigh of relief Morris removed his ear-muffs. Peggy
aped his movement. She had refused to wear Arab clothes, but
so did many Arab children and the Shaikhah had easily found
jeans and a Yogi-Bear tee-shirt to fit her.

"That was very much noise," she said gaily, in English. Once
again Morris marvelled at the accuracy of her ear—timbre apart,
it might have been his own voice talking.

"Too right!" said the pilot. "Jesus, what a dump! Do you
come here often?"

Morris grunted and climbed out. The marsh-waters had sunk
in the last four months almost to their lowest level, reducing the
humidity but raising the heat. All the acres of exposed mud
reeked of rot. For a moment he thought that the weeks of coaxing
and negotiation had come to nothing, for the rock seemed
deserted and he had been expecting to be met by the representatives of all eight clans. But as soon as the bee-hive basket was
handed out to him (on a shortened pole, to fit the cabin, and
empty, though the marshmen were not to know that) black heads
emerged from behind the cliff edges, wherever there was a foot-

hold out of sight. For a while they simply remained heads; they might have been stuck there, bodiless, after some tribal raid, a suitable necklace for Gal-Gal; but when Peggy and Doctor Knopf, the specialist in tropical diseases, climbed down a few of them began to climb up. From the cliffs nearest the landing-place a group of three men came cautiously towards him, the two on the outside looking comparatively intact, but supporting in the centre an old man with a disgustingly swollen leg. He was Qab.

"Thy buffaloes may rest in my wallow," said Morris.

"Half my cheeses are thine," said Qab. "Is this man also a great witch, Lord?"

"The words are thine, Qab. The man knows much of big legs and withered arms and weeping skins and belly-devils." Morris switched into English: "What can you do about a leg like that, Knopf?"

"Not much, by the look of it," said Doctor Knopf, a lean, yellow-skinned young man. "Can't tell for sure without tests, but when they're as bad as that you can usually only arrest the process and lessen the pain a bit. Grief, what a collection! What you've got here is a museum of tropical medicine. God! Is this a fair sample of the inhabitants?"

In silence the representatives of the eight clans hobbled, or crawled, or were carried towards the helicopter, their limbs swollen or shrivelled, their skins scaly or suppurating.

"The witches have been busy, Lord," said Qab. "You have said that you would bring great witches to Gal-Gal, witches not of the moon-world, who by their charms would undo this charm and that charm. Is this a true report?"

"It is true in part. My friend does not think he can make thy leg less big, but he ꟴan make it cease from growing. Moreover, he can ease the pain. But thy young men and thy sons—these he can protect from witchcraft, and drive out the charms that have recently begun to work . . ."

"We have been told lies," said Qab angrily.

"Who has told lies?" said Morris in a bullying manner. "Do I lie? Does the ninth clan lie? Who else has spoken?"

"You are an old fool, my uncle," said one of the men who was supporting Qab. "Witch, there is a foul charm starting to work at my back. Can thy friend drive it out?"

189

He swung round. Qab staggered and clutched at his other supporter. On the nephew's back, just below the left shoulder-blade, was a circular mess of yellow and orange pus, about two inches across, crusted brown at the edges. Doctor Knopf bent forward to examine it.

"Antibiotics should clear that up," he said. "It's hard to say. These people are teetering right on the edge of extinction. They were probably OK until about fifty years ago, with a bit of immunity to all the local bugs and uglies; but now the river's bringing them half the sewage of Asia. Still, that should clear up."

"My friend says he believes that charm can be undone," said Morris. "Listen, when I came to Alaurgan-Alaurgad thine uncle gave me a wife, a girl of no value at all, who had just such a charm working on her shoulder, and was sure to die soon. But I put a paste on the sore place, and behold, it is gone. I will show you. Qab will bear witness."

He turned to call for Peggy. She seemed to have disappeared, hidden by the ring of marshmen who stood or sat listening to the conversation. Then he saw her, above their heads, climbing up on to the mysterious stone slab which they called the House of Spirits. Really, he thought with exasperation, she's worse than Dinah.

All the heads had swung round to watch her, but Morris did not feel the wave of communal horror that flooded through the crowd. He was transfixed by the usual pang of longing for Dinah. She wasn't dead, but she might as well have been. Bin Zair's attack on her, at the very moment when she had triumphantly brought off a great feat of intellect, had destroyed her whole relationship with men, including Morris. Now her only acknowledgment of his existence was that she chattered at him for fruit when he showed himself in front of the cage; she was almost fully integrated into the chimpanzee group, leader of the younger females, scruffy and slouching, accepting the bullying by the males as a norm of life. Occasionally in the first couple of months Morris had tried to renew her interest in the plastic symbols, but she had scattered them about in hysterical rage. Since then he had drugged himself with work—annotating the fast-growing pile of tapes of marshmen's talk, and negotiating for the Sultan with the marshmen themselves.

With an effort he pushed all that out of his mind.

"There may be trouble," he muttered to Doctor Knopf. "You'd better get back into the machine. Tell the pilot to be ready to go."

But none of the tribesmen moved, or even looked at the white men. They stared at Peggy, waiting. Morris couldn't believe that she had climbed up there for anything except adventure, with perhaps an element of scorn for superstitions which she had grown out of. But as soon as she saw that she was a focus of attention she accepted her role, spread her arms wide, waited for several seconds, and at last began to dance. Now the marshmen crept towards her, silently, and it seemed unwillingly, like birds or small beasts hypnotised by the coiling and writhing of a snake.

Her steps speeded up. She whirled like a dust-eddy from one end of the slab to the other and then back to the centre, where she stopped abruptly with her arms raised above her head. She began to sing.

She sang in English. She had insisted that Morris should teach her his own language, and what right had he to refuse? What property had he in her marsh mind, as a research tool, if she chose to put it away? Besides, her will was stronger than his. All he could do was tape the learning process, to record whatever problems she faced in adapting to alien modes of thought. The answer had been almost none.

"You are fools," she sang to the marshmen. "You are a lot of stupid people. You do not know things. You do not know cause and effect. Cause and effect."

It was Morris's own voice, piping triumphant and scornful through the steamy air.

"Soon all you fools will be dead. Cause and effect. Cause and effect. Cause and effect."

PANTHEON INTERNATIONAL CRIME